Sand & Mistletoe

CHAUTONA HAVIG

ISBN: 9781790341238

Chautona Havig lives in an oxymoron, escapes into imaginary worlds that look startlingly similar to ours and writes the stories that emerge. An irrepressible optimist, Chautona sees everything through a kaleidoscope of *It's a Wonderful Life* sprinkled with fairy tales. Find her on the web and say howdy—if you can remember how to spell her name.

Cover photos: fabianschmidt/depositphotos, Sunagatov Dmitry/depositphotos, Ezhevica/depositphotos
Cover Art: Chautona Havig
Edited by: Haug Editing

Connect with Me Online:
Twitter: https://twitter.com/Chautona
Facebook: https://www.facebook.com/pages/justhewriteescape
My blog: http://chautona.com/blog/
Instagram: http://instagram.com/ChautonaHavig
Goodreads: https://www.goodreads.com/author/show/2946954.Chautona_Havig
BookBub: https://www.bookbub.com/authors/chautona-havig
Amazon Author Page: https://amazon.com/author/chautonahavig
YouTube: https://www.youtube.com/user/chautona/videos
My newsletter (sign up for news of FREE eBook offers):
https://chautona.com/newsletter

To my girls who learned ASL and as a result, learned to love the Deaf community as well.

Note: Because this book deals not just with someone who is "not hearing" but someone who is a part of the Deaf community, most, but not all instances of the use of the word "deaf" have been capitalized as per their preference. When speaking *only* of a medical condition, I left it lowercase.

Also, the places in this book are mostly based on real places in Ventura. I placed Sandpiper House approximately where the old Pierpont Inn resides (it's now a Wyndham). Beach House Fish on the pier, McConnell's ice cream, and Le Petit Cafe Bakery all exist, and I recommend trying them.

Reese's house on Pierpont Blvd. is also real—I lived there when I was nine. The annual parade of lights and the Olivas Adobe Candlelight tour both happen just as described, but… a little earlier in the month. I had to make that change to fit the timeline of the story.

Finally, the awesome ship at Marina Park at the end of Pierpont Blvd. is home to some of my favorite childhood memories. I whizzed down that zip line more times than I can count. They took it down, in 2016 or 2017, but they're working to bring it back. If you search "Awesome Boat Zip-line at Marina Park Ventura, CA" on YouTube you'll find videos of it. Of course, *we* did not have a rubber stopper to keep us from slamming into the pole when I was a kid, so I left that little safety feature off. Because I can.

Oh, and at one time, if you dug in the back corner of the sand, waaaay down, you might have found a white sweater with small chicks embroidered in squares on the front. It *might* have been buried there accidentally-on-purpose by a ten-year-old girl who really didn't like that scratchy old thing. This is not a confession.

ONE

Frustrated? Oh, she'd expected that. Overwhelmed? Had she considered it, certainly. Portia Spears stood in the rather grand entryway of Sandpiper House and held onto the handle of her rolling suitcase. This she did in an attempt at keeping it safe from being sent careening across the slick floors by her nieces and nephew. While sharp voices pierced the air from all corners of their home—for the next two weeks, anyway—Portia took in the architecture, the beachy furnishings, and the emptiness.

"It's cold. Impersonal. There's not a stitch of anything that feels like home." The words sounded overloud, even as she muttered them under her breath.

An argument broke out in the kitchen regarding who would sleep in the downstairs mini-suite and who would be upstairs in the master suite. *Jessica will win. Why do they even bother?*

Voices grew louder—loud enough that her nieces and nephews raced past to watch. "Five… four… three… Yep." Sleeping arrangements failed to hold their attentions, and she gripped the handle of her suitcase harder as the kids dashed past once more, eager to get away from the drama.

Her oldest sister, Cressida, the birth order anomaly and family peacemaker, made a play for just asking their parents where they'd prefer to be. At that, Miranda backed down. Desperate to get away from it all, and to attempt a bit of deflection, Portia hurried into the kitchen to get her room assignment.

Cressida lunged at her, all hugs and smiles. "You made it."

Before letting Portia go, she hissed, "Save me."

"You're on your own. They never listen to me." A glance at the other sisters told her how to proceed. "I need just twenty or thirty minutes alone after the traffic. Where's my room? Put me in a closet, I don't care, but I need to close my eyes."

Miranda flung bleached-blond hair over one shoulder and hurried to her side.

Uh, oh. She's looking for reinforcements.

"All the rooms are marked with a sticky note. I think you are up the stairs and two doors to the left—great view of the ocean. I put Mom and Dad in the suite at the end of the hall so Cressida and Austin can have the first-floor suite. No kids falling down the stairs at midnight."

Jessica protested. "It's not big enough for all those kids."

"They can sleep on the couch, then!"

Mouthing an, "I'm sorry" at Cressida, Portia slipped from the room before someone else tried drag her into the fray. She grabbed the side handle of her suitcase and carried it upstairs, to the left, and two doors down. *Portia* stared back at her from a yellow sticky note on a closed door.

Just the push of a lever-styled door handle and the door swung open to reveal a wall of windows. The room—bigger than their living room at home. The view? Well, Miranda hadn't exaggerated. Across the 101 and… She pulled up Google maps from the trip down. "Right. That's Harbor Boulevard…" According to the maps, the road paralleled a long stretch of beach. To the right, the pier jutted out into the water. To the left, houses after what the map said the "state beach" ended.

Christmas at the beach. If it had to be away from home, couldn't we have gone to the mountains? You know… snow*? I mean, at least that* feels *Christmassy. There's nothing Christmassy about sand and salt air.*

Still, she leaned against the windowsill and gazed out over the ocean. Several cars sat in the parking lot by the beach. A handful of surfers rode large swells. *It's got to be freezing.*

An accusation punctuated with an expletive rang out below her just as Portia saw something below. She leaned closer, her forehead pressed against the glass. Was it? Heart pounding, she bolted from the room, down the stairs, and out the door. With one eye on her phone, she groaned as she jogged down the steep drive to Sandpiper House and out onto Vista del Mar.

Her lungs screamed for mercy. *Need. To. Work. Out. More.* Honesty forced her to amend that. *Fine. Need to* start *working out.* Under the 101 Freeway. Her legs now protested in not-so-lovely harmony with her lungs. Still, she pushed forward, concern overriding her under-toned body.

Once the little boy she'd seen was in sight again, she called out, "Hey, are you okay? Buddy, what are you doing out here alone? What—?"

He didn't respond. He just stood along a wet strand of sand, wearing rain boots and digging in the sand each time the tide pulled back from shore. "Hey!"

Only as she reached him and touched his shoulder did he turn to face her. Eagerness vanished and fear replaced it. He stepped back, eyes darting about him.

"It's okay." Portia held up her hands. "I just wanted to make sure you're okay. What's your name?"

The boy shrugged. When she pressed, he backed away, his index finger swiping from ear to mouth. *He's Deaf!* Just to be certain, she pointed to him and made the sign for Deaf again to ask. He nodded in synchronization with his fist bobbing.

Portia grinned and rotated hers in front of her mouth to signify she was hearing and held a hand to her chest and introduced herself. She spoke aloud as well. "My name is Portia." Lowering her eyebrows, she reversed the sign asking his name.

Eyes bright, the boy signed D-u-n-c-a-n. A moment later, he formed the letter D and slid the palm of that hand over the other. A question in his eyes told her he didn't know if she'd understand.

"I see." Portia imitated the sign. "Your name sign is…"

After that, the boy's hands and fingers flew.

They shouldn't be bothering me about this stuff on my vacation. Reese Whitaker shot an apologetic look at his son, but Duncan's eyes sat riveted on the ocean before them. "Look, Gerry, I'm at the beach with my son. I don't have time to help you—"

His coworker pleaded again and Reese capitulated—as he always did. Duncan tugged his sleeve and signed to go dig for crabs. *You can see me,* the boy insisted when Reese signed that it wasn't safe. *I won't go where I can't see your head.*

His father's voice invaded his thoughts. *"You need to let him be more independent. If he could hear, you'd let him ride around the block. So let him do it now."*

Of course, he hadn't. If a car honked, if someone shouted a warning—if anything happened, Duncan wouldn't know until it was too late. But the boy made a good point. The beach spread out before him. Only a few surfers in the distance—not even another car parked in the "do not enter" area he'd entered.

"Go on." At the boy's surprised response, he grinned. "Go."

Gerry protested. "I need—"

"I was just sending my son out to the beach alone, so hurry."

In typical Gerry style, the question started out about one thing and finished up with another. All while he assured the guy that everything he'd called about could wait until after the first of the year, Reese kept an eagle eye on Duncan. *Dad's right. He needs this. No hovering. I'm turning into Mom.*

"—need the email about the planned outage on the twenty-seventh so I can get it to Lupe."

That he agreed with. "I think I can get that email for you. Hang on."

Email after email flew past as he searched for the right one, but it eluded him. He frowned, eying the phone. "I just saw it yester—oh. Wait. I know. I filed it…"

A sound from outside the car distracted him, but a glance up saw Duncan digging in the sand. *Loves those sand crabs.*

"Okay… I've got—"

A blur rushed past—a feminine one, he thought. Reese looked up just in time to see a streak in jeans and hoodie with crazy-long red hair tied up in a ponytail. The tail almost shot straight out behind her. And she was headed straight for Duncan. He had the door open and had made it to the sand before he remembered to tell Gerry he had to go. "Emergency. I'll forward that when I can."

He pulled up a few yards shy of the woman and his son. *She signs?* Relief washed over him. *He's safe.* Again he watched her. She spelled out her name. P-o-r-t-i-a.

As in Shylock and the others in Venice?

Her gaze rose and met his. An awkward smile formed. "I thought he was out here all alone."

"Yeah, not hardly."

"You can't see inside the car from the house. And he looked even littler from up there. So…" She backed away. "I'm—"

"Portia. I saw. You sign much?"

"Took two years in college." Even as she spoke, she signed for Duncan.

Reese couldn't help but ask. "Do you ever interpret?"

She signed her yes, even though Duncan had gone back to digging up sand crabs. "Not like my sister. She's the expert."

"You from here?"

After a glance over her shoulder, she shook her head. "We're just here for…" Her fingers hung air quotes. "'—Christmas.' Because that's what everyone wants, right? To spend their holidays in a strange house where nothing is familiar? Thrilling."

"You really should work on not repressing your feelings. It's not healthy."

A transformation came over her. One minute she'd been eager to chat ASL, and the next, she scowled at him. It reversed just as she said, "Who do—? Oh." Portia didn't have a pretty blush, but it faded almost as quickly as it came—much like the temper he suspected she had.

"Um… is your hair natural?"

"Yes and no."

"That explains a lot."

A chuckle—faint but present preceded a brief explanation. "I enhance my pale red. And yeah," she added, reading his mind, "I do have the temper to match. It runs in the family."

"The red hair or the temper?"

Duncan interrupted before she could answer. All attention shifted to the boy. Portia dropped to her knees in the sand and examined the handful of wriggling crabs, each no bigger than a Skittle. "They're so cute!" Her hands and fingers flew as she asked how he'd found so many.

"You've never seen sand crabs?"

"Didn't spend much time around this kind of sand."

He couldn't let that one lie. "Not many crabs in the desert?"

Gray eyes gazed up at him under light brown lashes. "How'd you know I'm from the desert?"

"How many kinds of sand are there?"

"Fair enough." She rose and dusted her hands off on her jeans. "Well, I should get back. Everyone's just arriving. I didn't even tell anyone I left. I just saw him and ran."

Though she hadn't actually done anything to help, she'd tried, and Reese found himself wanting to thank her—somehow. "You sure we can't talk you into spending a while here with us and then maybe a chocolate shake? I promised Duncan In-N-Out after we threw the Frisbee for a bit. I mean, you did try to save my kid. I should thank you."

Only when she blushed again did he realize how his invitation sounded. *It's like you're asking her out. Stupid.* But as she struggled to find an excuse to say no, Reese realized she'd known better than he. *Okay, so I did. I am. And I don't want her to say no.*

Mid-explanation why it wouldn't work, her phone rang. "Yeah? Well…" She gave him a second look and nodded. "I'll be back in a bit. I had to go do something. I'll explain later." Phone shoved in her pocket, Portia gave him a weak smile. "So that invitation. Has it already expired?"

"Nope. I'll go get the Frisbee." He took three steps before she called after him, asking his name. "Reese," he called back, jogging backward in the sand. "Reese Whitaker. Nice to meet you."

TWO

The first text message came after Reese had made his first throw. Duncan raced after it and tumbled in the sand. His giggles reminded her so much of her nephew's. *A.J. would like this. I need to get a Frisbee.*

Portia glanced over at Reese before pulling out her phone to see who'd messaged. Jessica. Without reading it, she shoved it back in her pocket and waited her turn to throw. Watching both of the Whitakers gave her a perfect opportunity to get a better look at Reese. *He's cute. Too bad Ventura's so far from Rosamond.*

The disc flew through the air and tried to lob off her head. Portia choked and grabbed at her neck. From the corner of her eye, she saw shock register on Reese's face, and instinct took over. She dropped to the ground, clutching her neck. And just as her head hit the sand, reason returned. *You don't know this guy! You can't do this!*

But she did. Both Reese and Duncan rushed to her side, much to her relief. She grabbed the boy around the waist and tickled him until he squealed. Reese just stared down at her. "When'd you realize you *weren't* going to wage a tickle war on me?" His upper lip twitched.

He needs a mustache to effectively use a twitch like that.

"Well?"

Duncan eyed both of them as if confused. Portia signed what his father had said and her response as she admitted, "Um, right about the time I hit the ground." Her phone buzzed again.

A glance showed Miranda this time. She shoved it back in her pocket and tried to right herself in the deep sand.

Reese's hand shot out to help her up. Only after she'd reached for it did Portia realize her mistake. *Cute guy with adorable kid plus physical contact equals danger zone.*

"Do you need to get that? I'm not one of those phone Nazis. Sometimes you have to answer."

"It's just my sister. She can wait." To cover the awkwardness, she snatched up the Frisbee and took off down the beach. Of course, Portia imagined herself running gracefully as people did in movies, but the way her feet had to fight for each step hinted that she probably looked more like a drunk orangutan.

After the sixth ignored text, Reese crossed the distance and folded his arms over his chest. "What does your sister want?"

"Which one?"

He eyed her. "How many do you have?"

As she translated for an only half-interested Duncan, Portia decided that's where he'd decide she was more trouble than a milkshake on Christmas vacation was worth. "Four." Just to get the upcoming inquisition over with, she added, "Three older, one younger. Only one is married—Cressida."

"Five girls..." He eyed her. "Portia and Cressida... parents like Shakespeare?"

Duncan looked confused until she signed, *Old, stinky books.* The boy giggled, and she continued. "Classic literature of any kind, but we're the Spears, so they went with the Bard's heroines rather than the Bennet girls."

At the confused look on his face, her heart sank. Cute or not, adorable son or not, she wasn't sure she could even be "just friends" with a guy who wasn't familiar with one of her favorite book families. "That's it. I'd better go home. I can't be friends with someone who—"

"Doesn't have any compassion on your poor nerves?"

She gaped at him... gaped and forgot to sign as she said, "You know Austen? I mean, that's not the most well-known line from P&P."

"My mom's an addict." He jerked a thumb at Duncan and signed as he said, "She even makes him watch with her—bribes him with tea and 'biscuits.'"

"Closed captioning?"

Duncan read her hands and laughed. His fingers tapped a "no" and he explained. Her eyes probably got the size of gobstoppers, but she couldn't help it. "He really makes up his own stories to the pictures?"

"He says they're more interesting than the real one."

As hard as she tried to scowl at the boy, his impish face, the dark hair and eyes that told a deeper story than their short acquaintance could uncover, all made it impossible. "For you, I'll forgive." She eyed Reese. "But you..."

"Chocolate shake?"

That she couldn't resist. "Okay. This time it'll work."

Duncan's impish expression had only been a faint echo of Reese's. "I guess that means there'll be a next time."

It went against every sensible thought her more rational side produced, but Portia just shrugged and signed to an eager Duncan, "Maaybeee..."

Why he'd thought a girl he'd never met before would just hop in his car and drive a few blocks to In-N-Out with a total stranger, Reese couldn't have explained. So, when they reached his old Volvo, and he moved to open the door for her, Portia started jogging toward Vista del Mar. "I'll meet you there." She held out her phone. "What street? Don't want to go to the wrong one."

"Harbor Boulevard—that one. Just up the way like a quarter mile. I—" But before he could offer the ride he knew she wouldn't accept, she'd torn across the road and up Vista del Mar.

Duncan nudged him and signed, *"She runs like a girl."*

You're too young to know what that even means. Regardless, he had to agree. "She does."

He'd barely found them a table—outside, of course—when a dark Buick pulled into the parking lot, and though he couldn't have explained how he knew it, he did. It was Portia. *Big car for a single girl. Maybe she's not…*

Her lack of ring—yes, he'd noticed it. No, he wasn't prepared to consider what that might mean—hinted otherwise. Portia swung from the car with the carefree air of someone totally comfortable in her own skin. A smile at Duncan—she obviously liked kids. However, when her gaze met his, the confidence evaporated.

That slight stumble as she stepped up on the sidewalk—since when had he ever thought something like that was cute? *Apparently since now.*

"Did you order?" Without waiting for an answer, she scooted toward the door. "I can go get them. Just tell me what you guys want."

Every instinct said he could trust her with Duncan—that he could insist on going—but wisdom said not to. Instead, he pulled out his wallet. "Would you mind? That'd be great."

Portia protested. "I've got—"

He thrust a ten at her. "Please? I wanted to say thanks, remember?"

If he'd put money on it, he'd have been certain she wouldn't agree. But after searching his face for something, and apparently finding it, she reached out to take it—between two fingers. *No chance to see if touching her hand is as electrifying the second time. On purpose, or just habit?*

Duncan signed his opinion of the whole thing without consideration for the fact that she could arrive at any moment and know exactly what they discussed. He told the boy as much. *"She'll know what you're saying. It's not like most people. She understands. Just remember that. No secret language with her."*

A grin split the boy's face.

Uh, oh…

Then Duncan did the most expected thing at the least expected time. *"Can I walk to Grandma's?"*

Once more, his father's admonitions filled his thoughts, but Reese pushed them back. *I can ask Dad about it…* That did it. He zipped a text message to his father. DUNCAN WANTS TO WALK FROM IN-N-OUT. WILL YOU MEET HIM?

The reply came seconds later. WILL YOU SEND HIM BEFORE I GET TO HARBOR?

Busted. Reese thought for a moment and zipped back, I'LL CROSS WITH HIM FIRST, THEN I'LL LET HIM GO WHEN YOU SAY YOU'RE GOING OUT THE DOOR.

I CAN HEAD OUT NOW.

As tempted as he was to let it happen, the five-minute walk would be over before their shakes made it. *Talk about awkward. "Oh, hi, Dad. This is the girl I just met and don't want to let go home yet."* That did it. He zipped back another message. WE'RE STILL WAITING FOR SHAKES. I'LL TEXT JUST BEFORE WE CROSS.

Reese's nerves jitterbugged as they waited. Duncan swung his feet and kicked the table as if it were the most interesting thing anyone could ever do. He also avoided Reese's gaze. *What's up with you?*

Just in time, he glanced up at the door, and a second later, his gaze reverted back to it again. Ponytail, hoodie, and jeans—he looked away once more. *Wonder how old she is? Seems older, but she looks eighteen at best. Two years of college ASL says she's not.*

Duncan jumped up to go help carry drinks, which earned him praise and Portia's undivided attention. She hardly looked at Reese as she set his chocolate shake, three dollars, and a nickel in front of him. "Oh, napkins. Sorry."

"Emma."

She froze in place. Their eyes met and held. "What did you say?"

"I said Emma. Paltrow version. Miss Bates."

A muttered remark under her breath that sounded suspiciously like, "You could be dangerous," buoyed his spirits as she dashed to get the napkins.

She's shy—sort of. I can work with that. That same rational place in his mind questioned why he was so keen to "work with" anything. *You just met her.*

As she returned, Duncan signed again, asking to walk to Grandma's. Portia eyed him. "Your parents live close?"

"Just a street over. I grew up on Pierpont."

"Which way?"

"Toward the beach."

All attention shifted to Duncan. Did he like visiting the ocean? Did they live close to Grandma & Grandpa? And when she learned that they didn't live in town, she asked how long their visit would be. Duncan's head shook as his index finger flicked up and down.

"Until the—"

Portia's phone rang. One look and she answered it. "Hey, Cress—oh. Okay, on my way back. Just distract everyone when I come in, okay? I don't want to hear it….what? Oh, brother. Why can't we get both? People can—whatever. Be right there. Just hang on."

She'd already stood and grabbed her cup and napkin. With a "nice to have met you" to Duncan, Portia turned and thanked him for the shake. "Thanks for inviting me. You probably saved me a boatload of drama. So, thanks."

And before he could get her number, she was gone.

Deflecting the questions proved easier than she'd expected. Her nephew, A.J. dragged her through the kitchen to show her the infinity pool off the side deck. "It's so *huge!*"

One look at it and her breath caught. No, it wasn't that big, not really. Their above-ground in the back yard wasn't much smaller, but it was impressive—all that water just coming up to the edge of… nothing. "It's gorgeous."

"Grandpa says we'll go in the hot tub after dinner if Mom says it's okay."

She hated to do it, but Portia knew her father all too well. He'd agree to something like that to make things easier on Cressida and Austin, but driving always gave him a headache, too. He'd be tense and want nothing more than to go in… all by himself. "Hey, buddy?"

"Yeah?" The boy looked up at her, eyes wide. He always knew her inflections.

"Do you *really* want to go in tonight, or could you wait?"

"I can wait. Aunt Jessica said we could play games, but I didn't want to disappoint Grandpa."

You're a good kid. Portia squeezed his shoulders and whispered a suggestion to go ask Grandpa if he'd mind waiting until the next day. "If he says he wants to do it tonight, though, maybe you should."

"I will! I'll tell Bella, too." With that, he raced off.

"And there goes any hope of discretion. Great."

Miranda's voice called from the kitchen. "Dinner's here!"

Wonder what we're having… Mexican or Chinese? In-N-Out? That thought brought a smile to her heart. *He was a nice guy. And Duncan… so cute. Wonder how old he is…*

Miranda announced the choice of pizza *or* Chinese. "We'll go shopping for real food in the morning, but tonight, this is what you get."

A silent, *"Because* someone *is too stubborn to do something more interesting"* followed, but they all heard it. Loud and clear.

Portia jumped in, helping Cressida's kids fill plates and get drinks. The kids sat in a little breakfast booth at one end of the kitchen, while everyone else scattered around the family room. Portia chose to sit with the kids, keeping one ear out for where the day's drama had begun and if a truce had been called yet or if they were just gearing up for the next battle.

She'd just taken a bite of lo mein when her mom called out, "Found a tree lot. It's really close. We could go tomorrow."

Anyone who didn't know the Spears family would have

sworn the precursor to World War III broke out, but it wasn't even an argument. Debates raged on the kind of trees they should get, if going to a parking lot tree "farm" was good enough, or if they should drive to one of the cut-your-own places that Google advertised. Make new ornaments or use the ones they'd brought from home?

Friendly insults, loud protests, laughter. Austin, her brother-in-law, brought in his plate to sit with the kids. Their eyes met, and Portia grinned. "Getting too heated in there for you?"

"I keep wanting to fix it, but Cressida's laughing, so it's just friendly, right?"

"Yep."

"You'd think after ten years I'd have you guys figured out." He reached over to stop little Charis from shoving more pizza in her mouth. "Chew that first," he admonished.

"If more than one person's laughing, it's good." Portia hesitated. "Usually."

She knew the next question, but it would take Austin a few minutes to ask it. Sure enough, only as they cleared the table and sent the kids to wash up did he ask. "How do you stand it?"

It hurt to answer—it always did when a friend asked, but Portia forced herself to be honest. "Who's the worst, Austin? I always say I'll never blow up about anything again, but…"

"Cressida… your parents… they don't get all worked up about this stuff."

Jessica entered before she could figure out how to respond to that. Answering then would just spark new drama. However, later she climbed the stairs and locked herself in her room for the night. Standing at the window, she gazed out over a nearly full moon—waxing, if she recalled her astronomy classes correctly—dancing on waves and pondered the question.

"I guess they just don't take things as personally."

She'd prayed for control over her temper more than anything else in her life—even, her perpetually single state. Once more, she got ready for bed with a prayer on her lips. "Okay, Lord. I'm here again. Praying for the same thing. Again. There has to be a way to get past this. Somehow. Even if it's just that I learn to keep my mouth shut until I've had thirty seconds to pray about it. How's that?"

Just as she fell asleep, Portia added one last thought. *And thanks for letting me meet Reese and Duncan. He didn't want me to go. I could see that. It felt nice. So thanks for that, Jesus.*

THREE

The crashing waves on the beach mesmerized Portia as she stood at her window the next morning. With long, brisk strokes, she brushed her hair until it should have crackled with static electricity. So close to the ocean, it just hung limp halfway to her waist. *Someday I should cut this.*

Every minute or two, her gaze strayed to where she'd seen Duncan standing there alone. The beach remained empty—not even a single surfer out on the swells that emerged and rolled into shore. Still, even as she shifted her brush to the other side of her head, Portia watched.

A knock jerked her from her reverie. "Yeah?"

Her youngest sister poked her head in the room. "Are you going somewhere?"

"No… I think I'll just stay here and read."

The sight of Tami's disappointment nearly changed her mind. "That's what Jessica said you'd say. I think I'll go to walk around downtown with Mom and Dad then."

"Have fun." The girl's listless reply caused Portia to call out, "Take note of anything you want to see again. We can go back tomorrow or Saturday."

"Really?"

That perked up grin almost guilted her into agreeing to go right then, but a second glance at the beach shifted it once more. *I came to read books on the beach. If we have to have Christmas* here, *then I'm doing what I like for once.*

That decided, Portia grinned. "Yep. And keep an ear out for what everyone else liked."

"I'll find some good bookstores. Mom says there should be lots here."

"You're just trying to tempt me. I know you…"

It worked. Tami grinned, waved, and shot down the hall. Squeaks on the stairs hinted she might be vaulting them two or three at a time. "Either that or A.J. was with her."

Below, the house came alive as people called for others, protested, asked if someone knew where a phone, some keys, a jacket, sunglasses, and even a coffee mug had gone. First, the front door banged open and slammed shut—several times. Then, as if from far away, car alarms beeped and moments later, engines roared to life.

Portia grabbed the paperback she'd brought and hesitated. "If somehow Reese and Duncan show up again, I am *not* going to have a book with a romantic couple plastered on the front." She reached first for her eReader and then her phone. "I'll just read on this. Easy to tuck away."

She peered over the railing to the depths below and called out. No one answered. She tried again from the bottom of the stairs. Nothing. Carrying a lightweight throw from a basket by the couch, Portia let herself out the front door, checked to see it was locked, and then remembered a water bottle.

"Car. I'll grab yesterday's from the car."

The walk turned out to be less chilly than she'd expected, and a glance at her phone told her it was a balmy sixty-four degrees. *Not bad… it's colder at home.* She strolled down Vista del Mar, across Harbor Boulevard again, and past the "Do Not Enter" sign.

Of course, once she reached the sand, "strolling" became impossible. Instead, she trudged through the mini "dunes" in search of some place to land. It took a few tries to find a comfortable reading spot. Her favorite meant the stiff morning breeze blew her hair out of her face—and occasionally kicked up sand, too. Her next favorite was a little too easy to miss… should any interesting people just happen to come walking along the beach.

I'm so pathetic.

Portia's only consolation was that she determined she was honestly just as eager to see Duncan as she was his father. "Or am I just happy to have someone to talk to who doesn't make me want to dump my coffee on his head?" Her voice sounded overloud—as if she'd tried to make it carry across a room. Quieter, almost in an under-breath, she added, "And book guys are safer. They have flaws you know all about up front, they never stink unless, again, you have fair warning, and there's no awkward moments—not for you, anyway."

So, resigned to a morning alone with her latest romantic friends, Portia spread out the throw to protect her from excess sand-age, curled up in a ball, and read her story. Well, she also tried *not* to hope that her poison green shirt would be visible to anyone who might happen to be wandering the beach.

"Chase Grahame," the hero of *The Cowboy's Demise,* had just learned he'd lost his job when a shadow fell over her. Without looking up, she muttered, "It's just wrong when the *beach* is overcast—even in December."

"Yes, it is. But it is—often."

"Wha—?" Portia tore her gaze from the phone screen and looked up into Reese's smiling face. "Oh!"

"I hoped you'd come out today."

Not until *after* she'd glanced around behind him and asked where Duncan was did she realize it might sound as if she wasn't happy to see him. "I mean, it's nice to see you, too, but I thought you brought him here so…" She swallowed at the raised eyebrows he gave her. "…he could… dig for crabs?"

"He went to Bible study with my mom." Reese hunkered down on his heels and gave her a sheepish smile. "So, I thought I'd come see if you happened to come back."

She held up her phone. "The family's out shopping, but I wanted to read."

"To read?"

All the angst that she hadn't even tried to contain still piled up until it wobbled and crashed down around her. "Christmas. At the beach. Who thought this was a good idea? I'll tell you. My crazy sisters. 'Let's rent a beach house,' they said. 'It's probably our last Christmas with just us,' they said."

"'It'll be fun,' they said?"

There, her face flamed. "Yeah. Something like that."

"And you didn't think you'd enjoy a week—"

"Two. Two weeks." She shrugged. "If it was June, sure. But for *Christmas*?"

He sank back on his backside and sat cross-legged before her. "And you were out-voted?"

With her phone stowed in her pocket, Portia stared at the sand before her, occasionally scooping up big handfuls and watching it pour out again. "They were—Miranda and Jessica. No one else wanted to come."

"And yet, here you are. Majority loses in your family?"

That's when she got her first good look of the day—at him, anyway. Still the same darkish, semi-wavy hair. Still the same piercing eyes—were they blue? Green? Gray? Pale brown? *Is that even a thing?* She couldn't tell. *Probably gray, then. Like me.* But today, Reese had a fair amount of shadow on his face. *Must have to shave a lot.*

"Portia?"

That snapped her out of a momentary lapse of self-control. *You cannot think he's cute. You're going home. He's staying here—or going wherever he lives.* Of course, after that thought, she'd lost him again. "I'm sorry, what'd you say?"

"I asked," a small smile played around the corners of his mouth, which only reheated her cheeks again. "—if your family goes by the 'majority loses' standard of voting."

"Oh, no. But this whole trip is their gift—well, plus Mom's contribution, which is probably pretty hefty."

"So everyone else gave up what they wanted so they could give a gift that no one wants." He leaned back on his hands and eyed her as he added, "I don't think I get your family."

If he'd sounded mocking or judgmental, she might not have accepted it so well, but that wasn't a sentiment Portia could argue with. "Yeah, well, I don't either."

They gazed at each other—not quite allowing their eyes to meet. After a few more awkward seconds, Reese rose and held out his hand. "C'mon. Let's walk. I'll show you my favorite place."

Every instinct said walking alone with a guy she didn't know was a great way to become the next victim of human trafficking, but Portia did it. And she'd forgotten her reaction to him taking her hand—even for the brief moment he did. *So not smart.*

They'd made it halfway to where the tide rolled in before he shook out her blanket, folded it, and draped it over one arm. "Okay, tell me about these sisters—and your parents."

"Why?"

After a sidelong glance her way, Reese shrugged. "I don't know. They sound interesting. Not everyone has a family who would give up what they want for the few who want something else. Besides, I don't know anyone with five daughters."

Portia looked for a way to get out of it, but a glance his way stopped her. "Well, Cressida's the oldest. Rumor has it Dad threatened to buy a Toyota Cressida if Mom went through with that name." She shrugged at his chuckle. "It's supposedly true. She's married to Austin—ten years almost. And they have three kids. A.J.—he's about Duncan's age."

"Eight?"

She nodded. "Yep. I thought so. And then Bella. She's five. Charis is barely three."

"A.J…."

"Stands for Austin James—after his dad and grandpa."

"*Bella*, and then *Charis*. Are they going to have a David, Ethan, and Fiona?"

Not everyone caught the names unless they saw the letters spelled out. "Nope. Cressida says she's done. They're moving to Idaho this spring, so that was part of the reason for the big Christmas."

"Ahh… and who comes next?"

"Miranda. Mom and Dad were going to do the alphabetical order thing, too, but then Mom discovered that Shakespeare coined Jessica. She never really liked the name until that. So… we have them mostly in order. Miranda's twenty-eight and is a social worker for the elderly."

"Married?"

She shook her head and bent to pick up a shell half hidden in the sand. "No, but she's engaged. Gavin's coming down for Christmas afternoon."

Reese repeated it all as if studying for a test. "And Jessica?"

"Twenty-seven. She just found out she passed the bar exam—works for legal aid in Los Angeles."

"Didn't you say she likes to argue? Sounds like she chose a good job for that."

There, Portia couldn't disagree. "Dad always said that her childhood was preparation for her career, and now that she passed, she can call it an occupational hazard." Loyalty forced her to add, "If you get in a bind, you want her on your side. She's relentless and fierce in her pursuit of justice." Something about that description seemed harsher than Portia meant, so she added, "She's also the beauty of the family."

Reese stopped, gave her a definite once-over, and shrugged. "One *of*, maybe." And before Portia could deflect, he continued. "And she's… married?"

"Single. Has an on-again-off-again boyfriend. We all hope more off than on."

"Don't like him?"

That wasn't a fair assessment, but Portia had never been able to articulate it. "No, he's a really nice guy, but…"

"So, you don't like him for her… or maybe her for him?"

The tide had moved up the beach a bit, and as he steered her closer to the looser sands, she considered that idea. "Yeah. Actually, I think that's a great way of putting it."

"Then there's… you? You said you had a younger sister, right?"

"Yes. I'm next and then Tami."

"So you're what, twenty? Twenty… one?"

"Twenty-five, actually." She started to move on with Tami, but Reese insisted on hearing more about her, too. "Well, I run the daycare at our church. We serve the community—have for the last forty years or so. I took over once I graduated. I love kids." As she spoke, she realized where they were going. "The pier?"

"Favorite spot. Anyway, your love of kids shows. Duncan keeps calling you 'the friendly lady.'"

They had another hundred yards to go before reaching the pier–more than enough time to tell about her little sister Tami before they reached the pilings. "She's fourteen." Portia braced herself for the response. *So help me, if you call her an oops, I'm outta here.*

"Quite an age gap there. Is it rude to ask if it was by choice? I never know if you're supposed to pretend you don't notice or what."

"Well, that was better than the usual, 'Oh, an oops baby, huh?' So rude."

They walked several more yards before he spoke again. "I doubt most people mean to be, but that's got to be hard for a kid to hear over and over."

Once more, she relaxed. "Yeah." Then, the story just spilled out. "Actually, it wasn't unplanned, just unexpected. They never tried *not* to have kids. But after me, none came for three or four years." She swallowed a lump at the memory of the series of miscarriages that followed. "Mom lost a few after that—for several years. Then she thought maybe she was going through early menopause, but nope. Tami came along."

"No Shakespeare for her?"

Surprise stopped Portia in her tracks until she realized she hadn't used Tami's full name. "It's actually Tamora, but no one calls her that. She'd probably refuse to answer. None of us love our names, but she… totally not a fan."

"Spoiled?"

Despite all efforts to remain neutral, she couldn't. Portia bristled. "If you ask Miranda and Jessica, yes. Dad's trying to keep her too little too long. Mom's not pushing her hard enough. But she's a lot like Cressida was—young in some ways, way mature in others. And she's so *nice*. We don't want her any different. She's just a *nice* girl. And there aren't enough of those, you know?"

By the look of him, he didn't know, so Portia reinforced it. "Trust me. Fourteen-year-olds are awful half the time. Tami's not. We'd rather keep her that way."

As they reached the pier, Reese led her under it and up the stairs on the other side. "C'mon. You'll love this."

"Only if you promise to tell me about you… and Duncan." She swallowed hard at realizing something she hadn't actually considered until that moment. "His mother?"

"That's a long story."

A glance down the beach showed their path—looked like half a mile or so. *That didn't seem that far when we were walking it. Odd…* As they reached the top, she gazed out over the boards. "It's a long pier."

Reese shoved his hands in his pockets and nodded. "Okay…"

FOUR

Gulls flew overhead, crying out for whatever they wanted. The pier, aside from them, however, was deserted. Reese shot Portia a sidelong look and swallowed a lump in his throat. Telling his story seemed to be a perfect way to run off the first girl who had interested him since the day he'd learned he was a father.

"If you don't want to tell me, I get it. I tend to just blurt out whatever I'm thinking without considering the other person."

"No, it's not that." He dug his fists deeper into his pockets and gazed out over the water. One step. Another. Once a rhythm began, so did he. "Graduation week in college. I'd landed my dream job and was crazy excited. Did a bunch of stupid stuff that included more alcohol than was wise and spending time with a girl I'd avoided all semester."

He felt it—the distance forming. Could he head it off by taking the out she'd offered? Common sense told him it would only push her away even more. "I don't have to tell you more—which is good. I don't remember much."

For two years he'd enjoyed the perfect job, the perfect church in the perfect town, and his perfect girlfriend—all the things he'd lost one Labor Day afternoon. "I just got this call from Corinne asking me to meet her at the McDonald's near our old dorms. I said no at first." The familiar lump that always formed when he thought about how close he'd come to never meeting his son nearly choked him.

"Oh, that would have been horrible, and you wouldn't have ever known it."

Should have guessed you'd get it.

"What made you change your mind?"

"I don't know. I just had this overwhelming sense that I had to do it, so I told her I'd be there in a few hours—holiday traffic and all." When he'd slowed to a slug's pace, he didn't know, but Reese forced each foot forward. "She was already there when I arrived—sitting by the window, watching for me."

They reached the end of the pier before he even attempted to continue. With the waves below and the gulls overhead, the familiar heaviness that came with each retelling of his story descended. He gripped the railing and prayed that she'd understand. Then he stole a glance at her and asked the Lord just why it mattered that she did.

Portia stood there beside him, hands gripping the rails only a foot from his, head thrown back, eyes closed, face turned toward the sun. "I see why this is your favorite place," she murmured. "I feel… peace."

"Isn't it great? Spent hours fishing off this pier when I was a kid—just me and Mom or me and Grandpa."

She turned to face him, eyebrows drawn together. "Your mom?"

"Dad doesn't fish, but he filets like nobody's business. Mom fishes—grew up on a farm, so…" As she turned back to bask in the sun, Reese continued. "I sat there in my car praying for something I couldn't articulate. I just knew something was wrong."

"How old was Duncan by then?"

"Eighteen months. I walked into that McDonald's trying to figure out if she needed money, was going to accuse me of something horrible, or just wanted to know about Jesus. I was hoping rather than expecting that one," he added with a sigh that he hated himself for. "I mean, I hadn't done a stellar job of treating her like a Christian guy should treat girls, you know?"

"Alcohol makes fools of the best of people," Portia

murmured. "I've seen it."

"Right?" Reese took a deep breath and leaned his forearms on the railing. "I came around the corner and saw him—Duncan sitting in one of those restaurant high chairs. Cutest kid you've ever seen."

"Well, duh. He's your son. Of course—"

Right about then must have been when Portia realized what she'd said. He turned toward her, head resting in one hand and grinning at her reddening face. "Oh, really?"

"Shut up and tell the story."

He did—in probably more vivid detail than he'd intended. As usual, each detail pressed against him until Reese almost couldn't breathe. The instant understanding, the way Corinne wouldn't look him in the eye, the way Duncan wouldn't *stop* looking at him—even when she got up to go get something from the car.

"Then he started crying. I didn't know how to make him happy, and she was still digging in the back seat, so I picked him up, trying to comfort him, you know?"

Portia moved a bit closer and laid one hand on his arm but said nothing.

The day relived itself in his mind and emotions as he told about the moment he'd seen her set a suitcase down on the sidewalk and jog around to the driver's door. "One second she was right there with us, and it was almost like the next she climbed into that car and slammed the door shut. *Then* she looked at me. I think she mouthed, 'I'm sorry,' but maybe that's just wishful thinking. A couple of minutes later, I got a text message telling me to go get the suitcase and that there was an envelope in the front pocket."

Maybe it was his imagination—wishful thinking and all—but Reese would have sworn she scooted a bit closer as she murmured, "I hate that women can do this—keep a child from its father like that."

"Well," he added, "you can figure out the rest. There was a letter and his birth certificate. She'd just learned he was deaf after a bout of meningitis that almost killed him. She 'couldn't take it anymore,' so she gave him to me. I could turn him over to social services if I didn't want him."

That did it. Portia turned to him, unleashing an explosion of opinions that ranged from criminal abandonment to gratitude that Corinne hadn't just put Duncan up for adoption without giving him a choice. She finished up with a question no one had yet asked him. "Was it hard to get legal stuff squared away? Like insurance and his name? Did she leave you a way to contact her?" And before he could answer that, she added, "Wait, didn't you say you had a girlfriend?"

"Yeah, I did. I'd even started praying about proposing."

"What happened with her?"

Reese turned around, leaned his arms back on the railing and stared up the length of the pier. "Nothing."

"Noth—like it was just over, or everything was normal and then…"

"We went nowhere fast. She wasn't ready to be a mom, and I'd become a packaged deal." At Portia's indignant huff, he urged her forward. "C'mon, she wasn't an ogre. It's one thing to have the Lord decide that you are who He wants to be a Deaf kid's parent. It's another to sign up for it just because you kind of like the kid's dad."

Portia rolled her eyes at him—deliberately. She stopped, made sure he looked at her face, and rolled them. "And that's what I think of that. She didn't 'kind of like' you if you were thinking proposal. What ever happened to 'for better or worse, sickness and health, deafness and adorability'?"

"Not sure that last one is in there, but even if it was… we hadn't made vows yet. I hadn't even asked her to." In a move that befitted longtime friends better than new acquaintances, he nudged her with his elbow and gave her a slight smile. "But it means something that you care. It does. Thanks."

It was the perfect time to do it. He'd been thinking about it for the better part of twenty-four hours. But how…? Would she think he was crazy? Creepy?

"Reese?

"It's—" He froze. "Yeah?"

Portia stopped in her tracks as well and shoved her hands in her hoodie's pockets. "Never mind. What?"

Though Reese knew he should insist she continue, he also knew he'd never get it out if he did. "First, are you hungry?"

"Yeah, why?"

"Beach House Fish has great red snapper if you like fish…"

She wrinkled her nose. "How about… chicken?"

Maybe *he* was the chicken, but Reese ran with that. "Oh, no. That could be a deal breaker."

A frown morphed into a weakly repressed smile. "What kind of deal?"

"I…" *Here goes nothing.* "Look, you're here until the second, right?"

"Yep."

"Me, too. Then I go home."

She gave him a wary look. "Where's that?"

"Newhall."

Surprise lit her face. "Wow, you're only like an hour from us."

Well, that's a good start…

"I just assumed you lived down here or were from out of state."

So you wondered where I lived. That's a good sign… With a sharp reminder to himself that he was just asking if she'd have time to get to know him, not asking her to marry him or anything like that, Reese blurted out, "So… not too far to hang out now and then?"

Her face fell. Without even trying to hide it, she just nodded. "Yeah, maybe."

"What'd I say?" Even as he asked, he knew she wouldn't answer.

But she did. "It's stupid. I mean, it's Christmas. I don't know what I was thinking. Yeah, sure. We could meet at a park and—"

She wants to see me here. Well, good. I was just getting to that. "I know Duncan would like that," Reese began, "but I was hoping for time just with you—if we got to know each other well enough to both want that after we go home." The words had been rushed and probably a bit incomprehensible, but he'd done it.

I don't remember asking a girl out ever being this hard.

"Wait. You want—what *do* you want?"

"Well… Saturday night, the Olivas Adobe is having their candlelight tour—luminarias, the kids do the journey of Joseph and Mary, music…"

They stood in front of Beach House Fish, the finest and only restaurant on the pier, Reese with his hands in his pockets feeling fifteen again, Portia with her arms half-crossed but her hands also still stuffed in her hoodie pocket. "So… you're asking me out."

"Yeah."

"While I'm on Christmas vacation with my family? I'm supposed to go out with a guy?"

Reese just smiled.

Smacking the smile off his face—Portia's greatest goal in life at that point. "Just what is that grin supposed to mean?"

"You are getting awfully worked up about something you are avoiding and irritated about."

A protest formed, but just as she began saying, "What do you think—?"

Reese continued. "I mean, your family is off shopping and doing other holiday stuff *together*, and you just happen to come out and sit where we met yesterday because you *don't* want to see me again and you *do* want to spend all the time you can with said loved ones. I see."

If only her hair didn't inspire a chameleon effect on her face. Portia glared at him. "Just because I wasn't excited about abandoning all our goofy family traditions so we could pretend to be people we aren't, while staying at that huge house for a couple of weeks, doesn't mean I don't love my family."

"Never said you didn't."

"And—" She lost steam trying to recall his other "accusations." Remembrance stoked the fire of her ire, and Portia kicked it into overdrive. "As for you—"

"I'm just the guy who enjoyed meeting someone who is transparent and authentic with people." He kicked a bit of sand between the boards of the pier and gazed at her.

Those eyes. Portia swallowed hard. They seemed to hold secrets she had to know. Still, pride said he just assumed she was chasing after him. *And wanting to see Duncan again isn't chasing anyone.* When her conscience protested that she'd revised that story a bit, pride kicked in double time.

Great speeches about how he'd convicted her about her attitude and she'd be spending the rest of her vacation investing in people she knew and loved filled her mind but refused to cross her lips. She stammered, took a step back, and like a five-year-old who got caught stealing from the cookie jar, fled.

Not until she'd reached her bedroom window did she stop, and there, while looking out over the wide view of the beach, she saw Reese walking back the route they'd come, head down, hands in his pockets. As he neared the house, he looked up and gazed at her window.

"Can he see me?"

At the road, he glanced back over his shoulder, presumably at the house, but kept walking along the beach until she couldn't see him anymore.

Portia flopped on the bed and rolled to her back. "I can't believe I just did that. Nice guy. Cute. Christian. Adorable son. *Deaf.* I'm so stupid." She dug for her phone until she remembered that she only knew his first name. Reese. From Newhall. She could hear him telling her his last name… jogging backward up that beach. But the name eluded her.

"Yep. I'm officially the stupidest person on the planet."

FIVE

The tree took up a significant portion of the center of the living room. How she'd managed to convince the family to move the coffee table and put that tree in the middle, Portia still didn't know. Had there not been an enormous "theater" and game room, it never would have happened. *The Spears can't be without their TV addictions.*

She'd even figured out how to hide the light cords so none of the kids—or their somewhat klutzy father—would trip. Popcorn and cranberries created "snow" all over the floor as everyone "sewed" lengthy strings of garland while she fiddled with lights to get out of doing it. Dad might be klutzy with his feet, but Portia and needles didn't mix well.

"Winter Wonderland" came through the bullet speaker just as A.J. brought her the first strand—all two and a half feet of it. "That's beautiful! Thank you. Go see if Grandma has another needle threaded for you."

The doorbell rang just as Jessica brought the next one. She practically threw it at Portia and dashed for the door. All peace and goodwill raced after her and slipped out while everyone in the living room listened to her greet Damon. Portia jerked the needle on Jessica's strand until it jabbed her in the hand. *So much for "off again."*

Miranda rose and stormed to the door. "Hey, Jessica. Can you come here a minute?"

"Damon just—"

"Arrived. We *know*. In the game room?"

The living room grew quiet—awkwardly, eerily, miserably, and a few dozen more adverbs that her English professor would have docked her for—quiet. Portia glanced at her mom. Lips thin, slow, shallow, deliberate breathing. *Not happy*. A moment later, she snipped off the end of the thread with more force behind those scissors than necessary—*oops*.

Just as Damon entered, raised voices did, too. While not exactly distinct, even Damon couldn't miss the gist. This was a *family* event, and he didn't belong. It didn't faze him—not even when Miranda's voice rose to a clear pitch. "—and my *fiancé* who *will* be family isn't even here, because *we* agreed that this was current *family only* until Christmas afternoon."

"Anyone have a spare needle for me?"

Mom just handed one over and asked how his drive was. Damon plopped a bottle of wine on the end table and began stringing a section with a grin and a short story about seeing a police chase. "No pit maneuver, though."

That is going to get knocked over, break, and we'll be paying a fortune to replace a couch or a rug. Seething, and without bothering to pretend she wasn't irritated to see him, Portia snatched up the bottle and carried it to the kitchen, muttering her opinions on leaving it where something could happen.

"Hey, thanks for protecting it. That's an expensive bottle."

At the doorway to the dining room, Portia paused and stared at him. *Are you really that stupid or that arrogant?* It only took half a second to decide on both. "I was talking about the couch. This can go in the garbage for all I care."

"You'll be paying for it, then."

She raised an eyebrow—she hoped. "Not hardly."

With the bottle on the counter, she dashed for the game room and stepped in. "What's he doing here?"

"He just was in the area and asked if he could come. No one cared that he was there last Christmas!"

Maybe it wasn't the most tactful response, but she frankly didn't care. "That's what you think. We *said* no one but family for the big stuff. Tree. Christmas din—"

Jessica's retort came fast, fierce, and with a razor sharp edge. "Well, maybe if you ever *had* a boyfriend, you'd think differently."

A million retorts fought for preeminence, which only meant that not one made it past her lips. She gaped at both sisters, clamped her teeth shut, spun on her heel and bolted. Through the kitchen, bypassing the living room, and straight up the stairs. "I'm just *done*."

As she stormed into her room, a few out-of-place items gave her the perfect excuse to vent her frustrations. Brush back on the dresser—with a bit of excessive force. Suitcase back in the closet—ditto. She heard footsteps on the stairs and raced to lock the door—just in time. The knob tried to twist before Miranda's voice called to her.

"Portia? We're supposed to be doing the *tree*."

"Yeah. Well, go for it. There are exactly the same number of people down there right now as there were ten minutes ago. Have fun."

Of course, Miranda's snarky comments about her childishness had merit. Portia wouldn't pretend otherwise. However, after a lifetime of watching the rules Jessica set up only apply to her when she decided they should, Portia had had it. She didn't respond.

Miranda banged.

The hoodie went on a hook by the door.

Miranda yelled.

Earbuds could solve that.

Her purse sat in the window—not quite wide enough for a seat, but definitely wide enough for the potted plant and her purse. As she dug for the earbuds, and ignored Miranda's insults and eventually her pleas for help, Portia set up her phone to play the same playlist she'd been listening to downstairs. She'd read that paperback she'd left behind.

A glance out over the water—the moon was larger tonight. Maybe she really couldn't tell, but it felt like it. Her gaze shifted left to where she'd first seen Duncan. And there, standing right in that same spot, was someone with an enormous sign. At least, she thought someone was behind it. The thing had to be as wide as a volleyball net and twice as tall. On some kind of poles, too. But no—right there in the middle were two extra but seemingly-connected poles. Legs.

She squinted, but the words on it looked a bit skippy. A snap with her phone camera did no good when she tried to zoom in. It had to be Reese. It had to be. Didn't it?

In a last ditch effort to read it, she snapped off the light to her room, ready to use her flash and see if that would work. She didn't need it. There in giant glowing letters came the message. *"A quarrel, ho, already! What's the matter? ~Portia"* Below that, *"Forgive me?"*

Fumbling for the flashlight app nearly made her drop her phone… twice. But she found it. She flashed it long at the window. Turned it off. Again. Off. And that's when she realized the light switch would work better.

Portia dashed to the door, flipped it on and off a few times. Fast. Slow. Fast again. Then she slipped on her hoodie, shoved the phone in the pocket, and listened at the door. A peek under it showed no shoes. Crazy? Probably. Still, she didn't care.

It took only a moment to slip through it. Half a minute later, she'd crept down the stairs. Little Bella nearly caught her as the girl dashed past, presumably for the bathroom, but in less than two minutes from the time she read that message, she'd slipped out the door and raced down the drive to Vista del Mar. Again.

When the first lights flashed, Reese didn't know for sure if it was a phone, a flashlight, or a TV show of some kind. But when it was followed by the whole room lights going off and on again, his hopes rose. Maybe she'd say yes to the festivities at the adobe. Maybe.

The crunch of shoes on sandy concrete reached his consciousness long before Reese saw her—and then it disappeared as she slogged through the soft sand to where he stood still rolling up the canvas sign his parents' church used to announce VBS every year. Moonlight looked good on her—too good. "Hey…"

"So, I was a jerk…"

They didn't have time for misunderstandings that took weeks to work through. Reese let the poles flop over and held out his hand. "Walk with me?"

Portia didn't answer, but she did put her hand in his and allow him to lead her closer to shore.

And some contrary, self-defeating part of him decided to say, "You really shouldn't be coming out in the dark to meet a guy you've seen twice."

"Tell me about it. That's what took so long. I had to go back for my taser."

Reese froze, gaping. "Wha—?"

"Gotcha."

Waves rolled in with that deceptive rhythm that always felt so precise—and never was. And as if she could read his mind, Portia remarked on it. "Is it true about waves?"

"What…?"

"That they come in groups of seven and that last is the biggest?"

Had she been reading up on surfing? Maybe trying to learn a bit to have something to talk about? That couldn't be it. She'd probably expected not to see him again. And that did it for him. "Short answer, no. Can I see your phone?"

It took effort not to read into the lack of hesitation as she pulled it from her hoodie pocket. "Why?"

Her asking *after* he took it proved equally difficult to ignore. Still, he added his number into her contacts, one-handed and slower than a kid eating liver and spinach, and passed it back. "This way if I say something offensive, you can send me angry text messages."

She held out her hand as well. "Come on. Give it over."

"I don't need yours if you have mine. You don't have—"

"Of course, I do." Portia took the phone and Reese tried not to be so hyper-aware of the second she released his hand to type the number in. As she passed it back, she added, "You never know when you'll have to resort to smoke signals to ask forgiveness. A text or call is easier."

Walking on the beach with a girl. He hadn't done it since he was about eight and looking for starfish—not unless you counted helping with youth rallies at his parents' church and showing some barely-a-teen how to get back to the van for her forgotten sunblock. Oh, and usually two hours too late.

There they were, walking along the shore in the moonlight, not talking even. And no longer holding hands. It hadn't meant to be a romantic gesture, taking her hands like that, but now…

Just as he was about to reach for it once more, she shoved her hands in her pockets and her whole demeanor shifted. "Damon showed up tonight."

"Damon's the… fiancé?"

"Jessica's boyfriend. It's supposed to be *family* only. It was even *Jessica's* idea, but there he is, just showing up as if he didn't know he wasn't supposed to be there. He *did*. He just didn't care."

Nothing he could say would help. Sometimes, people just do stupid, thoughtless, selfish things. Nothing anyone else can say will make it anything less. He racked his brains for the perfect line from one of his mother's movie adaptations. Austen and Gaskell both failed him. In his defense, he wanted to protest to no one in particular, he really didn't know much from them at all. However, a few lines here and there had become inside jokes between the Whitakers.

Probably need to confess that at some point.

Just as he was about to give up and ask for her hand again—it came to him. That movie with the heart transplant recipient. His mother had swooned over David Duchovny's line for days—possibly weeks.

It was stupid, too soon, and way too nerve-wracking to be

healthy, but despite every warning bell and alarm going off in his heart, Reese tried a paraphrase on that. "So… I feel about twelve and really pathetic, but I have to ask."

She stopped and stared at him, waiting. As if that wouldn't make it even worse—even harder. "Well? What?"

He'd meant to ask with every ounce of endearing charm he could muster if she'd consider allowing him to hold her hand again. It's what his mind devised as he gazed at her. Alas, his lips botched the translation and the request came out something like, "So, can I have your hand back?"

Things went from bad to worse as he added, "That's not what I meant!"

Portia eyed him with an expression too easily misread.

"I just—"

"Want to hold my hand. Got it." And without even looking at him oddly again, she pulled hers from her pocket and stared at it. "Why is holding hands so…"

"Connecting?" Reese waited for a nod—one that he didn't get—before continuing. "I think that's it. It connects people to each other. Sometimes just to show compassion or to help. Others because it's the only way to indicate a deeper connection. Then—"

"What's ours? Why'd you ask?"

Reese only had one chance to get it right, but he also didn't have time to consider much more. "That would be reason…" he counted. "Um, four. It's how some of us indicate a hope for a deeper connection… someday."

"But you just met me."

"And we only have eleven days to see if we even want to bother. If we were both from here, it'd be easy. It could take months just to go out on a date. No biggie. But once we're gone from here, unless we've taken time to figure out if we're interested at all, it won't happen." Reese stopped in his tracks and stared at her. "How come I couldn't articulate that earlier?"

"Dunno." She looked everywhere but at him until Reese decided she'd turn and run again. But she didn't. Instead, she shuffled her feet, turning a non-existent shell over with her toe or digging for a crab. "So, what time should I be ready tomorrow? And is Duncan coming? What do I wear?"

The grin he felt form probably made him look creepy in the moonlight, but Reese decided he didn't care—not at all. He started to turn back, but she tugged him the other way. "I'm not ready to go home."

"Good…" Giving her hand a squeeze—so natural he almost didn't realize he'd done it. "Dress however you like. I'll bring Duncan if you want. Pick you up—"

"Meet me at the do-not-enter sign that you like to ignore."

"Fine, I'll meet you there at five. We'll do the tour and maybe get something to eat afterward?"

Perhaps it was his imagination—Reese wouldn't put it past himself—but it felt as though she moved a bit closer, slowed her gait. Relaxed. "If there's no drama, yeah. That'd be great."

SIX

Telling Duncan that Portia would be joining them at the Adobe turned out to be a non-issue. He'd watched with careful attention, nodded, and signed his approval. *"I like her. She's nice. She's* really *nice. And she signs."*

Reese stood before the mirror, ready to shave and froze at his reflection. "Does she like beards?"

Even considering shaving off his scruff for a girl he'd just met and didn't even know couldn't be more stupid. Yet, the thought had passed through his mind. "That should either scare or amuse me…"

Their house was a small one—just two bedrooms, a bath, living room, and kitchen. Some of the houses on their street were worth minor fortunes, and compared to what his parents had paid for it over twenty years ago, theirs was, too. But the path from bathroom to kitchen had always seemed enormous when he'd been Duncan's age. Now, after a dozen steps, he could see his mother standing at the stove.

"Morning, Mom. Where's Duncan?"

"He and your dad went over to the donut shop."

"They'd better not come back without a maple bar."

She lifted a plate from over a bowl at the back of the stove and set the bowl atop it. "Oatmeal?"

"Sure. Thanks." She beamed as he kissed her cheek and whispered, "Still my favorite mother."

"Always my favorite son." It probably should have been a

hint—one of those ones that sends you running out the door before everything can go from sweet to awkward in one bite of oatmeal, but Reese was hungry, and his mom was swift. "So, who's Portia?"

Oatmeal flew across the table as his windpipe rejected the inhaled porridge. He coughed, she pounded, he gulped water, she folded her arms and stared. Reese had only one option. Answer. "A girl I met." Seriously, the woman should have been drumming her fingers on her arm and tapping one foot—both, even—by the intensity in her eyes. "On the beach."

A silent order to elaborate blasted him.

"So Duncan and I went to the beach. I got a call. Dad keeps saying I need to let him do things, so…"

The story spilled forth—all of it. Every single bit, from being surprised and relieved that she signed to what he'd been doing with the VBS sign the previous day. "Don't let me forget to take that back to the church tomorrow." Just as she opened her mouth, he added, "One thing bothers me, though."

"What's that? She sat opposite him, her elbows on the table and hands folded under her chin.

"I was so relieved when I saw her signing. It's like my brain said, 'Oh, she signs. She's safe.'"

She scowled. "That isn't healthy."

"That's what I'm saying! Why did I think that? I mean, I recognized it right away," Reese hastened to add. "I think that's good at least. But still. It kind of freaked me out."

"What do you like about her?"

Of all the questions his mother could have asked, she zeroed on the one that had the least satisfying answer. Several spoonsful of oatmeal disappeared untasted. "Um… it's hard to explain without sounding stupid."

"Try me."

Here goes nothing. He scooped up more oatmeal but didn't take that bite. Instead, he tried to find a better way of saying it—tried and failed. "It sounds so stupid, but I like that I'm interested. I haven't been—not since that day." Desperate not to remain as pathetic-sounding as he knew he did, Reese piled on everything he could think of. "She's really good with Duncan—natural. And she obviously loves her family but doesn't pretend they're perfect. Actually, they sound like a mess, but she's not, so how bad can they be?"

"You said she didn't want to come, right?" At his nod of agreement, she smiled. "Then everything they do will feel exaggerated to the negative, don't you think?"

Of course it would. Duh. "That's why you're the mom and I'm the kid."

Reese managed to finish his food, rinse the bowl, and pour himself a cup of coffee before the question he'd forgotten to expect emerged. "And when do we get to meet her?"

A reasonable explanation of why that wouldn't work formed on his lips and disappeared in the words, "If I can talk her into it, tomorrow. At church."

"Bring her over for lunch afterward."

Despite the pain of coffee burning his lips and tongue, Reese gulped down a bit to avoid responding to that one. *Ow!*

The scent of biscuits, sausage, and sizzling bacon greeted Portia as she emerged from her room gritty-eyed and cotton-mouthed. *Are they seriously making breakfast?* Bella raced past. "Hurry up! It's almost done! Grandma's making cinnamonies!"

Translation: Mom's making dessert and they're serving it for breakfast. So Mom has to make more.

Miranda greeted her with a hot mug of coffee, doctored with enough mocha powder, half-and-half, and sugar to please the most discerning mocha latte lover. "You slept in…"

It was probably an innocent comment, but Portia heard censure in it. "I thought that was what vacation is for."

"Yep. That's what I told Jessica and Tami."

Great. I just entered a battle and chose sides without knowing it.

"Can someone pour the orange juice?"

Before she could move, Cressida bolted for the fridge. "Got it."

It'd be a gauntlet that she didn't want to answer herself, but Portia tossed it down anyway. "Why are we making a big breakfast when no one eats one?"

"It's almost ten o'clock. It's more like *brunch*." Jessica eyed her with a look that said, "I dare you to argue."

And maybe if she wasn't looking forward to her first real date… *ever*… she might have taken that dare and lobbed it back in her sister's face. But the memory of her plans for that evening resurfaced just as the words registered—and memory won. "Whatever. I'm going out on the deck."

The sounds of cars and the ocean collided as she opened French doors leading to the deck. If she chose a chair nearest the cliff, she could even see a bit of sand and shore. And cars… lots of cars. Were people heading out of town to spend Christmas with family up or down the coast? Were some of those people coming to Ventura to be with family?

"Should've brought my book out here." She pulled out her phone to revert back to the one she'd attempted to read the previous morning, and saw a notification.

A text message.

From Reese.

GOOD MORNING.

Another one followed that. LOOKING FORWARD TO TONIGHT.

Her thumbs would get carpal tunnel issues if she didn't quit using them like needles knitting words together across cyberspace. HI. JUST WOKE UP. SOMEONE KEPT ME OUT UNTIL ALL HOURS.

A grin formed at the response. I SEEM TO REMEMBER TRYING TO TURN BACK SEVERAL TIMES.

If he only knew how insecure those turn backs had made her. Only the soft squeeze of his hand over hers had assured her he hadn't been trying to get rid of her each time she'd kept going.

And I only did it deliberately once—just once to feel that squeeze. The time after that, I let him turn us back. That counts for not taking advantage of the situation.

A voice beside her nearly cost Portia her phone. She fumbled as it flew into the air and managed to force it back down into her lap instead of over a cliff. "A.J.!"

"Hi! Mom wants to know if you want anything. She says there's rice cakes and cream cheese if breakfast is too much."

That she could get behind. "Please. Thanks."

"I'll bring it out. Grandpa's going to take me down to the ocean in a bit. Want to come?"

"Sure. I'll show you how to find sand crabs."

That stopped him mid-turn and made him plop over onto her legs. "You know how to *do* that?"

"Sure do."

"Be right back!"

Another message appeared just then. WASN'T COMPLAINING ABOUT THAT, BTW.

How was she supposed to respond to that? After a few false attempts, she tried deflection. WHAT ARE YOU AND DUNCAN DOING TODAY?

The deflection failed. Reese zipped back, IS THAT A HINT THAT I SHOULDN'T ASK AGAIN?

A.J. appeared just as Portia deleted her third attempt at a response. "Grandpa says he's going to take a quick ride, first, so take your time."

Portia heard it—disappointment. Remembering how much Duncan loved throwing the Frisbee, despite his inability to do it well, she made an offer. "Go tell him to meet us down there. We'll take a Frisbee. I saw some in the garage. I think we can use them."

"Yeah!"

He'd dashed off and returned before Portia managed to get her second bite of schmeared rice cake. "He says great. Mom says Bella can't come."

Translation: I don't have to share you this time. Portia's heart constricted. *How am I going to stand it when they move? Idaho is so far away. I shouldn't spend so much time with Duncan and Reese. I need to invest in my own nieces and nephew.*

"Aunt Jessica says we'll go fishing later—just her and me."

And that's why it's okay. There are four of us wanting one-on-one time. I need to leave them available and not be selfish.

"Aunt Portia?"

"Hmm…?"

"You okay?"

A glance at his little face with those wide brown eyes prompted a compliment he wouldn't appreciate—yet. "You're going to break hearts someday, A.J. Girls are going to cry themselves to sleep because you're not in love with them."

"Oh, gross. Some guys like that. Like Damon. He likes girls."

And that's one of many things I don't like about him. He likes girls, *not just my sister.* A.J.'s remark prompted a thought, though. "Hey, tell me something. If you were Deaf, what do you think you'd like to do most?"

"Deaf? Like I can't hear?"

Portia nodded. "You know… like how you like to play with Legos and ride your bike. What if you were Deaf?"

"Why does being Deaf have anything to do with it? I probably wouldn't like the piano as much, but maybe? Beethoven was deaf. Did you know that?"

"Yeah, I did. Thanks, buddy."

Of course, he was right. Her Deaf instructors would be offended at the implication—no matter how unintentional. *You're trying too hard.*

"I'm going to go find the Frisbees and get a jacket."

"I'll be out in a minute."

Her phone blipped again before she could recall that she'd left Reese hanging. SO, I'VE OFFENDED YOU?

This time, the response was easy. NOPE. AND I'LL GO SO FAR AS TO SAY THAT I HOPE THIS ADOBE THING IS KIND OF SCARY. YOU CAN FIGURE OUT WHY.

With that, Portia turned off the phone before she sent a "just kidding" after it.

SEVEN

By the time she returned from the beach with A.J. and her father, guilt had found a perfect plot of land in her heart and began to build a castle there—complete with a moat filled with frustrations. She only had one option left at that point, so complaining about the sand in her hair, down her pants, and between her toes, Portia bolted upstairs and begged Cressida to come talk to her while she showered.

The house? Empty, thankfully. So, while hot water pummeled her and warmed her through, she told her oldest sister all about meeting Duncan… and Reese. She did not share about the late-night walk along the shore, but guilt prompted her to confess the date.

"He asked me to some adobe thing—a Christmas in this old rancho place. I said yes."

"You have a *date?*"

"Um… yeah?"

"Sah-weet!"

Someone needs to tell her that no one says that anymore.

"When?"

"In… an hour and change?"

That's when Cressida figured it out. "Okay, what's wrong? Tell me you at least found out if he was a Christian? If you're not sure, you could take your own—"

"He's a Christian, and I trust him. Well, as much as you trust any guy you just met and decide to have coffee with or something."

"So what's the problem?"

Shampoo drizzled down into Portia's mouth as she told about the morning's conversation with A.J. and their subsequent fun at the beach. Between bubbly coughs and hacks, she pleaded for wisdom. "Am I being stupid to do this?"

"You can't put your life on hold because we're moving. Everyone wants to spend time with the kids. And frankly…"

Portia knew what her sister would say before the words filled the bathroom.

"…I want to get to watch this before I go. So have fun. Just text me now and then so I know you're alive."

"I'll give you his number, too."

Cressida asked a million questions, and in the process of her interrogation, got the whole story—the trip to the pier, the glow-in-the-dark Shakespeare quote, the walk along the beach—all of it. "Sounds like a neat guy. He really quoted Mrs. Bennet?"

"Yep."

"You have my permission to marry him. So, before we can make that happen, we've got to figure out what you're wearing." A squeal—one that only Cressida could emit—filled the bathroom and echoed off the stone-tiled walls "My little sister has a date! Yesss!"

As he pulled into the "do not enter" drive, with its perpetually-open gate, Reese stopped beneath the streetlight and gazed out over the moonlit water. *Thank you, Lord, for a full moon close to Christmas. That's awesome.*

The soothing lullaby of crashing waves greeted him as he climbed from his car. For the first time, he looked at it with the eyes of a girl… one he might want to impress. The older-model Volvo wouldn't impress anyone. *I didn't choose it to impress, though.*

It's supposed to be the safest car out there.

Movement in his peripheral vision made Reese turn, and there she came. This time, Portia's hair hung down in large, bouncy spirals—curls, but not. When she saw him, she waved. Hesitant. Shy again—just a bit—and as she neared, he saw her inching away from the circle of light beneath the lamp. *She's nervous, too.*

Reese met her half way, hands out to grab hers. "Hey, thanks for coming. You look great!"

"Had to tell Cressida about… it—"

"Our date?"

"Yeah." There it was again, ducked eyes and a hint of an embarrassed smile.

"Well, she decided I needed curls." Portia flicked her hair over one shoulder. "Like they won't be gone in ten minutes in this humidity."

"Most people say the humidity *gives* them curls."

"Yeah, well, my hair likes a *dry heat.*"

As he moved to open her door, he couldn't resist a bit of a tease. "Desert rat."

"Don't you know it." A hint of fragrance—indiscernible but clean and not too sweet—wafted past as she slid into her seat. And the minute he climbed in, she pounced. "Where's Duncan? I thought he was coming."

Reese started the car and backed out before answering. "He is. But he and Dad were playing Mario Kart, so he was late getting ready. Mom's helping him change, now. I'll just run by the house and honk." At her skeptical look, Reese added, "He can't hear the horn, but Mom and Dad can…"

"Oh. Duh." She shoved her hands between her knees and inhaled loud enough for him to hear. "I think I'm more nervous than I thought."

"I don't bite."

"I just want your kid to like me." While Reese tried to process that, Portia ran a hand over the door. "Nice car."

Relief kicked him in the gut rather than washed over him.

"You had me going. I bought it."

"Bought what?"

"The joke... you said you just wanted Duncan to like you... and then you said you liked the car."

"No joke. Love the car, and..." Portia gave him a sidelong glance. "I think Duncan already likes me—at least a little."

They'd already made it to Pierpont before Reese figured out what to say. "Well, my kid has good taste in women, so I guess I'll have to give you a chance."

She didn't seem to hear him. A glance her way showed Portia almost glued to the window, just like Duncan every time they visited. "These are some *big* houses."

"Yeah, don't get any ideas. Ours is tiny."

"I don't see any small—" Proof of his assertion came before she could finish. "I stand corrected. These have to be close to the beach. It's just right—"

"One block over. And that's Mom and Dad's place." He pulled up in front of the tiny two-bedroom bungalow that he'd called home for most of his childhood and honked.

The door banged open and Duncan tore down the walk to the car. Just as he reached for the door knob, Reese locked it. A mock-indignant howl followed. Portia protested as well and hit the unlock button. He locked it as fast as possible. It took three rounds, but Duncan eventually got it open before Reese could lock him out again.

The best part—Portia laughed just as hard as Duncan and he did. "You fit right in."

She twisted in her seat to sign something to Duncan, but his son tapped his arm, holding out a hand. Reese passed back his phone and winked over at Portia. From the confusion she showed, and the way she eyed him, Duncan's text message would surprise her.

If the groan that followed a blip on her phone meant what he thought it did, he was right. "Oh! Not one of the girls." She flipped around and gave Duncan a thumbs-up. "That's smart! I wouldn't have thought of that."

"It's better than getting a crick in your neck while riding. But beware. He uses the predictive text way too much. Sometimes it gets interesting." The temptation overrode his reticence. "And no flirting with him. You're *my* date."

Could anything be more awkward than a first date? Probably, but Portia didn't know what it would be. Texting with Duncan had distracted her at first, but it didn't last. By the time they'd left the car and made it to the courtyard, Portia had begun to wonder why cultures had ever given up on arranged marriages.

However, the sight of the clay pot luminarias spread out over the courtyard arrested all thought, and for a time, all awkwardness. She stopped mid-stride and gaped at the display. "Oh, wow…"

Reese's hands on her shoulders might have frozen her a moment earlier, but lost in the wonder of it, all she could do was lean into them just a bit as he murmured, "Isn't it amazing?"

"Totally." A moment later, she realized they'd left out Duncan, and she signed her enthusiasm for him.

Once more, she turned back to gaze at the little pots shining in the moonlight. "I bet this is even more gorgeous when the moon is hidden." Then it hit her. "Wait! Are they arranged to look like a star?"

"I think it's supposed to be the star of Bethlehem."

As they advanced toward the doors, it became harder to see, but looking back, there it was again—an unusually shaped, but exquisite, star of clay and light. "It's kind of like Jesus, isn't it?"

Reese eyed her with an unconvinced expression. "How so?"

"Clay and light. Jesus is the light of the world, and He came to earth to be born like us—just clay in the hands of The Potter."

Immediately, Reese dropped to one knee and began signing to Duncan. He pointed to the pots and explained what Portia had just said, but one of his signs looked off. Before she could ask about it, Duncan replied, again with an off sign—a different one, though.

"What is he saying about hair and Jesus? That sign is different than I know."

"He's saying that he likes that you know Jesus."

That's not what she saw. "What about Jesus' hair had anything to do with it?"

Duncan moved closer, signing again asking what hair—sort of—was saying.

"What is that hair—?" She stopped. Hair, but made with the letter P. A name sign. "Is that what he's calling me?"

"Well, tonight. Earlier it was…" Reese signed the word "sign" but with Ps instead of index fingers. "He's so enamored with you being a signer. I thought it would stick, but now your hair…"

She smiled at Duncan and thanked him for the compliment, but when he turned away, she murmured, "It's just hair."

"It's beautiful and longer than any I think he's actually seen… and certainly redder."

"A name sign…"

Portia didn't realize she'd spoken aloud until Reese signed as he asked, "You didn't have a name sign?"

"No… my sisters do, but no one's given me one yet. I'm not as much a part of the Deaf community, though," she hastened to add. "I didn't mean to complain or anything. I just…" She gave Duncan a bright smile before continuing. "I was just happy to have one—and from this little man. That's special."

Duncan slipped his fingers into hers as they moved inside, and it sparked a thought. "Is it… I mean, do you know if there's any significance to a Deaf person being willing to hold your hand when it limits his ability to communicate?"

"I don't know about other Deaf people, but Duncan never will unless he's in a familiar and comfortable place. He usually has lots of questions about everything." Duncan's head swung from Reese to her and back again, nodding as his father explained. "You're so good about including him. Even my parents and some of the people at church forget."

There, Duncan broke away and began signing something about the woman who waited for the group to form. Before she could ask for clarification, the tour began—and so did the questions. From seeing the rooms where the family heard the Christmas story to watching *las Posadas*—children acting out the journey of Mary and Joseph to Bethlehem.

I know she was young—although probably not as young as we think. Poverty and a hard life often delayed their periods and stuff, but still. She was a teenager, almost certainly. God sent His Son to a teen mom. Between that and the prospect of being stoned for saying, "Yes, Lord," she had it rough.

"You okay?"

Reese's question came just as Portia realized that a few tears slid down her cheeks. With an impatient flick, she brushed them aside and smiled over at him. "Yeah. It's just overwhelming to think about all He went through so I could avoid all I deserve to go through."

It sounded stupid to her ears, but Reese didn't seem to think so. He did that same shoulder squeezy thing that, once more, sent her pulse racing. *I can't like you. Not yet. Too soon. Wwaay too soon.*

Duncan signed a plea to go home. Portia gave Reese a quick look, but he seemed just as confused. "I told him we could go to Tony's Pizza..." He gave her a weak smile. "Not the most romantic place for dinner, but I knew Duncan would like it and it's *really* good..."

"I like pizza!" To herself, Portia added, *Not as much as half my family, but I like it.*

No one who'd seen one of Bella's physical displays of objection would call Duncan's response a tantrum, but Reese treated it like one. He shut down the jabbed signs and the scowling face with a few quick gestures that must have meant something to them but were signs she'd never seen before. *Probably special just to them or something...*

In the end, Duncan did apologize for an outburst she didn't even understand, and Reese took the boy home. The car hadn't fully come to a stop before Reese's phone dropped into the front seat area, the boy's head squeezed through between the seats, kissed his father's cheek, kissed hers, and out the door he went.

"Well, goodbye to you, too."

"I think he 'overheard' my parents talking about the date."

It made no sense, even with the air quotes. "I don't get it."

"Sometimes he can tell by their faces that something's important, and he manages to convince them to share." His head slammed against the headrest. "Who am I kidding? Sometimes? He's always watching. He can't read lips as far as I can tell—not at all. But he sure can read their faces, and they won't tell him no if they think it's remotely related to learning or it being 'fair' to keep from a Deaf kid when a hearing kid would know it."

"But what would your parents have to do with anything?"

Something in the way he responded—or rather, *didn't* respond—hinted at what he'd say before he blurted out, "They didn't think I should bring him. First date should be just us." Again, he hesitated before continuing. "You should know..." Reese gave her a sidelong glance, as if gauging her reaction. "They're hopeful... about the possibility of an us."

Her heart had begun to sink, but lifted and floated back into place at that turn of phrasing... *"... the possibility of an us."*

"I like how you put that. It's not..."

"There's no pressure, Portia. Sure, I'd love for things to work out. I think most people do when they first meet someone who interests them at all—if they're honest with themselves. But if you're honest with yourself, you also know that we meet a lot of people who aren't as interesting on second, third, twenty-third encounters as they were the first."

"True..."

"And hey, I've made it through three and am still interested."

Her underused filter insisted that she *not* ask. But when had she ever listened to that filter before? "And after twenty-three?"

"I'll ask you to marry me."

Only the wink saved him from a slug in the arm and her bolting from the car. *Calm down... just a joke... whew! Can I be ten again? Ten was such a nice, uncomplicated age.*

EIGHT

Spending over two hours hogging a restaurant table on a Saturday night—rude at best. Reese finally asked for the check and signed away his "blow money" for the week as an apology to the server. Still, it was only eight-thirty when he opened the car door for her. "Ice cream?"

She hesitated before sitting. "I'm still kind of full from the pasta..."

"Are you up for a walk on the beach and *then* we get to McConnell's before they close?"

For one miserable moment, Reese thought she'd say no. Sorting through his arguments on why she should reconsider almost made him miss her, "Sure, why not?"

"Wh—oh, great!"

A sidelong glance, a fledgling smile, a... well, you couldn't call it a giggle, but it was the closest thing to it. "You thought I'd say no."

"Yep—was mounting a defense or preparing an argument, or whatever lawyers do to convince someone of something."

As he slid in behind the wheel, she asked, "So what's McConnell's?"

She said yes without knowing for sure. With as much finesse as he could manage, he fumbled to get the key in the ignition as he forced out, "Our favorite ice cream place."

Taking Portia to "their" stretch of beach—not smart. It might give her the idea that she should go home instead of going for ice cream. Not only was he not prepared for the date to end, Reese also didn't quite know what to think of that. So, he drove down past the pier and pulled into the parking lot at Surfer's Point. There, they could walk along the Ventura Promenade without getting sand into Portia's shoes.

They'd made it three steps from the car before she turned and sighed. "I'm cold. I need my sweater. Sorry."

"There's no reason to be sorry. Let me get it." Her thanks hinted that she saw it as a gentlemanly response, but Reese had to use those few seconds to evict the idea from his mind that he would be more than happy to keep her warm. *First, inappropriate. Second, you don't even know your own mind. Third, you don't want to run her off before you know your mind, so cool it.*

Cool it. He couldn't help a smile at the semi-irony, and Portia noticed. "What?"

He could fake it, lie, tell her, or… No, he couldn't do any of that. So he went for blunt honesty. "I amused myself with something that would mortify me to share… yet. Ask me when I've known you for a month or two."

"Like you'll remember."

"Trust me," Reese insisted. "I'll remember."

They'd made it out of the parking lot and onto the promenade before Reese mustered the courage to tug on her sleeve in a bid for her hand. "It's tradition now, you know?"

"Tradition? I've seen you like three times, and we have a tradition?"

"Yep."

In the palm tree-filtered moonlight, her expression revealed little. A moment later she laced their fingers together and scooted just a tad closer. Still they walked along, hand-in-hand, still not speaking. Just *being.*

A man walking a dog wearing a service jacket passed them, and then Portia spoke. "Whenever I see service dogs, I wish I liked animals more." What could pass for a huff of disgust or a sigh of despair followed before she added, "But… I don't. So, oh well."

"Maybe you'd like them more if they were *yours*?"

There, she stopped and stared up at him, hand still intertwined with his. "Okay, you should know something."

"What's that?"

"If you're some huge cat lover who won't live without a dozen feline kings patrolling your place, then you might as well just take me home now. Not a fan."

He couldn't resist asking. "Of a dozen cats? How's just one…? Or four?"

"Four?! Why?" She clamped her jaw shut, pressed her lips together, and shook her head. "I should not be allowed in polite company."

That's when Reese realized she still held his hand. "Who wants polite company anyway?"

With a nod but not another word, she set the pace again—slow, leisurely, even. Only after the third shiver did Reese lead them in a wide U-turn and back to the car. Portia hesitated before climbing in, and they stood there. Just the car door separating them. "Sorry…"

"What for?"

"Cutting us short. I should have brought a jacket or something. I knew better, but my sweater looked nicer and—" With that, she plopped down into the seat and slammed the car door shut, nearly removing a couple of his fingers in the process.

She wanted to look nice. For me? For her? Do I care? It only took Reese long enough to reach his door to decide. *Nope. Don't care. She wanted to look nice on this date.* This *date. Her first. And it's with me.*

If he hadn't seen her blush before, he might not have known that Portia's face glowed with glaring mortification. Only a hint showed in the streetlight. But he saw it. He knew.

"I just want to say something."

The sound she made in reply could have been anything from, "Huh?" to "What?" to a grunt or groan.

"Thanks for letting me be your first date. That's something special. I don't want to take that yes for granted."

Weak street lamp light or not, he knew a glare when he saw one. Reese had almost asked what he'd said to offend her when she blurted out, "Seriously? Can you be a jerk now? I kind of need a jerk. I know how to handle that. You take me home, I'm ticked at you until morning, and then you disappear from my life faster than chocolate on my period."

Reese was pretty sure his snicker drowned out her gasp.

"I did not just say that."

"You don't want me to be a jerk? Good. I'd rather not. And taking you home now means no ice cream. I really wanted to drop some off for Duncan…"

She eyed him, and though he couldn't see it, Reese *felt* a hint of a smile. "You could do it after you took me home and I stormed into the house—slammed doors. All that good stuff."

"I'd be too broken hearted to want ice cream."

"You're so not a girl."

Reese started the engine as if he didn't expect her, at any moment, to demand that he take her home anyway. And he did. Still, once he'd backed out of their space, he figured out the perfect response. "Nope. Not a girl. I think even if you were mad at me, even if you *did* want me to take you home—please-say-you-don't—and even if you never wanted to speak to me again—too horrible to even imagine—you still would be glad that I'm not a girl."

"I don't know… There's no pressure if you're just another girl."

That he knew how to answer. Without even asking or hinting, Reese took her hand and squeezed it. "There's no pressure now—not from me. So if you feel pressure, take it off. You're the only one who can."

It felt rude—and a bit clandestine, if truth be told—but Portia insisted that Reese drop her off at the non-entrance sign. Of course, she hoped *he* would insist on walking her up to the drive of Sandpiper House. She wasn't disappointed.

"It's supposed to make me look good, but it's selfish," Reese admitted.

I hope that means that you wanted to string out the date a bit longer…

"—hope it wasn't too boring for a first date. I mean, it wasn't that exciting. I should have thought of that."

Portia, jerked out of her own thoughts on the night, slipped her hand back into his and took tiny steps toward the road. "And I was just trying to figure out how to thank you for a perfect first date without making me sound cheesy or pathetic."

"I did figure out how I could see you tomorrow for a bit without taking a lot more time from your family…"

She refused to admit, even to herself, that she'd been working on the same dilemma. Instead, she managed a nonchalant, "Oh?" as they began the climb up Vista del Mar. *When will I ever pull off nonchalant again? Probably never.*

"You could always come to church with us tomorrow. Duncan would love it, and you know I would."

One of the arguments that had foretold the drama that would ensue with a "destination Christmas" had been where they'd spend Sunday and Christmas Eve/morning for worship. Cressida and Austin wanted to stay home, read appropriate passages, sing a few carols, and play nativity charades. Tami had voted for that one the moment she heard it. Miranda and Jessica had argued for finding a church with a cool program planned—maybe a different one for each day, even. Tami had also lobbied for that.

Working at a church-run preschool meant that Portia had strong ties to her church and wanted to attend a sister church in Ventura. Tami thought that sounded cool, too. *Not as cool as the other stuff,* Portia mused as she listened to Reese talk about the church he grew up in.

Their parents, however, had no strong preference as long as the music wasn't too loud and they avoided obvious conflicts of theological interests.

Even as she mulled the options again, his words registered.

"Wait, what church?"

"The church of Christ up on—"

"Oh, wow." They'd arrived at the base of the drive, and someone stood in the doorway—someone who looked an awful lot like Cressida, even in the shadows. "Look, I've got to go. If they haven't come to a consensus, I'll come, but don't expect me."

He nudged her elbow. "Is that one of your sisters or your mom…?"

"Cressida. I think."

The idea of standing at the end of the drive, shivering in the cold and chatting no longer sounded like fun. Portia squeezed his hand, whispered, "Thanks for inviting me," and exhibited every ounce of control she could scrounge up as she strolled up the drive when she ached to dash to the door. As she turned, he waved and sauntered away.

"Looks like you had fun."

"I really did. It was cool."

Though she reached for the door, Cressida didn't open it. "If he asks you out after you're home, would you go?"

She'd been wondering the same thing all night, and she still had no answer. "I don't know, but I think I'm definitely closer to yes than I was when I left."

"Good."

Cressida still did not push down that lever to open the door.

"Okay, what happened while I was gone?"

"As Miranda put it, 'Since Portia isn't around, we'll just have to do this without her.'"

"Great."

Cressida's sigh gave away her opinion before she could speak. "And… we're going to mass at the mission—for both tomorrow morning and Christmas Eve."

"Mass? We're not Catholic."

A shrug—at least, that's what Portia thought it was—spoke where Cressida didn't seem able to. Then she found her voice. "Apparently, it's a cultural thing we've been denied, so we're embracing the cultural and spiritual relevance all at once."

Portia pulled out her phone and tapped out a text. CHANGE OF PLANS. I'M COMING. She then showed it to her sister before hitting send.

"What's his church?"

"Get this…" She still couldn't believe it. "Church of Christ."

A low whistle preceded Cressida's opening the door. They crept in to the sounds of an action movie filling the downstairs. "What are the odds?"

It was a question she'd pondered since Reese told her. "Right? Not many people worship there, but I'm both comfortable while still being challenged—at least at ours."

She hugged her sister, kissed Cressida's cheek, and whispered, "Thanks for the warning. See you tomorrow."

And the moment she closed her bedroom door behind her, Reese's reply came. CLASS STARTS AT 9:45. WORSHIP AT 11:00.

A minute later, another came. CAN'T TELL YOU HOW HAPPY I AM THAT YOU'RE COMING.

NINE

At seven-to-one, not including nieces and nephew, Portia was sunk, and she knew it. Still, she *had* to give it a fighting chance. "She *wanted* to go to everything more than one of 'my' churches, and suddenly Tami's dying to go with me? C'mon. What's going on?"

But even her usually neutral mom couldn't argue. "Look, you're the one who didn't want to go with everyone. Why should she want to? Is there a problem with her worshiping in the same building as you? It's just a building, isn't it? Does it *really* matter?"

"Of course, not! I just feel like I'm missing something here."

"If you don't object," Portia's father announced, "then why aren't we all getting ready?"

Without bothering to add warmth to her tone, Portia eyed her little sister and said, "If you're not ready when I am, I'm leaving without you."

Tami sat waiting in the car when Portia slipped out the side door a few minutes later. Google led the way across town and to the traditional-looking church building. As if oblivious to Portia's ire, Tami gushed about how "adorable" the church was. "Like in those cheesy Christmas movies or on Christmas cards."

Maybe if there was snow somewhere—and a candle in the windows. It doesn't look at all like Christmas should. Portia's conscience tried to get her to admit that neither did her church at home with its sandy surroundings and utilitarian facade. She refused.

Duncan greeted her at the edge of the parking lot, his signs so fast and excited that she stumbled over a couple. Tami eyed her, curious, and looked back. When she couldn’t keep up, Portia lost patience. “Just tell him he’s signing too fast.”

“I don’t remember how!”

“You… Sign… then jerk your thumbs toward you for fast.”

Reese met them in the foyer—or, rather, he met her. Duncan and Tami tried conversing all the way in. “Who—Tami?”

“Yeah. She insisted on coming. I think we have a spy in our midst. I just can’t figure out how someone found out about you.”

“Cressida seems the obvious choice.”

“I know it seems like it.” Portia called for Tami to hurry. “But um… no. She wouldn’t.”

Tami dashed up, “Duncan wants to know if I can sit with him. I think that’s his name.”

“It is.”

Again, Tami shot her a curious look but said nothing. She signed a “yes” and let the boy lead the way. A couple sat in the row of chairs that Duncan led them into—Reese’s parents. Between his mother’s smile and the intensity of his father’s eyes, no one would doubt the relation.

She whispered under her breath, “Why didn’t I realize that this would mean meeting your parents?”

“I mentioned it…”

Before she could panic further, the woman hopped up and enveloped her in a hug. “Hi! So happy to meet you—Portia, right? I’m Kendra…” She stepped back and the man offered his hand. “This is Brian.” She smiled at Tami. “I just don’t know who you are…?”

“Tami. I’m the youngest.” Tami gave Portia that *look* again and said, “I didn’t know we knew anyone here. No wonder you wanted to come here instead of the mission.”

It took excessive effort *not* to say, “‘We’ *don’t, and I barely do.”*

And it became even harder as Tami’s expression clearly said, *So this is where you’ve been going.*

Fortunately for her, worship began with the first song. While Portia, and sometimes Tami, sang from memory, Tami tried signing the words she knew for Duncan. The song became a jumbled mess that looked a lot like, "Jesus gave lots. We Jesus. Wash snow."

Portia gave up trying to focus on preparing her mind and heart for worship and helped her sister sign. Duncan's patience took on greater heights when she struggled to remember the sign for "redeemed" and he supplied it for her. Tami giggled and tried to copy it, but the rest of the song—lost to her.

A glance at Reese turned into a gaze when she caught him watching her little sister and his even younger son. Only when the minister rose to take his place behind the pulpit did Reese smile down at her. The passage was announced, and everyone in the auditorium began rustling pages in search of Joshua.

As he flipped to the right spot, Reese leaned close and whispered, "She's the neatest girl. Most young teens ignore him."

It only took one glance over to where Tami pointed at a page and failed to sign "verse" and Duncan worked with her to figure it out before Portia had to agree. *Yeah. She is.*

All through the sermon, the introductions to more people than she'd ever want, much less *hope*, to remember, and halfway home, Portia fought pride and anger. *I'm not even mad at her or them anymore.*

"Has Duncan always been Deaf?"

"No…" Though she tried to recall exactly what he'd said, she couldn't. "All I know for sure is that around eighteen months his mom found out he'd gone deaf after being sick and couldn't take it. So she sent him to live with Reese."

"You like him."

Portia nodded. "He's a cute kid. Sweet. Crazy patient when people don't understand him."

"No… Reese. I can see it." Tami pointed at the exit. "Hey, is that ours?"

Ms. Google informed them to take the next exit

"Good call." Portia did, however, ignore the bit about her liking Reese. If she got derailed now, she'd never do what had to be done. A glance over as her sister watched the hillside whiz past almost made her chicken out. Almost. "Hey, Tami?"

"Hmm…" When she didn't continue, Tami turned her way and stared. "What's wrong?"

"So, I was kind of a jerk this morning," Portia began. "Um… okay, a lot of a jerk. It hurts to admit it, but that was wrong, and I'm sorry." She glanced Tami's way and offered a smile. "I know Reese and Duncan were really glad to meet you."

"Yeah…"

They pulled into the drive, and before Tami bolted from the car she shot one last grin at Portia. "His parents were happy to meet you, too."

Mortification, thy name is Portia—or some mixed up Shakespearean nightmare like that.

Duncan's hands signed a mile a minute, stopping only long enough for a bite whenever he'd finished the last. It made for choppy conversation—much like any child with food in his mouth. "At least," Reese muttered, "we aren't treated to half-masticated PB&J when he talks with his mouth full."

His parents laughed, and he tried breaking into the signed rhapsodies about Tami to explain the joke. Duncan still didn't get it. *"It's just that when you sign and chew, your mouth stays closed. When kids* talk *and chew…"* Reese over-emphasized the "talk" sign, *"we get stuck seeing all that gross food moving around—and spraying us."*

That did it. Duncan snorted, snickered, and managed to lose part of his sandwich in the process.

"I retract my statement."

Duncan burst out laughing.

Reese eyed his parents, his son, and his parents again. "I didn't know he knew what that meant."

Duncan laughed even harder. Then his mom snickered—his dad.

"What?"

Duncan pointed, and a glance down showed a piece of ham dangling from a button. "I guess I was talking with *my* mouth full."

"I think," his father began with little attempt to stifle a snicker. "Our Reese is desperate to keep talking so we can't ask questions about Portia."

Truth had never sucker-punched harder.

"She's a beautiful girl, Reese—inside and out, from what I can see."

Picking up on the sign for beautiful, Duncan began a new tack—the wonders of Tami. *"She's smart. And she's nice. She should have a name sign that is smart and nice."* His first attempt wasn't smooth, but by reversing it and making nice go before smart, he managed the sign well enough. *"That's Tami."*

Under her breath, his mother murmured, "I think someone has a bit of a crush."

Reese nearly choked at that. "He's *eight*, Mom!"

"And you fell in love with Bitsy Baldwin when you were four."

"She hated to be called Bitsy."

A shrug, a hint of a smile… His mother wouldn't give, and he knew it. "Well, she was a tiny little thing. You always liked them petite… until now."

"C'mon, Mom! Portia isn't exactly an Amazon."

"Compared to Bitsy, she is."

"Liz is almost fifty, married, and with the way her daughter was making out with that boy at the youth forum, on her way to being a grandma." Despite his protest, Reese couldn't argue that Portia had nearly a foot on not quite five-foot tall "Bitsy."

With his plate pushed aside and his arms folded over his chest, Reese's father leaned back in the chair watching. So while his mother chattered about potential date ideas, Reese hardly took note. He just watched… and waited.

"Will you ask her out again, son? Soon?"

"We're going for donuts in the morning—early. Six o'clock." The memory of Portia's snarky, biting response to the hour prompted a smile. "I get the feeling that she gets up early often—that it wouldn't be hard to do—but that she is *not* a morning person."

Duncan asked to be excused—to play Mario Kart. His father rose to go, too. He paused by Reese's chair as he passed by and said, "Pray, son. If you have questions, pray. If you think you have answers, pray. When you think you don't need to anymore, pray even harder."

Where it came from, Reese didn't know. He looked at his mother, but she just nodded. "What?"

"Reese, honey, you're conflicted. You might not be able to see it, and you might not know why… not yet. But you are. Your dad's right. Pray."

He would have gathered plates from the table and put away the leftovers, but she shooed him out the door. "I see it in you, son. Go walk and talk with your Father."

"You like her, though?"

"I think it would be easy to like her, Reese. She's kind, she is obviously interested in Duncan for his own sake, and if the way she watches you when she thinks no one is looking counts for anything, she's interested in you for yours, too."

That thought occupied Reese's thoughts as he kissed her cheek, signed his intention to go for a walk, and took off down the street. *Mom's never wrong, Lord…*

It might not be true, but had always felt like it. Down to and around the corner, he strolled along Bangor Lane, past small houses, tall houses, plain and remodeled to the end of the street where steps took him up to the sand and shore. How many times had he done that as a kid… weekly? Daily?

Prayer, though. His father couldn't have been more right. He needed to bathe the idea of a relationship in prayer. But where to begin? The heaviness in his heart lightened as he remembered something his youth minister had told him once. *"When you don't know where to begin is where you begin—admitting that to the Lord. It unlocks that part of us that tries to pretend He doesn't know anyway."*

"I don't know what I'm doing here, Lord."

Waves of emotions rolled in, one after the other, but words and thoughts stayed far out beyond the breakers of his heart. As that thought formed, Reese relaxed. *That's my problem, isn't it? I don't know what to do with emotions that I'm not even sure I should feel yet. That's where I begin. Clarity. I need it, Lord. For me… for her. For all of us.*

Cold air whipped at him even as the sun did its best to warm the shore. Reese shoved his hands in his jacket pockets and inched closer to the damp sand as the tide pulled away from shore, bit by bit. And there… there he prayed. Waited. Listened.

A glance back showed a single row of footprints, and the old poem that had been decoupaged to a piece of wood and had once hung in their tiny hallway came to mind. *A single row of footprints… always…* Confidence soared. *That means the poem is really just reminding us that You always carry us. Should have known. If You'll carry me, You'll carry all of us. Through all of this. Always.*

A gull soared overhead and came in for a landing a few yards away. *Thanks.*

Settled, confident, *prayed*, Reese turned back home. The certainty that the Lord had his life under control, that things would work out just as they should with Portia, that she might just be more than a "nice girl," lasted right up until his mother brought popcorn into the living room for their Sunday night movie.

She passed a bowl with light butter to him and passed his dad the heavy butter version just as his phone blipped. Portia's smile greeted him on his screen, but her text message swiped the smile that had begun to form despite every effort to disguise it.

"What's wrong, Reese?"

He turned the screen around and tried to stuff down his disappointment—tried and failed. The words still burned themselves into his mind.

CAN'T COME IN THE MORNING.

His mother spoke first. "Oh, Reese…"

"Everything okay, son?"

"Portia sent him a text canceling their date—rather abrupt one."

"She can be pretty forthright…" Common sense told him

that he didn't know her well enough to be this disappointed, but a glance at Duncan's confused expression gave him the out he sought. *It's just that Duncan really liked her, too. Not everyone takes time to get to know him.*

His phone buzzed again before he could convince himself of that idea. EXPLAIN LATER.

"What is it?" His mother leaned over to read it. "Well, that's more like it. Probably some family thing."

"At six o'clock?" Reese steeled himself against the hope she seemed determined to instill. "I don't think so, but thanks for trying, Mom."

Again, the phone preempted the movie. This time, it held just one word. PRAY.

TEN

Lights flashed in the drive, in the street, and large, portable spotlights shone down on the rocks below Sandpiper House. Portia's teeth chattered as cool air, a stiff breeze, and what a more alert part of her suggested might be shock buffeted her. An officer asked the question again.

"So he was in the hot tub…"

"Like I said," she snapped, wincing at the cry of pain blown up from below. "He was in the hot tub with the kids. He's blind without his glasses, you know. He stepped out of it and slid right off and down the cliff." A shudder washed over her. "It was horrible."

"They'll get him to the hospital and be sure he's all right," the woman assured her. "Now why wasn't the light on?"

Portia tore her eyes from where two firefighters held ropes that helped the others down to where her father lay on rocks—unconscious, they thought. Glaring at the officer, she didn't bother to keep the bite from her words. "There are no lights—and that ledge is slippery. I almost fell down myself trying to get to him."

"Had he been drinking?"

Seriously? You're going to try to make this about fault? My dad just fell down a cliff and you're what, going to cite him for public intoxication?

"Miss…"

"My dad doesn't drink—ever. Hates the stuff."

Jessica appeared and draped an arm over Portia's shoulder.

"Everything okay?"

"I think she's trying to make this Dad's fault somehow."

The officer made no indication that she'd just been insulted. Jessica offered an apologetic smile—one that irritated Portia, of course, and said, "It's just her job. She has to take a report if she comes out here. It's okay."

But it wasn't okay. Nothing was. Her father was hurt—who knew how bad it was?—and an already pathetic excuse for Christmas had just become even worse. "That's your take on it. Can you finish this? I'm going to go see if A.J. is okay."

The officer started to say something, but Jessica preempted her. No one could deny Jessica's skills at managing people and getting them to do whatever she wanted. *And she'll go to the hospital with Mom. She's good at that stuff.*

A.J. stood alone, arms folded over his chest in a perfect imitation of his father, jaw set. "Hey, buddy…"

"Is Grandpa going to be okay?"

"That's what the firemen are here for—to make sure he is. They said he's breathing and his heart is steady." *Fast, maybe, but steady. You don't need to know that part, though.*

"Mom says we might have to go home."

Two days before Christmas. We don't even have everything done yet. Tomorrow is the stockings run. They can't go home!

Two firefighters pushed past and took up places at the ropes. Portia showed A.J. how they'd pull Grandpa up the cliff and then carry him out. "If he'd fallen father down, they might have been able to just go up from the road down there, but they'd be blocking it for a long time if they did it that way, so they're doing this."

Cressida arrived, ready to talk to him and assuring him that all would be well… eventually. "Dad and I are going to the hospital in the morning, but Aunt Jessica is going now. She'll send us messages, so you'll know what's going on. I promise."

After what seemed like hours, the stretcher with Larry Spears strapped down, neck in a brace, and arms rigid at his side appeared. One glance at A.J., sent Portia in motion. She knelt beside him, an arm around him, and tried to explain.

"They have to do that because they're pulling him up a hill. They don't want to hurt his spine. They did it when he had the truck accident, too. Remember? He joked that they strapped him down because the ambulance ran him off the road?"

The boy's tears didn't slow.

"I'm taking him inside," Cressida murmured. "Let me know if you hear anything from Jessica."

A hollowness remained behind as the door shut, leaving her all alone. *Ridiculous. Mom's over there by the stretcher—Jessica, too. Miranda's talking to the officer now—and Austin.* That prompted a thought. *Where's Tami…?*

It took two sweeps of the area to see her little sister shivering at one end of the ledge separating the hot tub from the cliff. No towel. Just a swimsuit in the stiff breeze that kept Portia freezing. She snatched up the nearest beach towel and hurried over. "You're going to freeze."

"He fell."

That's all it took. Portia pulled Tami from the ledge and pushed her into the house and up the stairs. Bella and Charis stood in the bathroom, brushing their teeth, but Portia shooed them out. "Go spit that out in your mommy's sink. We need this one."

It took a few shrieks of protest and Portia shouting for her sister to get Cressida rushing down to shush the girls. "I told them to finish in your bathroom. Tami's been sitting out there all wet and in her swimsuit. She needs a hot shower."

Tami apologized, as if she needed to, and stepped into the shower—swimsuit and all. Just then, the ambulance blipped and a siren wailed as it drove away from the house. Heart sinking, Portia stood just outside the bathroom door and zipped another text to Reese. I'M SCARED.

The text came through at nine-thirty. GOT A MINUTE? Before Reese could reply, a second one popped up. BEACH? NOW?

After zipping a promise to be right there, he eased from the couch, tucking the blanket he'd shared with Duncan in beside his son and whispered a, "Portia sounds desperate," to his mom.

"Not to be insensitive, son, but Duncan can't hear you. You don't have to whisper."

"Yeah, but Dad can, and he's about to start snoring any second." The first ragged snort of air punctuated his assertion. "I rest my case. See you soon."

"I'll keep praying."

That stopped him. Reese took a moment to hug his mother, inhaling the comforting, familiar scent of apple shampoo and Dawn dishwashing detergent. "Thanks, Mom."

Three steps down Pierpont Boulevard—that's all it took for him to reconsider and dash back to his car. With the streets empty, he managed to make a U-turn, zip down the road, and arrive at the beach non-entrance in record time. Portia stood there, a pillar in his headlights, arms wrapped around herself, head down, and he suspected, eyes closed.

Reese's heart constricted, and all doubts that something terrible had gone wrong vanished. He wished them back again as he shut off the engine and climbed from the car. Hair whipped by wind in random swirls, she reminded him of a sentinel in a fantasy movie. With a cape and a torch or a sword, he'd have cheered with the audience, confident that no one would get past her.

Portia's gaze met his just as he reached her—pain-filled—obvious to him, even in the half-covered moonlight. All doubt fled. Reese pulled her close and held her. "What's going on?"

"Dad—" She choked, unable to continue.

Lord, please no. Don't let him have died on Christmas *vacation with the family. The possible* last *Christmas vacation together. Please…* But she waited for him, either unable or unwilling to continue without some response. "Heart attack? Stroke? Is he—"

A giggle followed—nervous, but better than the wracked,

emotional silence. "Not quite that dire… I don't think. A fall out of the hot tub and down a fifteen to twenty foot cliff?"

"You're kidding me."

"Nope."

No other option made sense, so he asked the obvious. "Did the railing give?"

"There's no railing." That did it. Anger supplanted fear, and Portia raged. "What idiot rents out a house with an infinity pool and hot tub and *no* mats for the slippery, fenceless *ledge*? You know, the *drop off* to the rocks and road below. Those rocks kept Dad from rolling into the road down there! He'd be crushed with all those cars!"

There wasn't any response that would help that, so he pulled her close again and held on. "I'm so sorry."

"He wasn't moving, Reese." A shudder followed before she repeated herself in soft, hoarse tones. "He wasn't moving."

Again, Reese started to apologize, but his walk with the Lord that afternoon shifted it. "Lord, please hear us now. Portia's father…"

It took a moment for her to pick up the cue. "Larry."

"Right, Larry needs Your healing touch. Because You've told us to pray for the sick and You will raise them up, we're praying and asking for healing for Larry. I also ask You to comfort the family. Mrs. Spears—"

"Pat."

"Right," he continued, "Pat is probably worried sick. Please give her wisdom and clarity to work with the doctors to give him the best care. Help each doctor know what is best and be careful not to interfere with the others…"

Unsure what specifically to pray for, Reese started with the head, went to internal organs, and moved to bones next. He would have begun praying for Cressida and her family after that, but Portia murmured, "Tami is really scared. I'm worried about her."

That's all he needed to hear. "For Tami, we ask for comfort and confidence. Please let her know, without a doubt, that You have all of this in Your hands. You can and will work for Your glory, and that's all Larry wants, I know. Help her accept what she doesn't like, and trust where she's weak—"

A sob cut him off… and broke his heart. He lowered his head to her shoulder and held fast. "Lord, please…"

He couldn't be certain, as much as he wished he were, but Reese thought he heard Portia whisper, "Don't make me love you."

"What?"

"You did not hear that."

A gentleman never argues—not about affairs of the heart. This much, Reese remembered from his father's lessons in understanding women. None of them had been accurate, as far as he remembered, but he'd try it again. This once. "I heard nothing. What'd you say?"

The giggle that followed much outshined that sob. "Oh, man. You're dangerous."

Instinct insisted that a walk would be perfect. She'd go. He knew it. He also knew that she'd berate herself if they got far down the beach and someone sent a message telling her to hurry home. If he didn't do *something*, she'd go home, and instinct again had an opinion on that one. *She needs distance for a bit.*

His mother's favorite psalm came to mind, so with one arm still around her and his other hand shoved in a pocket, Reese leaned his head against hers and recited all he could remember.

"I will bless the LORD at all times;
His praise shall continually be in my mouth.
My soul will make its boast in the LORD;
The humble will hear it and rejoice.
O magnify the LORD with me,
And let us exalt His name together.
I sought the LORD, and He answered me,
And delivered me from all my fears…."

He reversed a few words here or there… one verse he skipped. But with the music of the ocean as accompaniment, Reese went through Psalm 34 once, twice, and part of a third time before Portia fumbled for her phone, sighed, and turned to face him.

It hadn't been a romantic moment—not in the traditional sense, but with only a few small inches separating them, everything shifted. *In a movie, I'd kiss you right now.*

"I have to go."

"I'm praying. My mom's praying. When Duncan and Dad hear, they'll pray. And I'll put it on the prayer chain at church."

A tear glistened on her cheek as she whispered, "Thanks." Reese would have wiped it away, but she pressed a quick kiss to his cheek and fled down the street.

Warm, more confident than he should be, Reese followed. She must have heard him, because at the front door, she turned, waved, and slipped inside. Her text message came a moment later. THANKS.

ELEVEN

Charis' screams ripped her from sleep for the third, fifth, five-thousandth time that night. Except now light peeked through the window, as the soft lights of dawn stretched over the ocean and into Sandpiper House. Portia struggled to a seated position on the living room couch and blinked. Across from her, Tami stirred.

That's all it took. She bolted into action, taking stairs two at a time. She and Cressida arrived at Charis' bed almost at the same moment. The contrary child reached for Cressida and then wailed louder when her mother picked her up.

"I've got this," Portia insisted as she took her niece and headed toward her room. "Get some sleep while you can."

"Mom sent a text a while ago. Said Dad's conscious."

Unease and relief mingled in her heart as she waited for more.

"That's it." Cressida shrugged. "She'll send more when she knows it."

"What did Jessica say?"

"That Mom's not pushing enough for answers, that Dad is pretty banged up, and that they keep talking about some pain he has in his left shoulder and the spleen."

Every medical show she'd ever seen treated spleen injuries as life or death. *What if they don't catch it because Mom won't get in their face when she needs to? He could die?* Her eyes rose heavenward for a minute, and Portia shot up a plea for answers.

Comfort came immediately. "God doesn't need Mom to do things our way just so Dad gets the help he needs. God's bigger than that."

What else could be said? She gave Cressida a hug and carried Charis to her room. Snuggled down in the blankets, Charis rolled over, back to Portia, stuck her thumb in her mouth, and snored inside twenty seconds. *And this is how the species continues… adorableness.*

A fumble on the nightstand did not produce her phone as expected. She shifted, listening for a change in Charis' breathing. The kid didn't even slow her miniature snore fest. But as she rolled over, the phone still eluded her.

On the coffee table where I left it.

It took three times as long as usual to creep from the bed and settle the blankets so no cold drafts woke the semi sleep-deprived child. Once she made it from the room, Portia bolted downstairs, eager to read the text messages for herself. The phone showed one text message from her mother plus four others. Before she could click on the plus four, another came through. From Reese.

WE HAVE A DATE.

Irritation mounted, but another followed.

WAITING FOR YOU.

She zipped back a reply. I CANCELED. REMEMBER?

On the heels of her reply came, KNOCK. KNOCK.

Heart jumping into her throat, Portia dashed for the door. She flung it open, but no one stood there. A glance down showed a box—a small, pink pastry box. Inside, four donuts. One maple, one chocolate that looked chocolate filled, if the tiny hole on the side meant what she thought it did, one mini apple fritter, and a plain glazed.

Without even picking it up, she zipped back a text. AM I THAT BIG OF A PIG?

A rustle nearby preceded another text by a fraction of a second. TWO ARE MINE. At that, Reese stepped from behind a pineapple-shaped palm tree and brushed through odd grasses to meet her at the door. "Is it safe?"

"Safe?"

He reached for her chocolate donut, but Portia batted his hand away, grabbed it, and took a bite. Reese's chuckle hinted that he'd bought it… just for her. "You've been reluctant to introduce me, so…" He snagged the plain glazed.

"You remembered my favorite donuts."

A small smile belied the nonchalant shrug. The man was pleased with himself. Still, he ignored the semi-compliment and asked, "You okay this morning?"

Before she could answer, a series of squeals grew closer and closer as A.J. and, if she guessed right, Bella raced down the stairs. Reese looked ready to kiss her—forehead, cheek, total lip-lock? She didn't know, but it was there—whatever *it* was.

That "it" defined itself as he exhaled and stepped back. "Keep me posted. Let me know if you need anything." Another step back…another. "I'm just a call, a text, and a street or two away, okay?"

"Thanks!" she half-shouted, half-whispered as he reached the drive and waved back at her.

"Now, how do I hide these from the kids…?"

Thanks to Skype, group text messages, five determined daughters, one confused brother-in-law, and two overwhelmed parents, Christmas Eve had a plan by ten o'clock that morning. Portia was on kid duty until Cressida and Austin returned from a visit to the hospital. "We'll take the kids up the coast or to one of those tree farm things or something." When Portia protested, Cressida stepped closer and shook her head. "I need to get everyone out of here for a while. They're kind of going stir-crazy, which makes Austin jittery, and that's not good for any of us. Trust me."

"Gavin's coming!" Miranda tore through the living room in search of some lost item and retrieved it without really looking much. "We'll go buy one of those box Christmas dinners and finish up everyone's shopping, so get your lists submitted now."

That stopped Portia in her tracks. "What do you mean finish up everyone's shopping?"

No one heard her. Miranda called for text messages with lists of needs, and Cressida promised to do it on the way. A.J. pleaded to go with his parents and protested at "request denied."

At one end of the enormous island, Tami watched, growing visibly more agitated by the second. And that did it for Portia. "Excuse me! *EXCUSE ME!* Shut up!"

Silence reigned. The nieces and nephew gawked at Aunt Portia "swearing" while Miranda scowled. "Just send it to my—"

"No, no, no. What are you *buying* when you're out shopping?"

"Everything. Wrapping paper since no one remembered to bring any, the food, the *thing* Cressida wanted for that *certain person* but couldn't find it—whatever?"

Though she felt her eyebrows draw together, and her vanity said she'd develop that deep crease between her eyes just like Granny Vogel, Portia didn't care. Almost. More important things were at stake. "When will you be back?"

"Who cares? You stay here and watch the kids—keep Tami from getting bored—"

"Thanks!" Tami gave them all a disgusted look, raced from the room, and pounded up the stairs.

Miranda took a step… two. "What's wrong with her?"

"I'm not sure," Portia snapped. "It could either be feeling like an imposition for having to be *watched* like a little kid, or maybe she's just scared and wanting to see her dad, too?"

"Well we can't just invade the hospital *en masse*! You can take her up once I get back from the stores."

Backing down—not an option. "It's Christmas Eve, Mandy. I have to go buy *stocking stuffers*."

The argument exploded from mild irritation to abject

frustration. Miranda wanted family tradition changed. "There's no reason we should be waiting until Christmas Eve to buy this stuff!"

"We've *always* done that," Portia protested. "It's what we do. Deal with it."

"But now we're in a bind—"

Tami appeared. "If she can say it, so can I. Shut. Up!" The entire group might have turned on her, but Charis took that moment to echo. "Shut up!"

Bella protested. "Don't say 'shut up,' Charis. We're not allowed to say, 'shut up.' 'Shut up' is a bad word…s."

Desperate to get the topic off words that her sister had worked *hard* to keep from her kids' vocabularies, Portia asked Tami what she needed.

"Cressida is coming back soon. Then Portia and I can go get the stuffers. We were going anyway. And maybe when we're done, we can stop by the hospital?"

Everyone's phones went off at once—Cressida. The message a simple one. LET'S POSTPONE CHRISTMAS UNTIL DAD IS HOME. GET THE STUFFERS AND GIFT STUFF WHILE WE CAN, BUT WE'LL BUY FOOD AND MAKE A REAL CHRISTMAS DINNER WHEN THIS IS ALL SETTLED DOWN.

Without even waiting to hear the consensus, Portia bolted for the stairs. "Don't leave until I get out of the shower!" From somewhere, a protest rang out. She ignored it in favor of hot water and shampoo—*lots* of shampoo. Of course, the moment she stepped out, she remembered.

"Great. Now Gavin and Damon both are invading before our Christmas dinner. Shocker." She couldn't help but grin and add, "I should invite Reese just to throw things off even more."

Not for the first time, Portia wished the curses of

Shakespeare's plays were real and that she could evoke them without getting in trouble with the Lord for the action *or* the attitude that prompted it. This time it was prompted by the house—the great, enormous house full of things that the nieces and nephew couldn't touch and without all the things at home that they could. No one wanted to go near the hot tub for obvious reasons, and it was too cold for the pool. Even A.J. found playing pool difficult, and if she played ping-pong, the girls got into trouble.

When all games had been exhausted, and all the kids wanted was screen time, Tami stepped in. "We could take them for a walk on the beach…"

A glance at her phone showed it almost two o'clock. "I thought of that," she whispered back. "But what if that's what they have planned for when they get back—if they *ever* get back."

"Well, they should have told Miranda no. We have stuff to do."

It wasn't that Portia disagreed, of course. And she agreed even more as she dashed across the room just in time to save a pottery jug from becoming a mosaic on the tile floor of the kitchen. Still, how often did Cressida and Austin get time alone…ish?

Three o'clock inched closer and closer. Reese sent two texts, each half an hour apart—on the dot. If she hadn't been afraid he'd stop, she would have teased him about an alarm. Just before three, Cressida texted. CALL ME. TELL ME THE KIDS NEED ME NOW. SAVE ME.

That's all it took. She tapped the screen. "Hey. So, should we take the kids to the beach or something? They're about to tear apart the house, and I don't want Miranda to lose her deposit…"

As expected, finishing their late lunch quickly became of massive importance. "We'll be home in twenty. Thanks for letting us know." Cressida's follow-up text message read simply: THANKS.

Guilt-free, Portia doled out Kindles and searched for movies… just in case. She needn't have bothered. The blissful sounds of disgruntled children who lost games that Portia didn't hope to understand filled the room. A ding from Reese followed a few minutes later. TONIGHT'S THE ANNUAL LIGHT SHOW AT THE HARBOR VILLAGE. DAD'S GOT A COLD. NOT GOING. MOM'S STAYING HOME, TOO. DUNCAN AND I WONDERED IF YOU AND TAMI WANTED TO COME. A few seconds later, a second text showed up. THAT WAS MY MESSED UP WAY OF ASKING YOU OUT.

With no news about her father, Portia couldn't guarantee that Tami would be there, but a few seconds of thought was all it took to answer for herself. PICK ME UP HERE? WHAT TIME? WE'LL SEE ABOUT TAMI.

Just as Cressida burst in, ordering the kids out to the car, his next text came. FOUR O'CLOCK? DRESS WARMLY.

Tami appeared at her shoulder. "Ready?"

"Let's go." Still she didn't move from her spot on the couch. SIX? WE'RE JUST LEAVING TO GO SEE DAD AND DO STOCKING STUFF.

His reply came just as she climbed into the car. CARNIVAL STARTS AT 5:00.

That's all it took. I'LL BE WAITING AT TEN TILL?

TWELVE

That annoying, placating voice over the hospital loudspeaker greeted them as Portia and Tami reached their father's room in the Ventura County Medical Center. A curtain blocked their view, but they inched around it. Larry Spears had never looked worse. Bandages covered most of his head, scrapes to his face and arms—some bandaged, others not. He looked like he'd been in a fight for his life.

I guess if he'd gone any farther and hit the road, he might be.

Their mother noticed them first. "Hey…"

Tami rushed for a hug and reassurances that Dad would be okay. "They're taking him back for another CT scan in a bit. The doctor can't see anything wrong with his spleen, but he's got classic symptoms of a rupture."

At that, Tami blanched. "I thought spleens were like death if you didn't get them fixed. You bleed internally, don't you?"

"They're watching hemoglobin and all that," Mom insisted. "They're taking good care of him."

"He is right here, awake, and capable of speech, even." Though Dad's voice sounded weak, his quirky humor still showed.

That has to be a good sign.

Jessica burst into the room a moment later. "The guy from radiology is coming." She eyed Portia and Tami. "What're you doing here?"

Tami just buried her head in Mom's shoulder, but Portia

eyed her sister with a less-than-warm look. "We heard this strange guy got hurt and decided to show up and convince him to repent before he dies."

A snicker, cloaked in coughs, made the coming verbal backlash worth it. Except it never came. Jessica rolled her eyes and began moving stuff out of the way. "While Dad's getting scanned, I'm going to get some real food somewhere. Anyone want anything?" The silent addendum rang loud and clear, *And by anyone, I mean Mom.*

The radiologist's assistant arrived with a wheelchair just as Tami asked if she could come back after stocking shopping. Dad cried out as they tried to help him sit up, gasping through the pain. After a second try, Portia decided to get Tami out of there and sent Jessica a look that said, "Call me the minute you know what's going on."

A nod.

And that's why Jessica is so good at this. She knows how to keep everything going smoothly.

A second cry sounded as they reached the door. Jessica stepped in, demanding help. "Can't you see he's in some serious pain? Do something."

Though tempted to go back, Tami's panicked expression made her pause and reconsider. "Well," Portia began as she hurried them down the hall. "Looks like Jessica will keep those guys in line. She's good at that."

"Yeah…" Tami sighed. "Is she going to be mad if I come back?"

Some things should never be spoken, and questions like if anyone would be angry that a girl wanted to be with her father ranked right at the top in Portia's mind. That latent part of her that wanted justice for all—doled out by herself, if you please—strongly suggested a return to the hospital room and a relinquished piece of mind. However, one of those rare times she listened to the Lord's prompting *first* appeared out of the proverbial thin air.

Portia punched the elevator button when they arrived and

turned to Tami. "She's not here to keep us away. She's here to help us—*all* of us, not just Dad. So, if you being here helps you, and I know it'll help Dad, then she's going to want you right there with them. Trust me."

If only it were that easy to convince a fourteen-year-old girl to trust an older, and somewhat wiser sister.

In the elevator, a woman fought back tears. Red eyes, quivering lip—Portia knew the signs better than most. Her own voice shaking, she smiled. "Are you okay?"

"No."

At least she's honest. A glance at Tami showed her sister watching—listening. *Gotta do this. Going in, Lord.* Portia stepped a bit closer and offered to pray for the woman. "I'll under—"

"Please."

"Anything specific?"

Tears rolled down her cheeks. "That my husband's passing is swift and peaceful." The last few words Portia could only guess at, broken as they were.

"Um, Lord, please be with this woman... and her husband. I'm so sorry he's not doing well, but You can do all things that should be done. Please comfort all of them and give the doctors wisdom." A few seconds passed—seconds that felt like hours. No matter how hard she tried, Portia couldn't think of another thing to say. "Please, Jesus... *Please.* Amen."

The woman hugged her as they reached the first floor. "Thank you. That was... thank you."

All the way to the car, Tami watched her. But when she started to pull out, and her sister still stared, Portia lost patience. "What?"

"How'd you do that? Just pray for some stranger?"

"Prayer."

Exasperation shut Tami down. Portia saw it in the way the girl snapped her head and looked out the window, ignoring her. By the time they'd reached the exit to the parking lot, Portia understood.

"I wasn't blowing you off, Tami. I keep praying for stuff like that. I say I'm a Christian, right? I say I want to care about people like Jesus did. Well, I don't—not naturally. So, I pray that Jesus will give me those little moments to practice."

"Really?"

The hint of awe in Tami's voice and the wide eyes hinted that her little sister needed a clearer picture. "Yeah. But I miss about half of them, I'm sure. And half of what's left…" She flushed. "I ignore.

"But you did it this time. That counts."

I guess…

"Do you really think Jessica won't mind if I go see Dad again?"

"She might *act* like she minds, but she really just wants to take care of him. And you'll do that. It'll be okay. You'll see.

Not until they'd reached Target did Tami finally admit that *maybe* Portia wasn't *all* wrong. *Nice of you to finally decide I have a brain.*

The madhouse began in the parking lot and crept like a slow tide toward the front doors. Carts? What carts? Tami had to rush all over the parking lot to find one while Portia stormed the front door battlements. The Dollar Spot? Cleaned out of almost anything worth looking at. Empty shelves in the candy and snack aisles.

When she found employees—a near miracle, it seemed—they all said the same thing. "All merchandise in stock is on the shelves."

They did find a few mini Lego sets, and subsequently, her conversation with A.J. prompted Portia to pore over the larger sets while Tami dashed to the restrooms. Choosing the right one—almost impossible. *How do I know what he has? What he likes? If he even likes them?*

Just then, she saw a pirate roller coaster. Beside it, Batman. A lone Star Wars set stood cockeyed on a shelf below. And beside that, Hogwarts in all its four-hundred-dollar glory. *I don't think so.*

"Doesn't A.J. have *enough* presents already?"

Her reach for the box with the roller coaster ended up with her hand smashed into the shelf. "Ow! Don't sneak up on me like that!"

"I didn't! A.J. has that. Remember? He saved up all summer for it."

"I wasn't buying it for him… but it is kind of pricey…"

"No offense," Tami began in a tone that told her all was well with her sister. "But I don't really want a Lego set…"

Despite her fake laughter, Portia pushed back the box. "I could buy Hogwarts for you…"

"Done." Tami reached for the box, but Portia tried to push it back. "If I was rich, it'd be yours. Meanwhile, I search."

When Tami had left to wander around, as well as how long she was gone, eluded Portia. And once more, she jumped and nearly whacked her head this time as Tami asked why she was still staring at Legos. "I thought you weren't getting him one."

"It's not for A.J."

"Then who?"

Why it sounded so awkward, she couldn't explain—even to herself. "I was thinking about Duncan."

"You hardly know him!" When Portia didn't respond, she continued her objections. "You're the one who always tells me that we don't have to buy gifts for everyone we meet."

"Well, you *would*. I just thought it would be nice to do something for Duncan. He's a great kid." Once she got going, Portia seemed incapable of stopping. "I really like him… a lot. So, I thought maybe I should do something for him for Christmas, since who knows when I'll see him again."

"Yeah?"

She sighed. "I don't know… Maybe I shouldn't."

"Mom always says that we should err on the side of doing more instead of less, right?"

"So, which one? I want it to be special." Portia ordered her face not to flame as Tami shot a look at her. "I mean I want him to remember me, you know?"

At this, Tami snorted. "No one forgets you, Portia."

Still, Portia reached once more for the pirate roller coaster—twice what she'd hoped to spend but way more fun than the cheaper sets. Tami shoved Hogwarts at her. "Get him this. It's so cool. Of course, I'll hate you forever for not getting it for me, but still…" Whatever else Tami might have said vanished as she twisted the box and reached behind it. "Hey… look at this."

As the box appeared behind the oversized box containing a deconstructed Hogwarts, Portia knew it was just the right thing. "I—I love it. It's perfect. I mean, I met him on the beach, and we walk there sometimes. It's…"

"I've never seen a ship in a bottle out of Legos. A.J. would go nuts."

"I'll get him one for his birthday. This one's mine—for Duncan."

Almost an hour—they'd almost spent an hour in Target, buying half a dozen things at best. And her phone alarm had gone off twice. She'd have to get home and have Miranda drop off Tami. And the girl wasn't going to like that. Who could blame her?

"So how come you didn't take me on the beach? I could have practiced talking with Duncan."

"Duncan?" Portia nearly ran into the back of a car as she stared at Tami instead of the road. "What are you talking about?"

"You said you guys walked on the beach sometimes."

I did? Uh, oh…

The long, steep driveway that had been filled with cars all week now stood empty. Reese waited. Five o'clock crept closer… and closer. *Should have brought Duncan with me. Saved time.*

Maybe he should, but they'd almost pass the house on the way to the marina anyway. It had seemed so logical to at least give Portia the semblance of a regular date and pick her up first. *She liked it last time, but now…*

Her dark Buick shot up the drive just as he reached for the ignition. Portia bolted from the vehicle, reached into the back seat, and grabbed a bag. Even before Tami had made it out her door, Portia had disappeared into the house. A text message followed a few seconds later. JUST GOT HOME. BE OUT THERE IN LESS THAN 5. I HOPE. SORRY. FAMILY.

Sure, Reese could have gotten home and back in five—maybe. But the single purple rose on the seat beside him told him not to. It wasn't Christmassy, but the florist had been out of everything else remotely romantic that wasn't *red.* His mother had been adamant about that one. *"Don't go with red. If she reads a lot, she might make more out of it than you mean. Unless…"*

Of that, he'd reassured her. Yes, he felt like Portia *could* be "the one." But that could was a very tenuous and definite, *could.* For now, anyway. A moment later, Tami appeared again, but she went straight to the car and began carrying in bags. The door opened just as the girl reached for it, and the two sisters collided, sending bags flying and contents tumbling.

Portia did an impressive sidestep, one-footed hop as she dodged the melee, holding a gift over her head and shouted something indiscernible to her sister. A protest followed, but Reese only heard Portia's retort—most of it, anyway. "—told you to wait until I was gone!"

With that, she dashed down the drive, hair streaming out behind her, one arm in a coat and the other fumbling to find an empty armhole. How she managed not to drop said gift—he could only attribute to her experience in working with toddlers. She came to a skidding stop before him, and brushed her hair from her eyes. "Hey."

Reese kept glancing over Portia's shoulder, watching Tami try to stuff everything back in bags. "Does she need help?"

"Probably, but maybe now she'll listen. I nearly broke something coming out that door with her in the way."

He'd known it would happen. At some point, sooner than later, he'd assumed, she'd show some flaw or another—something more serious that made him think twice. He'd be concerned if she didn't—concerned about his own discernment. *I don't expect her to be perfect. I mean, I'm not, but Lord, I didn't think she'd be so… harsh.*

"Am I obnoxiously late?"

The question snapped him from his prayerful reverie. Reese, still mulling his questions, opened her door, reached in, and presented the rose anyway. *No red—good choice, Mom.*

"Oh, it's gorgeous!" She inhaled, apparently soaking in the rosy goodness. "So many purple roses have red undertones. This is such a blue purple. I love it."

That was the Portia who had come to invade his thoughts more often than not over the past week. The one delighted with life. The one who loved children. *Tami's hardly a child. And you don't know what kind of issues they're working with. Stop judging… for now.*

He thought she'd said something as he pulled away, but not until she touched his sleeve and asked, "Are you okay?" did he give her his attention again.

Reese turned onto Pierpont before sending her a sidelong glance. "Sure. You?"

"You're just quiet. I wondered… Sorry I was late. Tami needed to visit Mom and Dad, and then there was this thing with the CT scan person. Then Target was *crazy*. Oh, and I have a gift for Duncan." She tapped the box in her lap with one hand while sniffing the rose again.

"That's nice of you. It wasn't necessary, though. My parents spoil him, of course—only grandchild."

"Well, I love gifts, and…" She fumbled with her rose as if unsure what to do or say.

You're being awkward, and she's feeding on it.. That did it. Reese pointed to a bottle of water he'd brought. "It's no vase, but I figured it would keep the rose hydrated until you got home."

"Oh! That's a cool idea."

Portia's tone sounded both sincere and over the top all at once. Again, it was his "fault." He'd have to do *something* to fix it—soon. *Just ask what's up. She'll tell you. She doesn't seem to be excessively reserved…*

He pulled up to the curb in front of the neighbor's house, where Duncan wouldn't see them. "I think we should have helped Tami. It's bothering me that we didn't."

"If she'd just *listen*, it wouldn't have happened." A tirade—what else could you call it?—began, starting with Tami bringing in bags she'd been told to leave alone and ending with being sick to death of her family discounting her opinions and wishes on things.

Maybe it wasn't his place. Scratch that, he knew it wasn't. Still, the hurt look on Tami's face wouldn't leave him, and he had developed a quick and deeply soft spot for the girl. "So, are you really upset that she didn't want to leave stuff in the car, or are you really upset about past hurts and injustices and using this as an occasion to vent them?"

A cold silence didn't bode well for his plans for the night. He could only put it one way. Portia Spears was ticked—possibly at him as well as Tami, now. "I'll go get Duncan?"

"Yeah."

The choice presented was say what he really thought and possibly make things worse, or keep his mouth shut and let the light show be the end of things. *Disappointing, but not the end of the world. Better now than later, I suppose.*

Before he could decide if he should move the car up yet, the tirade began again. "If I would have gone off and did my own thing at her age, I'd have been required to scrub some part of the house as a reminder of how to do what I was told—*how* I was told. But no… she's the baby, so she can get away with anything."

"Sorry." Maybe he'd just get out and walk to the door. Give her time to cool off. *Yeah… because the extra fifteen seconds is really going to make a difference.*

"And then I bet Miranda doesn't take her to the hospital. So, I'll have to when I get back. Because she needs to be there. She's a daddy's girl. And of course, it'll be late. So I'll have to wait until she gets done there, because she won't get to stay long. And I—" Portia cut herself off.

The turmoil roiling in her heart showed in the fidgets of her hands, the pursed, lips, the rigid stare out over the street. Silent. Angry… angry but hurting, too.

Eyes closed, she whispered, "I can't believe I just said that."

"Sounds like you've been under a lot of stress…"

A sigh escaped Portia's lips just as he started the car and inched it forward to rest in front of their house. She shot him a glance. "Sorry, I need to call Tami."

As much as he wanted to hear that conversation, Reese used the gift as an excuse to dash inside and give her the privacy she obviously craved. Duncan raced out the door just as he arrived. He stepped in front and let his son barrel into him before signing for Duncan to take the red and green-wrapped box inside.

Portia waited by the car, eager for a hug when they returned and blushing at Duncan's signs of how beautiful she looked. "Thank you."

"He's right, you know." Reese held her still-open door again and waited for her to seat herself. "That green coat—gorgeous."

"I decided I wouldn't freeze tonight."

The tapping on his shoulder hinted that Duncan already wanted his phone. "Mr. Talkative is in rare form today. He hasn't stopped talking about how much you'll love the lights, the food, the games…"

At Seaward Avenue, Reese nearly forgot to turn left. Just as he pulled up behind a pickup, her phone blipped and a moment later, Portia sighed. "Everything okay?"

Her thumbs flew over the keys. "Yes. I—now I wonder if I should have pushed Tami to come."

"She didn't want to?"

"She was so determined to go see Mom and Dad again that I didn't ask. Then I bit her head off for doing what one of the others probably—" her phone dinged again, cutting her off. "Yep, Miranda sent her out. I told her to leave everything in the car, but Miranda wanted it all in the house—safe."

In his book, she sounded both irritated and remorseful—at the same time. "I'm going to have to apologize." Portia shot him a glare. "Note, in case you care. I don't like to apologize, and I *really* hate to admit I've been wrong." As he worked on a response, Reese could have sworn she added, "Baby steps, baby steps…"

THIRTEEN

The cheesy carnival rides wouldn't impress most kids on most days, but with the scent of funnel cakes and popcorn mingling with salt air and flashing lights, all corniness turned to magic. "I'm riding the putt-putt-plane with Duncan!" Portia urged the boy to the back of the line and added, "I can't believe it's free!"

"They're getting their money's worth." Reese gave her the first genuine smile she'd seen from him all evening. "I'm going to go get us burgers at The Parlor. Do you want cheese or not?"

"What if I'm vegetarian?"

"Then you shouldn't have had chicken alfredo when we went out to eat."

She elbowed Duncan and signed, "Busted." It was a word he didn't know, so, after telling Reese she wanted cheese on her burger and extra fries, she proceeded to do her best to explain "busted" to a little boy who didn't know why she wanted to break something.

"It means someone caught you, and now you're in trouble."

Duncan shook his head. *"No trouble. You forgot."*

Sarcasm—it never was easy to make hers understood to the Deaf—another reason her interpreting abilities never commanded the same interest as her sisters' did. However, despite multiple failed attempts, Duncan finally signed busted… twice. Then he winked.

They'd reached the front of the line before Portia got it.

"You little stinker!"

He giggled—sort of. His laughter sounded more like a cross between a guffawing giggle when he tried to repress it... and totally adorable to boot. He started to sign something, but the carny urged them forward to their planes. That's all it took. Cheesy and about as terrifying as swinging on a kiddie swing set, they floated around the swimming-pool-sized ride. Up... down... at one point, the guy pulled a lever and every airplane spun in place.

A memory prompted Portia to try something. She spun the wheel at the front of her plane and it twisted in place—just like tea cups at a county fair. It did infuse a bit more excitement into the ride, and once Duncan saw her, he managed to send his own little plane into a "tailspin."

Head flung back, Portia closed her eyes and allowed every bit of *joie de vivre* she could feel to fill her. *I really should have asked Tami if she wanted to come. She could have seen them tomorrow...*

Guilt demanded she do something about it. So, the moment they climbed out of the planes and stumbled toward the gate, Portia grabbed her phone and zipped a text message to Tami. A reply came back almost immediately. THANKS, BUT I JUST WANT TO WATCH A MOVIE AND GO TO BED. MIRANDA WOULDN'T TAKE ME OVER, AND NOW JESSICA IS MAD AT HER BECAUSE SHE SAYS IT'S TOO LATE—OR ALMOST.

Drama. Why did it have to ruin everything? And why did she let herself get involved? *I always say I won't... then I do.*

"Everything okay?"

Portia's phone bounced a few feet away—in the grass, thankfully. She dashed after it, brushed it off, and checked function before she responded to Reese's apologies. "It's not you. I'm just trying to decide if I should talk Tami into coming here. Miranda would bring her. They aren't taking her to the hospi—" A new message appeared.

"Scratch that. It seems that Jessica is bringing Mom home for a shower and Tami back for a while. They'll swap out. Good."

As he handed her a burger, Reese asked one more time, "Are you sure? You seem..."

"I'm ticked off, but mostly at me. I should have been more assertive for her. I just seethed instead. And look where that got us. Now there's going to be a bunch of drama over how Miranda didn't take her."

Crowds half-drove them toward a terraced seating area, but the noise made it hard to hear what Reese said. *If only my hands weren't full. I could talk anyway…*

But once seated, Reese prayed over their food and set his aside for a moment. Hands clasped before him, he gazed at her. "We can go get her—take her to the hospital. That's the more important thing."

Every time he said or did something that touched her heart, Portia stuffed it down—habit combined with defense mechanisms, she thought. This time, she couldn't. Instead, she stared at her burger, suddenly not hungry anymore, and tried to force down the emotions that choked her. Words finally surfaced—weak, ineffectual, but words nonetheless. "Thanks. No, but thanks."

"I've got one more thing to say."

This is it. This is where he tells me that he's glad we met but we probably should just stick to friendship…

"This isn't on you. You're not responsible for making other women adult."

His words shoved aside her fears as the opportunity to tease appeared with them. "Ooooh… my mom would kill you for that. 'Adult is not a verb. Stop using it like one.'" Somehow, and she'd consider the ramifications of that later, Portia had managed to sound exactly like her mother.

"Sometimes, it just works. And it does here." He nudged her knee with his and nodded at the burger. "Eat. Trust me, you'll want to. We'll get hot chocolate fudge cake after—"

That's all it took, Portia took an enormous bite and signed, *"Yummy,"* to Duncan. He grinned. *"Cake good."*

Of course, by the time she put away the entire burger and every one of the amazing fries, Portia didn't know if she'd ever eat again, much less cake in an hour. "I'll do my best," she promised with hand raised as if in court.

As music floated over light-dappled water and crowds of ooohing children accompanied it all, Reese stood with one arm around his son's shoulder and the other hooked around one of Portia's. Lost in thought, he hardly noticed the jerking about that her signing to Duncan did to his arm.

Lost in prayer, he didn't care.

Portia's, "Oh… wow…" did pull him out eventually.

Across the water, one cruiser had decked itself out to look like three separate ships with white lights creating "sails" against the night sky. Music drifted over the distance—a children's acapella choir singing, "I Saw Three Ships."

She pulled away, moved to Duncan's side, and began signing the words to the song. Once she'd given him an idea, she invited him to put his hand on her throat as she hummed. As she caught Reese's eye, she grinned. "One of many great things about Deaf children. They don't complain if you sing or hum off-key."

"It is pretty cool…"

As if it decided the whole contest, Portia leaned back against the rail, looped her arm back through his, and waited for the next. "That one gets my vote, though."

It did, too. Despite a dozen more that she cheered over and remarked on different elements, when it came time to cast votes, "Three Ships" got hers and by default, his. He couldn't *not* help her help it win. Duncan, however, voted for the "Santa ship." A thirty-foot sailboat with the "fattest" light display he'd ever seen, all displaying an enormous girth as it glided past.

The final boat, often a spectacular sight, looked quiet and unassuming until fireworks erupted. "See," she insisted. "They're celebrating that the ships won. I'm going to get cotton candy. Anyone else want some?"

Duncan declined, as did Reese. "Sure you want that? Chocolate cake…"

"Oh, ugh! You're not a nice man." Even as she spoke, Portia moved closer, leaned back against the railing, and grinned up at him.

"I'll remember that you prefer men who leave you to settle for inferior desserts that you have to pay for yourself."

"I always thought it wasn't fair that guys had to do all the hard work—ask someone out *and* pay for everything. Just doesn't seem right."

He waited for her to continue, but Duncan hurried over and signed a need—bathroom. *"You can't wait?"* The boy shook his head. That meant leaving. Now. *Someday, he'll get over that public restroom phobia. One accident when he was six and doomed for life is not acceptable but…* A glance at his son's hyper-concentrating face was all it took.

He had no choice. Reese turned to lead them through the crowds to try to escape before the rest. "I kept waiting for you to continue."

"And say what?" Portia signed to Duncan, asking if he enjoyed the lights while she waited for an answer. The boy just nodded and made a face. "What's wrong with him?" she asked as she signed, *"You okay?"*

"He needs to use the restroom. And," Reese continued, "usually when a woman tells me it isn't fair for guys to have to pay, they end with how guys think it entitles them to certain… *favors*, as my mom calls them."

She stopped in her tracks, staring. He didn't notice for several steps, but when Reese turned to ask if there was a problem, Portia growled at him. "Wait. Is that a thing?"

"Is what a thing?"

"Guys expecting girls to… what? No, wait. I don't even want to know. My imagination is probably sufficient and inadequate at the same time."

Duncan pulled Reese's sleeve and lunged toward the parking lot. He nodded and took off at a jog. "Sorry, we need to go… like, *now.*"

"If he has to go, surely there's a restroo—"

"He won't go in a public place. We need to hurry."

They did manage to avoid the influx of leaving cars. Reese shot down a four-lane road at speeds Portia insisted would get them pulled over. He heard every single unspoken word about it.

They heard the seatbelt snap back at the door frame just as Reese pulled up to the curb, and Portia shot out a reproof. "Don't unbuckle until the car has completely stopped! It's not safe!"

But Duncan had already dashed from the vehicle before she finished. Reese grinned at her, shaking his head. "He can't hear you, Portia."

Her hand clapped over her mouth. "Oh, how stupid. Still, we need to tell him." She reached for the door handle, but Reese stopped her.

"He'll be out in a minute—to say goodbye. You can tell him then."

The silence around them pressed closer with each second. Reese said nothing. Portia replied in kind. And silence gave birth to a healthy baby it named awkwardness.

Just as she blurted out something about how much she liked the plane ride, Duncan dashed out the door, wiping his hand over his forehead and shaking it out. *"Whew!"*

"Does he have accidents?"

Reese promised to explain, but urged her to tell Duncan to be safe. "Maybe he'll remember if his Portia tells him. Your word is pretty much law already."

Her "scolding" turned into jokes about becoming so flat he can slip between doors and doorjambs and how it would lead to a life of crime. *"Be smart. Unbuckle when cars stop. Only. No pancake Duncans."*

Duncan jerked open the door and flung his arms around her before stepping back and signing, *"I promise. I love you. Come Christmas dinner."*

"We'll see…" As she almost always remembered to do, Portia signed as she spoke.

Reese reached across her, gave Duncan a fist bump, and reached to pull her door shut. *"We're going for a drive and then maybe dessert. Tell Grandma I said you can have cookies if you want."*

"Does he know that we use more words than he does?"

As Reese pulled from the curb, he sighed. "He's still torn between pride in being more 'efficient' than we are and being cheated out of all the words. Someday he'll understand that for hearing people, the cadence and arrangement of words brings pleasure."

"Like poetry. Did you tell him that words can feel like music to people? He feels the beat of music, right? The resonance of the notes?"

"I hadn't put it that way, actually." Reese shot her what he hoped was a diabolical look. "I think I'll wait until he decides in favor of efficiency again. Then I'll tell him."

Her fidgeting prompted him to turn down Bangor Lane. "Let me show you one of my favorite places as a kid."

"This close?" The skepticism gave way to understanding. "Oh, the ocean?"

"Yep. *My* beach. Down where we met you," he explained as he wound through the tiny curved street and pulled up to a drive he knew would be empty all night. "Come on. We walk from here."

She met him at the back of the car—the first time she hadn't let him come around to open her door. *Is she more comfortable? Less intrigued? More eager to see me? Why?*

"So, where you met me?"

Maybe it was a little pathetic—he couldn't be sure—but seeing her *not* stuff her hands into her coat pockets gave him hope—hope that he actually wanted again. *We'll talk about it. That's all. We'll just have to talk, but not now. Too early.*

A nudge to his elbow reminded Reese that she'd resumed his story and he'd missed the cue. "Oh, right. That's *Duncan's* spot. When he heard the other was *my* favorite, we spent the better part of last Christmas break going to every single section of beach in a twenty-minute drive to find where he liked best so *he* could have his favorite. That was his." Reese took a chance and just laced his fingers with hers—with*out* asking or hinting first. "Want to guess why?"

They reached the steps up to the beach just as he saw her give up. But at the first step up, she laughed. "Because it says not to enter there. He feels like a total rebel or something."

"Yep!"

Once they sank into the deep, loose sand at the top, Portia stopped and gazed out over the moonlit water. The words came in a whisper—almost. Over the crashing waves of high tide, Reese had to strain to hear them, but no mistranslation could mistake it.

"If I tried to hold *your* hand, would that be awkward?"

"As in if I hadn't and you did instead?"

Portia turned away and tried to trudge through to the water's edge without answering. That wouldn't do. "Portia?

"I'm already embarrassed. Can we just forget I asked?"

"No."

That caught her attention. She turned and glared—even half-moonlight couldn't hide the ire in her eyes—at him. "Well, excuse me, but I'm going to, even if you won't."

Waves still crashed, the moon still hung half-hidden among the clouds, and despite a half-hearted yet successful attempt to retrieve her hand, they still walked hand-in hand, but now the sand grew harder as high tide inched back away from shore again and they followed the rim.

"I like you."

She shot him a quick look but said nothing. Well, not at first. But the words came eventually. "I think I like you, too."

"I wasn't looking for some kind of declaration, Portia. I just thought you should know it. It's why I wasn't willing to pretend like I didn't hear you ask if I'd be okay with you making a move on my hand. I liked knowing you might want to."

It worked. She shot him a *look* before squeezing his hand and shaking her head. "I think you really are going to be dangerous."

"Just thought you should know why." They made it another

twenty feet before Reese spoke again. "If we want dessert from Le Petit, we need to go soon."

Portia just held on tighter and kept moving forward, eyes on something—or perhaps nothing—in the distance. "If we want dessert, we'll go to Denny's. Pumpkin pie. Done."

"You like pumpkin pie?"

That lost him her hand. She stepped away, folded her arms over her chest, and yes—definitely *glared* at him. "If you hate even the sight or scent of pumpkin pie, it's a deal breaker. I eat it from October first through December—guilt free."

Reese just stared back, searching her for some sign of nerves. It came with a twitch to her eyebrow and a flare of her nostrils. Then he slapped his own face and turned to keep walking. "I cannot ask you to marry me over pumpkin compatibility. Tempting, though… very tempting."

There it was again—that little snort, so faint few people would have heard it, but he'd been listening. A moment later, Reese's heart turned to girlish mush when Portia's hand slid into his. *Oh, this is dangerous… way too dangerous.*

"That was good."

Now… now was the time. "Good enough to earn a visit for Christmas dinner tomorrow? We're late eaters—six o'clock." Only the waves and a gull who hadn't gotten the bedtime memo answered. "You're welcome to come anytime, of course."

That's so helpful.

"I mean, if you're up at six and want to watch Duncan open his gifts…"

Because that's every woman's dream. "I went out with this guy over Christmas, and he is so amazing! He even let me watch his kid open presents!" Lame.

No amount of self-rebuking worked. Still, Reese blathered on. "Just let me know in time and I'll make him save yours for last…"

Oh, Lord. I can't stop. Can you make *me stop? Please? I beg You.*

"We tend to read Luke between gifts and breakfast…."

Why not add, "And we can sing 'Away in a Manger' if it'll make us look spiritual enough!"

"And games in the afternoon, but I know you have family stuff, too."

In other words, I'm inviting you for it all, but I'm going to make you feel guilty if you actually come. Good one, Whitaker.

In a change he could only attribute to belated answered prayer, Reese said nothing for several yards. Just as he started to assure her she really was wanted, Portia said, "I wish I could hear you."

"Wha—oh, funny. Thanks. I should still feel guilty about refusing to ignore your question, but I don't."

She gave him a sidelong glance, but in the half-murky moonlight, he couldn't read it. "I—oh! No, I was just wishing I could hear what you were saying in your head. I could tell. You were carrying on a different conversation than we were."

Reese started to ask how she knew, but that would, of course, be a perfect way to verify her assertions—something he did not intend to do. "Well, I meant it. We'd love to have you all day—sleep over and wake up with us even." The words reverberated in his head until they battered some sense into him. "Um, wait. That came out—"

Laughter—loud, boisterous, utterly raw and unfiltered. It filled the night air. "Oh, if you—" she gasped. "If you could see your face…"

"Laugh… go ahead."

"I will."

As they neared the edge of the beach closer to "her" house, Reese turned her back again. "Don't want you seeing home and it giving you ideas about needing to go back."

"I probably should."

"Yes, you probably should," he agreed. He pulled her a bit closer and squeezed her hand. "I just don't want you to."

They'd made it halfway back before she spoke again. "I probably need to apologize."

"For?"

"I was rude to Tami—and it put you in a bad spot. Sorry."

I thought you didn't like to apologize. That was almost... almost... *an unnecessary apology.*

"Better take it now. It's a limited-time offer. In a few seconds, I'll deny it—as pathetic as that is."

"It took guts to do that. Thanks."

Again, they walked without talking, but that comfortableness just *being* that had always intrigued him in certain couples appeared. It permeated the way they walked, the way their hands swung between them with almost rhythmic movements—the way he could swear their hearts beat in sync with one another.

You need to go to bed. That's just...

"Do you feel it?"

Portia's words jerked him out of that wondrous place where new feelings are forged and into reality again. "Feel what?"

"Never mind."

Something deep within him told Reese not to let her run away like that. He stopped and pulled her back to him when she tried to keep going. Too soon? Probably. He didn't care. Hands at her waist, he rotated until he could see half her face. "Feel what, Portia?"

She gazed out over the water as if looking at him took more emotional energy than she had to offer. "It just felt like we were... connected. Like everything was in some kind of harmony." A huff followed that. "Oh, that sounds dumb. I don't know how to explain it."

"Like we're in sync?"

Her head nearly did an owl twist toward him. "Yes!"

"I thought so, too..." The light playing on her lips—much too tempting. *Get her home before you go overboard. Moonlight and waves are dangerous combinations, Whitaker.*

"Reese?"

He tore his gaze from her lips and met hers. "Yeah?"

"Thanks."

Not until he'd watched her disappear into the door of Sandpiper House and had driven away did Reese realize two things. First, the gift he'd bought... "Totally giving it to her. Time to quit second-guessing everything and enjoy this."

The second… he'd forgotten to get her to agree to come for Christmas dinner.

A text message buzzed just as he pulled up in front of his parents' bungalow.

COMING TOMORROW. NOT SURE WHAT TIME OR FOR HOW LONG, BUT I'LL COME AT LEAST FOR DINNER.

Another followed a few seconds later.

THANKS FOR THE BEST DATE EVER—AND FOR MY FIRST PROPOSAL. NOTE: YOU OWE ME A SLICE OF PIE WITH ENOUGH WHIPPED CREAM TO MAKE THE DAIRY FARMERS HAPPY.

FOURTEEN

Screams ripped Reese from sleep and propelled him face-first into the floor. He'd managed to struggle to a sitting position, still straining to see around him, when the door opened and the hall light blasted his unsuspecting eyes. "Aaak."

Mom stood there. "Reese?"

Despite the subconscious anguish of having a very pleasant dream snatched from him, Reese managed to climb up on Duncan's bed, wrap the thrashing, screaming boy in a blanket burrito, and hold the boy close. With his neck pressed against Duncan's temple, he hummed… just as he had those first weeks after Corinne had left their son behind.

The dreams returned when Grandma Whitaker had died a few years later—right after Reese finally made his son understand that the beloved old woman wouldn't be coming back. Wouldn't make a mess of her signs and say ridiculous things in the process—not ever again. *"In heaven, you won't need to sign. You'll understand each other perfectly."*

Maybe it had been the wrong thing to say.

The struggle shifted as sobs slowed. Reese recognized that shift—the move from frenetic flailing to desperate to free his hands. To talk. He untucked one corner of the blanket, and Duncan sat up.

Mom turned on the light, moved over, kissed Duncan's cheek, and after a fierce hug, turned away. The door clicked shut behind her. And Duncan signed.

Of course, it was the same dream as every time. The black shadow that crept over everything, the heavy, oppressive feelings, the giant claw that snatched at someone important. This time… Reese dreaded to think of who his son feared losing next.

"Portia."

It made no sense. He didn't know Portia well enough to miss her enough for nightmares.

"She's leaving," he insisted. *"I won't see her."*

All Reese could say was that they had phones and cars. It wasn't as dire as all that. Duncan seemed unconvinced.

Four hours later, they awoke, Reese with a crick in his neck, aching spine and legs, numb backside. Duncan had only one thought on his mind. *"Presents now?"*

"Coffee first."

His son dashed from the room, and his parents' door banged open a moment later. "Better make that two."

With the finesse of a drunken zombie, Reese made it to the kitchen and even so far as to pour the coffee waiting for them. After that, he lost track of his thoughts and movements. Mom found him staring into a mug of swirling coffee. "Did I put something in this?"

"Taste and see. If it's too sweet for you, I'll take it." She leaned her head on his arm. "Are you okay?"

"It was over Portia."

"Portia!" At least his mother didn't see some issue that he'd missed. "Why? He hardly knows her."

The coffee needed only a bit of half-n-half to make it palatable, but Reese took his time figuring out the perfect ratio before answering. "I don't get it, Mom. I don't. He's terrified we'll never see her again. It seems awfully soon to attach himself like that."

"That's what I thought. So why the—?"

Duncan arrived with Portia's gift in hand, cutting off all discussion. He shook it and signed permission to open before grabbing Reese's hand and nearly causing a second-degree coffee burn. Reese followed out of self-preservation alone.

Sort of.

With his parents on the couch just as they always had, and seated to one side of tree in case Duncan needed help, Reese kept his phone recording every rip of paper, every tear, and the enormous squeal of delight when the ship in a bottle appeared. Without prompting, Duncan began signing his thanks, his excitement at seeing her soon—all of it.

It ended with, *"Please don't go home. I'll miss you."*

That was Mom's cue to pop the cinnamon rolls in the oven. Dad excused himself for a bathroom break. Reese hunkered down on his heels and examined every bit of the box before Duncan was ready to listen. *"She doesn't live here. That's right. But neither do we. She lives closer..."* As he sometimes did for emphasis when usual methods didn't work well, Reese signed the word again, one letter at a time. *"C-l-o-s-e-r to us. It's only an hour. If she has time, we can go see her."* To himself, he added, *If she wants to. Please want to.*

Mom hurried into the room and pulled the neat, square box, that still sent Reese's heart racing at the sight of it, from beneath the tree and tapped it. *"That one next. It's from Grandpa."*

How many kids got presents from *just* grandpa or *just* grandma when both lived, and with each other? Reese suspected it wasn't many, but every year his parents split all but one gift into individual ones. *And you can tell who gave what without even seeing the tags.*

The moment Dad appeared, Duncan ripped the paper from it, once more in a dozen small pieces, his eyes widening with each one. *"I have a helmet? Why? What is it for?"*

And the Christmas hunt was afoot. Thirty seconds later, it also became a toothy Christmas, complete with blood, saliva, and other nauseating reminders that not everything about being a father was a joy. *Bodily fluids are proof of that.*

Duncan's new grin, however, proved that sometimes, that stuff was all worth it. *"I ride my new bike?"*

What else could he do? The kid *couldn't* ride a bike yet, but he'd end up a bloody mess by the end of the day trying. *Yay.*

The bedside clock glowed eight when Portia awoke. Had her phone not read, DECEMBER 25, she might have forgotten the day. Before she could even look at notifications, the thing restarted for reasons that she suspected meant she'd be buying a new one, soon. *Probably dropping it last night…*

Nothing about it felt like a *normal* Christmas. Nothing. From what she could tell, the kids weren't even awake yet. "It's *abnormal*! Kids should be bugging me to get out of bed and watch them open presents. It's what kids *do*. This is insane."

Not only that, but throwing off her light blankets didn't send shivers up her spine. Again, Portia protested. "I should be stupid cold! This isn't fair. This is so stupid unfair. Christmas should be cold!"

A shiver hit as she neared the window. "Well, that's a bit more like it. Still. Ugh."

Notifications hit her phone as it powered up again. The first from Reese, and something about that did silly little things to her heart—things she didn't know how to translate… yet. *But I will. I definitely will.*

MERRY CHRISTMAS.

Another followed on its heels. WHY DO I FEEL LIKE I SHOULD SAY, "CHRIST IS BORN!" LIKE SOME PEOPLE DO AT EASTER WHEN THEY SAY, "HE IS RISEN!" HE WASN'T EVEN BORN ON CHRISTMAS—NOT REALLY.

Her thumbs danced across the keyboard of her screen as she shot back a reply. BECAUSE GREEN TREES IN SPRING OR SUMMER AREN'T THAT UNUSUAL. IT'S MORE FUN IN DECEMBER.

As she read the next, a few lines about how much Duncan loved his "ship in a bottle," a text came through, bumping the other messages and at least two or three pictures out of the way. HUH?

Next came a coherent reply. OH. TREES. GOOD POINT.

UNLESS YOU LIVE IN AUSTRALIA.

She'd heard the argument, and while she felt bad for Aussies—something that would probably tick them off if they knew—Portia couldn't help but cling to her own traditions, preferences, and prejudices. Christmas *should* be in a northern hemisphere winter. And the southern hemisphere could gloat in knowing they were using the right… ish… season. "But most of the inhabited world is in the northern hemisphere… isn't it?" Remembering the existence of that little place called Africa hinted that maybe she might be wrong on that score. *But if China is northern… and I think it is…*

The picture of Duncan holding up the box with a cheesy gap-toothed grin stopped her heart. "When did he lose that tooth?"

The next showed a "Meerryy Chrismas, Portia" sign followed by a text from Reese. HIS SPELLING… TELL ME IT'LL GET BETTER. SOMEDAY. I'M PLEADING HERE.

Her instincts said he'd done it without telling anyone.

A video followed with Duncan signing about all his gifts… the bicycle and helmet, the movie, the pirate ship she'd decided was too much for someone she didn't know well. Zoo passes. If the signs she almost couldn't read meant anything, he *loved* the zoo and invited her to come every time they went.

The video panned to Reese's red face before a laughing Duncan signed that his father was embarrassed. "Mortified is more like it… but that was a smile, so he's not miserable at the idea. That's good… I think."

Noises around her hinted that the family was waking up. Portia spent five minutes trying to find somewhere to prop her phone so she could sign a message to Duncan. The latch for her window proved perfect.

"Merry Christmas, Duncan! I'm happy you liked your presents." She struggled for what to say next and finally finished with, *"I'll play that game with you as soon as I can get there."*

A knock came just as she pulled her phone down. "Coming…"

"It's your turn to make breakfast."

And you couldn't have told me last night, Miranda?

"I said I was coming!"

"And the kids are starving!"

"Then tell me that you expect me to do things next time! I didn't know!"

Miranda's next words she missed, but the tail end came through clear enough. "—going to take off all night!"

"I was home by ten-thirty!" Portia jerked open the door. "That's hardly all night."

Hair up in a messy bun and wearing a baggy long-sleeved tee, Miranda looked better than anyone should right out of bed. "For someone all bent out of shape because our guys came early, you sure are ready to dash off at a moment's notice to meet this one."

For just a moment, Portia managed to rein in words she shouldn't speak. But only for that moment. Then they poured forth with the force of the waves crashing against the jetties along Reese's beach.

"I didn't just pull him into our *family* time. After all, *you* guys said this was *just* for family. *You* wanted this one *last* time for *just* us! Well, I didn't bring him in, but you two did quickly enough."

Miranda shut the door behind her and leaned against it, hands on hips. "Yeah," she added, voice much too soft to be safe. "… and we *know* these guys. I'm *engaged.* Just a few months and I'll be *married* to Gavin. In that time, you'll have forgotten this guy's name."

Her gut clenched at the idea, but a retort flew out before Portia could consider the wisdom of it. "Because you've forgotten every guy you've ever been with?"

"No—"

"What about the 'pick up date' at college parties you went to? Do you remember any of *their* names? The guys you were so proud of because it was 'just a date—no strings'? What about them? Can you—?"

"This isn't about *me.* This is about *you* not even doing your part—"

Never before had she had the desire to slap any of her sisters—well, never so strongly, anyway. "Like you did last night? Taking Tami to the hospital *like you promised?*"

"Jessica—"

"Rearranged things to make it happen. Don't even pretend that it was the plan all along. I almost had to cut my date short to play chauffeur because you didn't keep *your* word."

"Like you kept yours about helping with the logistics around here?" Miranda's voice rose—a sure sign she knew she'd lose the argument.

Portia nearly crowed as she drove home the point. "I asked for a schedule before we even left home. You said you'd have it when we got here. I asked Thursday. Friday. Saturday. Sun—"

"Fine. I'll do it."

Miranda turned to go, but Portia lunged for the door. "No. That's not the point." Never had Portia ever managed to know how to word an argument before, but suddenly, she was full of loquacity. "The point is, you come in here and accuse me of not doing something *I didn't know I was supposed to do.* And you do this all the time. You and Jessica. You create rules for everyone else that you don't bother to follow yourselves. Well *I've had it.* Don't ever attack me for something I couldn't prevent again."

"I—"

Before Miranda could try to shoot her down, Portia rewrote that last line and delivered it with every bit of punch it needed, if she did say so herself. "Actually, just don't ever attack me again. If you can't just talk to me like you would some random stranger who tapped your car door with theirs, then don't talk to me. Those people get more kindness from you guys than I do."

With that, Portia squeezed past, opened the door, and slipped out, determined to get downstairs before the tears arrived. Miranda's voice reached her by the time she hit the first step. "Portia, wait…"

"I'm not—"

"I'm sorry."

While not every Spears found apologies as difficult as Portia, Miranda was probably third in line for least likely to choke one out—Jessica being second, of course. She looked up, and to her disgust, the first tear fell. "It's okay."

"No…" Miranda moved closer, slowly and without taking her gaze from Portia's face. "It's not. You're right. I was mad at myself for forgetting to do it, and then I forgot to text you a copy. We're so used to you being available whenever."

Do not go off on that. She just apologized. It's true, too. I am. Despite the pep talk, the words still stung. *It's like I'm that aunt in antique books—the one the family just assumes will take care of everything so the rest can go off and have fun.*

"—like him?"

Jerked from her thoughts, Portia didn't hear it. "What?"

"I asked if you really like him—this guy. Tami says his name is Reese?"

"Yeah. And yeah, I like him."

The crooked smile that gave Miranda an appeal that had attracted boys since the fourth grade appeared. "I'm not used to thinking of my little sister being old enough for a boyfriend."

"I'm twenty-five. I sure hope I am. I mean, I can rent a car now and everything."

Miranda reached her side and hugged her. "Go get a shower. I'll do breakfast. You take my dinner—"

"Can't. I have a date."

"For *Christmas* dinner? What happened to it being all *family*?"

She fell for it. With a retort about how they weren't *doing* Christmas yet all fired up and ready to fly, the twinkle in Miranda's eye gave it all away. "You're so dead."

"Gotcha." Miranda took a few steps down before calling back. "Still, I'll get breakfast. You can take my breakfast on Thursday."

"Fine…" Portia retorted. "But send me that schedule—*with that fixed!* I don't want to hear about how I missed my day for the rest of this vacation!"

FIFTEEN

There's something extra irritating about Christmas not happening on Christmas, but the rest of the world acting like it is. *Where am I supposed to get good paper for making cards on Christmas? Walmart and Target are being thoughtful, responsible employers and giving their employees the day off.*

Portia stared at the accumulation of stuff in hopes of figuring out something amazing. Her mother had contributed a set of colored pens. Cressida had a few pages of planner stickers that would work in a pinch—and a pair of scissors. The house had printer paper in the office.

Bella had a box of crayons.

Glue? Nope. Glitter? Thank-You-Jesus, nope! Colored paper? Not hardly. Not even a single *coloring book*.

Who doesn't have coloring books for their kids!?

Austin had fixed that one. He went online, printed out a dozen easy-to-cut-out coloring pages, and plopped them on the table. "Will that help? Glad they have that 'office' we can connect to."

"Works… we still need something to glue them to. And, oh. Glue."

"Supermarket?" Austin shoved his hands in his pockets and eyed the pile. "They sometimes have weird stuff in their stationery aisles."

She'd have bolted out the door, but Austin was ahead of her. "I'll go. You know what you're doing here. I can find paper and glue."

Thanking him took more effort than perhaps it should have, but by the time she got the older two kids coloring, she'd forgotten. "Remember, we're making *two* cards for Grandpa. One for Christmas and one to get well. You want them to be pretty and make him know we wish he was here."

For three minutes—three blissful, joy-filled minutes, the table looked as if it had been staged for a stock photo shoot. Charis' piggies sat perched on each side of her head, the bows looking as if freshly tied there. Bella kept her crayons in a perfect study of random scatteredness. It shouldn't have worked, but of course, it did.

A.J.'s helpfulness—Portia snapped a few of her own pictures of that. Charis' attempts to color "inside the lines," which meant fewer scribbles off the paper and onto the table. Bella's "mothering" of her older and younger siblings—a beautiful picture of familial bliss.

But at one second past the three minute mark, or so it seemed, everything disintegrated faster than a snowman in Death Valley in July. Screeches brought Cressida running from where she had been stacking the dishwasher.

"What's going on?"

"A.J. said my snowflake's ugly!" Bella's indignation caused a rather adorable mispronunciation of her Ls as Ws, producing more of a "snowfwake's ugwy" effect. And that prompted A.J. to mock said speech issues. Charis took sides. If only Charis hadn't done that. In tiny fists, she tried crumpling up everyone's cards. Portia dove for them.

Cressida marched A.J. from the room, stern growls following in their wake. *He's busted.*

And as if all that wasn't enough… a text message came through—Reese. HOPING ALL IS WELL AND WE'LL BE SEEING YOU SOON. A picture followed. One with a bicycle sitting on top of Duncan, rather than the other way around. THE KID'S GOT CYCLING SKILLS. THEY'RE JUST NOT USEFUL ONES. SAVE US.

Half an hour—it took a full half an hour to get them all

sitting back down and working on cards again. Now glue littered the table like an icing factory gone wrong. Crayons were broken and had been worn to a nub in spots—too bad the kids refused to tear paper away from the crayon.

That's when Charis gave up. She threw her crayon across the room, folded her little arms over her chest—sort of—threw back her head, and wailed. Portia zipped a text message to Reese. CAN I USE YOU? LIKE BE THAT PERSON WHO TOTALLY USES SOMEONE TO GET OUT OF SOMETHING?

The reply came almost instantly. PLEASE.

COME GET ME? KNOCK. ASK IF I'M READY? YOU NEED HELP WITH

Portia didn't even get that text finished before Cressida burst in, "Shush! Stop!"

Charis did *not* stop. Bella took up the battle cry—it had definitely become one of those. A.J. blurted out a half-hearted apology and went back to where his card had been. His protests began now.

Portia finished that text.

SOMETHING. HURRY.

Only the Providence of God and His kindness in her life kept her from hitting send with an addendum of, "I'll make it worth your while." *I can't even… thank you, Lord. Thanks.*

Someday, probably sooner than she expected, she'd tell him about that. He'd think it was funny. And it would be. Then. At that moment—not so much!

"Portia!"

Jerked from her panicked reverie, she stared first at each child before realizing Miranda had called her name. "What?"

"Don't you have to get ready for your date?"

That stopped Cressida's scolding. She turned to Portia, jaw agape, and sent darts of disapproval. "You have a *date*? On *Christmas?* Isn't that against everything you've complained about since this whole idea began?"

"Um… I wouldn't even think about it, Cress, but as far as *I was told*, we aren't celebrating Christmas today. This is just any other day. Did that change?" Hands planted on her hips as if of their own accord. Portia hoped she agreed with the move, now that it was too late and all.

Miranda inched closer and beckoned Portia to follow. "You really need to get ready, *don't* you?"

"I don't know!" Request to Reese forgotten, Portia stared down her oldest sister, fury drowning out everything else—especially her common sense. "I *thought* that I had one person here who supported me." Her hands began shaking as she turned to face Miranda. "I was just wrong about who it was, I guess. Thanks 'Randa."

With that, she bolted for the stairs. She'd just managed to swap out her shirt and brush out her hair when the doorbell rang. Practicality said to skip the lip gloss and save any hope of Reese still speaking to her again. Vanity silently begged Miranda to be the doorman and keep him from bolting.

The gift she'd managed to hide from Tami? She popped it in her purse and dashed out the door. At the top of the stairs, however, Tami came back to mind. "Where's Tami?"

Miranda waved her down. "Reese is here. I'll take care of Tami. It's fine. Have fun. See you later."

If her sister hadn't been waving her phone around as she spoke, Portia absolutely would have missed the not-so-subtle hint that a text would be forthcoming. *Gotcha. I'm so dense today.*

At the car door, Reese held it shut. "Are you okay? You sounded…"

"I refuse to ruin your Christmas just because my family is stressed." And that's when it hit her. "That's it, isn't it?"

"What's it?"

"No one wanted to come, so we tried to make everything perfect, which never goes right, and now everyone's worried about Dad and disappointed about Christmas. That's why the drama seems so much worse than usual."

Disappointment flickered in his eyes. He gazed at her, waiting for something—what, she couldn't imagine. "Do you need to stay?"

The first Miranda text arrived. TOOK TAMI TO THE HOSPITAL BEFORE I CAME TO SEE YOU THIS MORNING.

Relief washed through her and over her. A second came a moment later. SORRY I FORGOT TO TELL YOU. IT'S BEEN HARD ON ALL OF US.

She turned the screen around so he could read it. "Nope. I'm good to go."

All afternoon, he watched Portia—concerned. She cheered Duncan from the front of his bike, running backwards up the sidewalk and falling twice. Her hair became a windblown mess, and Reese loved it.

While she leaned against Duncan's handlebars, eyes sparkling and smile wide, he stood behind, hands shoved in his pockets. "You're beautiful." A dozen recriminations pounded his brain before he'd even finished speaking. *That's considered sexist these days, isn't it? And she won't be afraid to tell me exactly what she thinks about it.*

A few other self-attacks formed, but his mind zipped back to her being more than willing to speak her mind. *I like that. Weird… I don't think I've ever found that attractive before.*

"Reese?"

He snapped to present and saw Duncan grinning at him. Portia just looked worried. "Sorry, what?"

"I said thanks… Are you okay?"

"Not sexist?" He groaned aloud. "Ignore that."

"No way." At Duncan's quick glance, she winked. "I distinctly remember someone not forgetting something *I* said when I needed it."

What he would have replied, Reese couldn't decide. At that moment, Duncan turned to him and signed, *"You like her? Girlfriend? I like her."*

Reese couldn't possibly hope to answer that without her "over-seeing" the conversation. *"We'll talk about that later."*

"I can go…"

Reese, thankfully, never had a chance to respond to that. His parents appeared, ready to take a pre-dinner prep walk and determined to take Duncan with them. *Bet they would've taken a pre-dinner prep nap if she wasn't here.*

Duncan insisted that he be able to "ride" the walk. Being Christmas, Reese's parents relented after a torturous three and a half seconds. "You don't have to, Mom…"

"We'll be back in half an hour. Dinner's in two. You should take her down to Marina Park. She'd enjoy the zip line."

"Great idea. Should be pretty empty right now…" He eyed her. "Walk it or drive it?"

Portia seemed to test the idea. "How far?"

"A mile."

After a couple of seconds, she jerked her head toward his car. "Drive. We can walk the beach instead of a street, right?"

This girl's a romantic. Remember that.

Inside five minutes, Reese opened her door in a near-empty parking lot. The wide sidewalks that usually sported kids on bikes, skates, skateboards, and scooters, despite signs warning against such hooliganisms, were empty. Cold air blew in off the water, but Portia had dressed warmly, and even if he hadn't, Reese suspected he might not notice.

I guess I understand Duncan's fear. The idea of not seeing her again… hurts.

They trudged through sand, passing a die-hard beachcomber sweeping his metal detector in slow, wide arcs as he searched for items of value. "I bet that thing is worth more than my first car," Reese mused as he grabbed the rope and they climbed up in the park's greatest treasure—the pirate ship.

"Favorite thing as a kid—bar none."

Portia accepted the rope but stared across to the pole where the line ended. "Looks kind of low…"

"Put your feet up when you get near the middle."

With a decided shake of the head, she handed back the rope. "You take it. Show me."

The cry of gulls overhead, the wind in his hair—the magic of whizzing down a zip line. The title sequence of his childhood. For the twenty-second ride, he was eight again and so lost in the moment that he almost forgot to "pull up" and drop off in time. "Yeah!"

He jogged back to the ship with the rope and told her to wait until he could get to the end pole. "I'll tell you when to drop."

"If you let me slam into that thing…" Portia called out.

At least, that's what he thought she said. "I've got you. Go!"

Just like that, she went. Her squeals—just like every little girl he'd ever crushed on for the hour and a half they were his girlfriends. He'd found true love a dozen times by the time he was ten. *And not once in high school or college. Weird how that works.*

Right as she neared the end, instinct took over. He jumped forward, grabbed her around the waist, and jerked her away from the pole. As if ripped from a cheesy Christmas movie, they landed tangled in the sand, but instead of a lingering look of awareness followed by a long-awaited kiss, they resembled a Three Stooges audition. Facing opposite directions, Reese hit ground first, but somehow his legs ended up on top of her stomach. Her elbow, in a feat that hinted at a moonlighting job as a contortionist, landed in his rib.

Portia sat up, shoving him off in the process and shaking sand out of her shirt. She wiped it from her face even as she laughed. She also glared, and it struck him that only Portia Spears could both laugh and glare at the same time. "You could have *warned* me!"

He gasped for a full lung of air before laughing himself. "I didn't mean to do that. I was going to call out and tell you when to jump, but that dad-instinct kicked in."

A lump formed in his throat as Portia ran her fingers under her hair and shook out the long strands. The red glowed in sunlight in ways that he thought only existed in fantasy novels and movies. Her fingers combed through non-existent tangles as if determined to prove to him that the mess she thought her hair was… well, it was his fault. *Guilty, then.*

"What?!"

He blinked. "What, what?"

"You're staring. Do I have sand on my forehead?" She brushed off her shirt and her knees as if sand dared to linger. For one irrational moment, he nearly asked if glitter ran from her presence. "What?!"

"Glitter is scared of you, isn't it?" A groan filled his mind, and Reese prayed it hadn't escaped when he wasn't looking.

"Don't I wish. Why?"

"Just curious."

A step closer… two. She reached out and brushed sand from his temple. "What's wrong? Do I have bird poop in my hair or something?" She closed her eyes. "Please tell me I don't have bird poop in my hair."

"Any warm spots…?"

Her eyes popped open. "Ew! Um…" Relaxation followed. "Yeah, no. You're right."

"I said it before… and it's still probably so un-PC it isn't funny, but it's true. You are crazy beautiful." His more rational self told him he'd offend her if he didn't shut up. He didn't. "How are you still single?"

Her reply came faster than he'd expected. "I'm picky."

Every instinct screamed for him to risk it—to kiss her while he had the moment. Something deeper within whispered, *Wait.*

Reese opted for a compromise. He inched forward and brushed non-existent sand from her jaw. "If I didn't know that it's way too soon, I'd kiss you—if you'd let me." A sigh escaped as honesty forced him to admit, "Not true."

Disappointment? Is that what flickered in her eyes? He thought so, anyway. *Disappointment in that I didn't or that I said…* Then he realized how it sounded, and the temptation to test a theory proved impossible to resist. "It wouldn't matter if you 'let me' because I wouldn't ask. I'd just do it."

It looked as though she chewed the inside of her lip as she

mumbled, "Jimmy Stewart, huh?"

"Jimmy—the actor?"

Portia trudged over to the zip line and grabbed the rope. "That's what he did in *The Glenn Miller Story*. He got her to come to New York and had an itinerary for them to hurry up and get married before some gig that night, and she started arguing that you don't just show up and do stuff like that. So he kissed her, and the next thing you know, they're married."

She'd taken three steps toward the ship again before she finished, but then Portia froze. "That sounded more logical and less about marriage in my head. I just meant that he did it—kissed her. Didn't ask. Just did it. The rest..."

"I didn't hear." Reese hurried to catch her other hand and walk back to the ship with her. "Not this time."

Not until they'd climbed up onto the ship and she was ready to propel herself out over the sand did Portia reply. "I'm single because I'm a hermit... and according to my soon-to-be-brother-in-law, I intimidate guys because I say what I think."

With that, she kicked off and whizzed over the sand. Reese watched, heart pounding as if he'd run a marathon—or perhaps just for chasing after one thought. *Or because God had a plan?*

SIXTEEN

The tiny kitchen didn't allow for everyone to work together, but Portia kept busy as Brian and Kendra worked in that beautiful synchronization of a couple married for a long time. "How long have you guys been married?"

"Which time?" Brian gave her a wink over his shoulder and turned back to finish rinsing green beans in the sink. "Gotcha with that one, didn't I?"

Portia couldn't help repeating, "Which time?"

"They got divorced when I was almost fourteen," Reese said from the doorway. "Worst year of my life."

Kendra nodded. "Mine, too."

When Brian added, "Mine three," she suspected it was something they said whenever the story came up.

"Um… is it rude to ask what you're talking about?"

Duncan rushed in with his ship in a bottle set, begging to start it. Portia stopped setting the table long enough to sign, *"After dinner. It's almost time to eat."*

For a moment, she thought he'd protest, but Reese's hand on the boy's shoulder was all it took to change the cloudy face to resigned. *Need to learn what he does with that. Would be great to have in my "how-to-deal-with-toddlers" toolbox. If it works for littler kids.*

As quickly as he'd come, Duncan raced off, and Portia gave Reese a, *Spill the rest of this story* look. Well, it probably came out as more of a, *Don't make me have to ask and embarrass myself* look, but same difference, right?

"They got back together at my high school graduation," Reese said just as she'd given up and was ready to ask.

A look at him confirmed it. "You waited to tell me until I gave up."

"Guilty."

"You'll pay for that."

Her insides began a gymnastics routine as he grinned back at her and said, "I hope so."

The kind of swoony sigh that Portia reserved for her Austen and Gaskell adaptations sounded from the oven as Kendra pulled rolls out of a smaller section. "I'm thinking we need to move to Newhall, Brian."

Brian, however, appeared as confused as she was. "Huh?"

"I want to be close enough to watch this."

"Watch what?"

This time, Portia wasn't tempted to echo at all. She knew exactly *what* Reese's mom wanted to watch. Confirmation came three words later. "Reese and Portia."

Her cheeks warmed as understanding lit Brian's eyes. They'd probably turned a very bright pink by the time he winked and said, "Well, I'd say we'd want to move to Acton or something, then. Maybe Palmdale."

Warm turned flaming hot as Reese's arms came around her waist and his voice filled her ears. "Mid-way from my house to hers… so we can meet there and be properly chaperoned?"

"That'll work." Kendra winked at her. "Any excuse, of course…"

"I think I'd rather hear about how a divorced couple is married." Portia clapped her hand over her mouth to stifle both more words and a groan. It failed in the latter. "Um, so where's the butter?"

"Butter bell on the fridge. And it's my fault," Kendra began. "I kind of had an early midlife crisis. My kid was in high school, my husband had just gotten a promotion, and I was still just a housewife who didn't do anything special—no crafts or gardens or… anything. I just read a lot."

"Sounds like the kind of housewife I'd be—unless I had about fifty kids." Portia winked at Brian's shocked face. "Hey, I know what to do with a bunch of kids, but vacations are all about books and catching up on movies and TV shows."

She realized Reese hadn't moved—still stood there with his hands at her waist—and she still hadn't gotten the butter when he murmured, "And dating ruggedly handsome men?"

"I've never dated, remember? You were my first date, so no."

Brian howled. "Oooh, she got you. Guess you're not as good-looking as you thought, eh Reese?"

Kendra looked indignant but pursed her lips and seemed determined to say nothing. Portia just rolled her head back and tried to meet Reese's gaze. That utterly romantic move in books and movies, failed in reality when you weren't much shorter than the guy. She ended up craning her neck instead and winking. "Didn't say he wasn't good looking—or even handsome. But there's nothing rugged about him… thank goodness."

"Not a fan of the lumberjack types?" Brian grabbed the butter when her eyes shifted that direction, in an obvious attempt to keep her right there where he and Kendra wanted her. Right there in Reese's arms.

No complaints here.

"You wound me, Dad. I distinctly remember wishing I could grow up to be the Brawny man."

"Yeah, well, now she's a woman in flannel, so I'm glad you didn't."

Reese laughed, and that laughter did another tumbling workout in her stomach. *I like his laugh too much. Who likes a laugh, anyway?*

"Where's Duncan?"

"Probably watching something on his tablet while he thinks he can get away with it." Reese leaned way back but didn't loosen his hold on her. "Yep. I'll let it slide. Can't wait for you to hear the rest of this story."

And they told it, too. From Kendra's decision to kick her

husband out of the house and go back to school, to the day they sat side by side at Reese's graduation. Kendra pulled the turkey from the oven as she told her part. "I was so miserable the whole time. I'd just convinced myself that I was being stifled and oppressed by being 'stuck' in the house all day. I never *talked* about it with Brian. I just knew I'd go crazy if I didn't at least prove to myself I could do something more if I wanted to."

A soft sob tore at Portia's heartstrings, and she found herself leaning into Reese as Brian moved to take over with the turkey… and the story. But before that, he pulled his wife into his arms and kissed her without even the slightest trace of embarrassment that they had an audience. "Love you, Kennie."

"I know. Fool that you are."

"Fool for you." And as if he hadn't just played out every romantic moment Portia had ever watched or read about—every moment she'd ever *envied*—he turned to her and winked. "There we were, just standing next to each other at Reese's graduation. I knew her, better than she knew herself in some ways, and I knew she was miserable. Reese sat up on that stage looking out at us, and it killed me to see the pain he was in. I mean, there we were—just being his parents, you know?"

"Yeah…" Portia didn't know, but what else could she say?

"So I did the only thing I could think of. When they called his name, she jumped up and clapped, just like I knew she would. I jumped up, too, and the minute he sat back down and Kendra started to seat herself, too, I wrapped my arms around her and kissed her."

"You didn't!"

"Yep. That was one of the things I suspected she'd needed and I'd never given her. I was shy back then…"

Reese's spit take would have drenched her had he actually been drinking. Kendra snickered and gave her husband a reproving look. "*I* was the shy one… about affection, anyway. I'd killed that spontaneous part of him with my embarrassment over it."

"And now is when they argue who was more at fault for

what their marriage counselor called a breakdown in communication that led to a break*up*… in fellowship." Reese's interjection earned him a snap with a kitchen towel, but still he didn't move. And still, Portia didn't want him to.

"By summer's end, we'd gotten a marriage license and brought Reese and my mom in as witnesses for a private ceremony in the minister's office."

Beautiful… Only when she realized she hadn't actually said it did Portia repeat herself. "That's just beautiful." She gave Kendra a weak smile before asking, "If you could tell your younger self one thing, what would it be?"

"Tell your husband everything—even the stuff that you think makes you look foolish. Actually…" The woman met Portia's gaze and held it. "*Especially* then. I think when we hide stuff from our 'other half…' that's when we start listening to the lies of the world."

Saying goodbye after a perfect day… Reese didn't know how people did it. Yet they both leaned against the back of his car, hands stuffed in their pockets, doing just that. Well, one could argue that they were decidedly *not* doing that at all.

"I don't want to go in, but I do. I want to see the kids and find out if it's my turn to go to the hospital, or if Dad actually has to have surgery or not… all that stuff. I just don't want to say goodbye."

He draped an arm around her shoulder and pulled her a bit closer. "I know what you mean."

"Too soon for that." She turned to face him, her eyes darker in the shadows—or was it with emotion. "Right? It's too soon not to want to say goodbye for what… hours? I mean, we can see each other in like twelve hours if we want. How stupid—"

Reese couldn't let that continue. "It's only stupid if we don't actually want to, right? When you find a new TV show, is it stupid if you binge watch it?"

"So that's what this is? Binge dating before LifeFlix takes it away again?"

"Life... *flix*?"

Portia shrugged. "Work with me here! I'm just trying to make a point. I'm trying to agree with you."

"Absolutely. LifeFlix it is. I hate it when sites remove my favorite shows. It's so annoying."

She glanced up the street before turning back to him. "Reese, we have to talk, you know."

"I know."

"Because I don't know if I can keep seeing a guy who doesn't like my favorite shows, or who likes stupid ones like *The Bachelor*."

"I'll watch anything you want as long as you watch big games with me—playoffs, World Series, Super Bowl..."

Music that sounded suspiciously like the opening strains of a recently released, romantic Christmas song jingled from her pocket, but Portia silenced it before she even got it out of her pocket—and before he could verify that suspicion. It hadn't been her ring tone the previous day. Good news? He hoped so.

"It's Jessica. Gotta take it." She leaned close, gave a feather light brush of her lips to his cheek, and dashed off, calling, "Thanks for Christmas *on* Christmas. It was great!"

She wouldn't answer until she finished her call, but Reese tapped out a text, anyway. DAD SAID ONE OF THE THINGS THAT HE LEARNED MOST FROM HIS "FOUR YEARS IN SIBERIA" IS THAT YOU TELL PEOPLE WHAT'S IN YOUR HEART. ALWAYS. SO I'M TELLING YOU. I HOPE YOU OCCUPY A PLACE IN MINE UNTIL I DON'T HAVE ONE TO KEEP YOU SAFE IN.

Reese stared at the words, hesitant. It made no promises—no declarations—but it did share a hope. It fit his father's criteria perfectly. It spoke his heart even better. He had to try—had to. Before he could talk himself out of it, Reese tapped the send button.

It's on you now, Lord.

The drive home—prayerful. He climbed from his car, still not ready to go inside and work on Duncan's bottle again, and being Christmas, he knew he'd never say no when his son pleaded with him to finish, "just the ship…" Especially if that plea included, "For Portia?"

And it would. No doubt about that.

So, with a quick text to tell his parents where he'd gone, he took off at a quick clip back up Pierpont to Bangor Lane. At eight, he'd been convinced that his teacher was wrong when she said Bangor, *Maine*. Duncan still thought that uproariously funny. *Kids today are so grown up—and yet they're exactly the same, too. Weird.*

He climbed the same steps they'd climbed together the night before. He walked the same stretch they'd walked. It's no wonder he wished she was there, and part of him wondered if maybe she might be right. Binge dating?

So, with nothing else to do, and disgusted with himself for waiting for that moment… again, Reese began to pray. For her father's health? Definitely. For a family dynamic that he'd thought broken but now wondered if he just didn't understand. Would she want a family where everyone got all heated over little things?

It wouldn't be good for Duncan, Lord. Or would it? Would it be better if he saw that people can argue and get upset but still love each other? Not leave *each other? I've figured that much out, anyway. No matter what she says or how upset she gets, she loves those people like I've always wanted to be loved—fiercely. Unconditionally and yet… conditionally, too. How's that even possible?*

Portia might think his mother was teasing about moving so she could watch a romance sprout and bloom, but she wasn't. Reese prayed about that, too. *Help me find a way to include Mom. Somehow. I need this house right where it is. Duncan needs it. The memories…* The picture of their tumble in the sand and the way Portia smiled at him—her *zest* for everything they did— filled his mind. *New ones as well as old. Unless they just don't like it here anymore, unless Dad needs a new job or something…*

Prayers transformed into dreams—a life in Acton near the peach farm. Duncan could work there as a teen. Portia would be closer to her family. Instinct told him that would be important. Practicality told him to stop being so ridiculous, but as usual, practicality lost. Little girls? Boys? Both? With four siblings, would she want a larger family? Smaller? She'd want at least one more child, wouldn't she? Adopt, maybe?

An international family formed in his mind—Chinese, African—or maybe Haitian. Russian? Did they still need families for Russian and Romanian orphans? His mother would be over the moon.

No matter what happens, I need to try to make this a thing, Lord. Somehow. Maybe a remote job? That might work, even if I wasn't married. I should talk to Duncan sometime. See if he'd like that. Or, maybe I should talk to an adoption attorney—see if it's even possible. Yeah…

He might have gone on to create an entire ministry focused on giving unwanted, older boys a permanent home if a text message hadn't come in from his father. DUNCAN FELL ASLEEP. WOKE UP SCREAMING. COME.

The last word wasn't necessary, of course. Prayer-slash-dream time cut short, Reese sprinted to the steps and scrambled down them. He jogged down Bangor Lane just as he had as a boy when he'd forgotten the time and knew he'd be in trouble. Just at the front gate, Portia's text came through. Two simple, absolutely inadequate words. He loved both of them.

ME TOO.

SEVENTEEN

For a blissful twenty minutes, Portia thought things with Damon might be at a beautiful end. As she came downstairs to see if anyone needed help with breakfast, she found him pacing in the kitchen, obviously talking to Jessica at the hospital, obviously peeved. Riddled with guilt—for at least fifteen seconds, anyway—Portia flattened herself against the dining room wall and listened.

"—am sorry your dad got hurt, but he doesn't need *you* to be his sole medical advocate. Your mom's perfectly ca—"

Maybe it wasn't fair, but Portia couldn't help creating her own version of Jessica's side of the conversation. *"That's what you think. Mom's all about letting everyone make their own decisions—even when they're not capable of it. She won't 'interfere' and then stupid decisions get made. They're talking about sending him home today!"*

"And no one but you can be there, right? No one else can say, 'What are the side effects of this medication?' or 'What restrictions will he have?' Your mom has already done all that, hasn't she?"

"Thanks to me! I was the one who said something. She only asked after that. I told you about the CT scan! They were hurting him, and neither one of them did anything about it. That was before *they caught the ruptured spleen..."*

"It's probably best if they don't do that surgery, Jess. The spleen is more important than people think."

Portia couldn't help but snicker at how close she must be,

and she almost cheered when Damon made the stupid mistake of trying to guilt her sister out of doing something Jessica thought important. Fortunately, Damon was ranting loud enough that he couldn't hear the near-giveaway.

"—didn't give up on Christmas with *my* family to have you play doctor. If you were the only daughter, I wouldn't be complaining, but c'mon, Jess…"

"Everyone's doing their part, Damon. I'm here to help Mom and Dad. Miranda's keeping the house from being torn up by Cressida's kids, Portia is keeping Tami from being worried, and she's also helping Cressida with the kids… it's what we do. It's called family."

Portia turned to go. Whatever else would be said didn't matter, because even if Jessica hadn't said any of it, it was true. All their wackiness and determination to be right—to have things how each of them thought it should be—it's what made them Spears. It's why their mother didn't get involved. It's why even after weeks of animosity over something or another, if anything happened, everyone dropped everything to be there. Tami's piano recital. Jessica's presentation at a university in driving distance, Miranda's commendation from the governor… all of it.

The sound of something crashing in the kitchen sent her rushing back. "Everything okay?"

Damon stood there, holding two pieces of a plate in his hands. "Got ticked. She won't listen."

"Jessica?"

"Yeah. She's determined to *be* there no matter what."

"It's what she does. Tami's appendectomy, Mom when Tami was born, Dad's back surgery a few years ago… It's how she says, 'I love you.'"

He dropped the plate pieces in the trash before digging into his pocket and pulling out a ring box. He dropped it to the island counter. "That's how I wanted to say, 'I love you,' but she's thwarted every one I've come up with. Looks like another plan down the drain."

"What was this one?"

He shrugged. "What's it matter now? Maybe it's God telling

me no."

"Or maybe it's you showing her and all the rest of us that you really want this." She stepped forward. "You know I like you. And you know I don't like you for *her*. Prove me wrong. Fight for this."

With that, she took off upstairs. At her window, she pulled out her phone. HELP. I JUST CHALLENGED DAMON TO PROPOSE… I THINK.

Reese had to have been on his phone, because a reply came back in less than twenty seconds. HOW SO?

She took a chance that he'd answer and called. "Hey…"

"Morning…"

"You, too." Why she'd called? Portia didn't remember.

"So, you challenged the guy you don't want to be your brother-in-law to make that happen?"

It sounded worse when he said it. "Um… kind of?"

"Why?"

The story came out… eavesdropping, the whole shebang. "I think I wanted him to prove me right. To get all worked up and take off. It's just the kind of thing he'd do. But…"

"But?"

"Well, it doesn't matter what I want, does it? What matters is what Jessica wants."

Reese's silence hinted she might be right, but a sigh caught her off guard. "I planned to try to get you over here today, but I think you should call Jessica and volunteer to take over at the hospital."

"She won't do it. She thinks the rest of us are incompetent."

"Then promise to call if anything comes up that she might want to weigh in on. Tell her that you all need her at her best in case things get serious again."

Every word she tried to say wouldn't convey what she wanted it to. After a dozen false starts, Reese broke in. "Hey, Portia?"

"Yeah?"

"The Lord and I had a nice talk last night—prayed for your

dad, by the way. Can't wait to meet him. Anyway, we talked a lot about you. Mostly, I talked and He listened. But I learned something last night—something I think we both need to remember."

Her heart still a puddle of goo at the idea that Reese had included her in his prayer time, Portia almost missed the cue. "What's that?"

"If this thing we've started is what He wants for us, if we continually seek Him in this, if we're prayerful and watchful, it'll happen. In *His* time. And that's all we can ask for, right?"

The goo got gooier. "Yeah." She gave a long, slow exhale to steady herself. "I should call Jessica, I guess."

"Before you go, I just have one question…"

Please let it be will I go run through a Starbucks drive-thru with you…

"How do you feel about adoption?"

Outside the hospital room door with call buttons and cries for help disrupting them every second, Jessica gave Portia a rundown on every nurse and aide. Never had Portia's fingers flown as fast as they did while she typed up notes.

"And that physical therapist? She's not careful enough with him. All he needs to do is walk so he doesn't get pneumonia or blood clots. That's it. So, don't let her push him to go faster or to sit in the chair if he doesn't want to."

"Got it." After a quick hug, Portia pushed Jessica to the door. "Go surprise Damon. He's really down."

"He's really selfish, you mean. This is *family*."

"Yeah, and he's been treated like one of us for ages, but he's been left out of this. Give him a break."

Suspicion furrowed Jessica's forehead into a giant, invisible question mark. "You don't even like him. Why are you so—?"

"Oh, come on. Maybe I just want you to see how wrong he

is for you. Maybe I just want bonus points with you for when I bring Reese to meet everyone. Who knows? I just felt bad when I overheard that conversation and thought it was time you had a break. We want Dad home tomorrow!" Each word grew louder until Portia had to drop the last sentence into a hiss to keep it from being overheard. "Now just get out of here. Sheesh."

Mom sat in the chair by Dad's bed with a ball of cotton yarn and a crochet hook. *When was the last time I saw that?* Portia couldn't remember. "Get any done?"

Reaching into a drawer beside her, Mom pulled out three crocheted dish cloths—plain and ugly as anything, but serviceable. "Almost done with my fourth." She jerked her head at the doorway. "Did Jessica get off?"

"Yeah." It seemed wrong to spill Damon's plans, but it also felt wrong to keep it from her mother. Portia went for a semi-compromise. "I think Damon's going to propose."

"That's what I figured. He didn't bat an eye when she missed his big birthday plans for her while Tami was in the hospital."

How much do you know about me and Reese?

Her father asked how the grandkids were holding up.

"Bored stiff. It's too cold to spend all day at the beach, especially when you can't get wet, Cressida won't let them near the pool—small wonder—and you can only play so many games that you've already played so many times before you're bored."

Dad gave her a *look*. "And the preschool teacher doesn't know how to keep preschool kids entertained?"

"A.J. is hardly preschool age"

Her mother's near-unison prompted giggles from both of the Spears women. Unfortunately… it also prompted the wrong move—those giggles. Dad just eyed her with that, "I've gotcha" smirk of his and leaned back. "So… tell us about this guy, then."

"I've been thinking maybe A.J. just needs more 'big kid' time. He is stuck with the girls a lot, and he's good with them, but he's still a kid."

It didn't work. Her father just laid there, arms folded.

"Oh, and you've got to read this story he wrote about how

you got hurt—better yet, maybe I'll call him and have him read it to you."

As she fumbled for her phone, Dad just grinned. "He's that great, huh?"

All ineffectual distractions ceased with that one.

"Yeah." She glanced at her mother, back at Dad, and sighed. "I don't want to be stupid, you know? At first I thought I just liked him for his kid—great kid."

"What's so great about him."

Portia nearly didn't stop herself in time. The words, *"He's Deaf, for one"* sounded so superficial and stupid when put like that. But she'd seen a patience in the kid that she'd often observed in Deaf people. All theories of it being more resigned than genuine had fled in the wake of meeting Duncan.

"He's got a great personality—fun sense of humor. And determined! He got a bicycle for Christmas yesterday. Can't ride it to save his life. But blood dripping down his legs, he gets back up on it and keeps going. Every. single. time."

This time, her mother piped up. She dropped the crocheting in her lap and eyed Portia with that curious look that meant she'd been thinking already. "Could it be an equilibrium thing—with the hearing? How'd he go deaf? Was he born that way?"

"No… meningitis before he was two." Her mom's guess made sense. "You think?"

"Probably. I know sometimes the Deaf have imbalance issues. I think viral things are one of the causes, but I don't remember. Too many college paper edits ago." Mom shoved the crocheting in the drawer and stood. "I'm going to go grab a Coke. Anyone want anything? Chips, beef jerky, Snickers?"

For you not to go?

Dad asked for cheese puffs, but Portia just shook her head and dug for a buzzing phone. A text from Reese brought a smile—one her mother missed, fortunately. Her father didn't—equally *un*fortunately. "What's up?"

"He said to tell you he's praying for you."

A skeptical look on Dad's face prompted her to show him

the text. A new one popped up before she retrieved the phone again, and this one prompted a big grin. "Interesting..."

She snatched it up, expecting something rather mundane like, "The temps are higher today" or "We're cleaning the gutters."

Instead, a rather lengthy text appeared. DARE YOU TO TELL HIM THAT I CONFESS TO HAVING MUCH MORE THAN A CASUAL INTEREST IN YOU. I'D LIKE A CHANCE TO MEET HIM—TO MEET ALL OF THEM. WE'D OFFER DINNER AT OUR HOUSE, BUT IT MIGHT BE CRAMPED FOR YOU GUYS. WHAT IF WE DID A DINNER INVASION—SHOW UP WITH ALL THE FOOD BUT YOU PROVIDE THE SPACE?

Another one followed quick on its heels. DON'T BREAK MY HEART AND SAY NO.

"What'd he say now?"

She pretended to read it again and look disappointed. "He changed his mind."

"Liar."

"A girl has to try."

"Tell him Sunday night."

"Tell who Sunday night?" Mom entered with empty hands. At Portia's pointed look, she shrugged. "Forgot to bring change. What's happening on Sunday?"

"The boyfriend wants to meet the family."

As if she wasn't even there, her mother took up the mortification process baton. "Sounds serious if we're jumping to families already. We didn't meet Gavin's until the engagement party."

"This guy seems old fashioned. He wanted her to talk to me for him."

"Old fashioned or a coward. Should have asked for your number."

Dad didn't agree. "No... I think he has figured our daughter out pretty well. He *dared* her to tell me."

"And she did?"

Here Portia piped up. "Not intentionally!"

From around fifteen or sixteen, the girls' parents had made a habit of *not* giving them directives. So when her father said, "Give him my number," well… she did. Maybe if he'd barked orders over every little thing she could have justified saying no, but Portia just couldn't.

"I might hate you."

"You'll get over it. You always have."

The mortifying truth of it was… he was right.

"Now, I really might hate you."

Here, he grinned and dug for his phone in the tray by his bed. "The best daughters do." He held it and waited.

Portia prayed for an over-eager physical therapist to arrive right about then. Instead, the phone rang.

EIGHTEEN

She'd arrived at nine o'clock. By noon, Portia just wanted to go home. While her parents spent every minute tormenting her with questions, observation, teases, and *looks*, Reese sent a text message every fifteen minutes with ideas of what they could do when she was "sprung from the hospital" that evening.

So, when two o'clock came, and along with it an oddly-acting Jessica, Portia zipped back a, MINIATURE GOLFING SOUNDS FUN. WHAT TIME? text to the latest idea.

IT'S MORE FUN AFTER DARK, SO NOT BEFORE 5. DINNER FIRST? WALK ON THE BEACH?

Five o'clock—too early for dinner. Beach walk—maybe. She zipped a message back. LET YOU KNOW WHEN I GET HOME. NEED TO SEE WHAT THE FAMILY IS DOING IN CASE THEY NEED ME FOR SOMETHING. GET BACK TO YOU IN 30.

She nearly melted at the, IS THIS WHERE I SAY I'M COUNTING THE MINUTES? IT'S TRUE, YOU KNOW.

"Okay, does anyone need anything before I go?"

Dad spoke first. "No… but nail the windmill for me. I've never gotten that one in one shot."

Portia bolted for the door, and might have made a getaway if Jessica hadn't followed. "You're going putt-putting? Really?"

She'd been through a lot, she told herself—endured massive teasing and torment. So it might have justified her response—just a little. "From the one who *always* complains that I don't do enough when we go places. From the one who managed to find a date at every vacation spot we went from the time you were fourteen? From—"

"Whatever. Glad you're so concerned about Dad."

That she made it "home" without causing a sister-rage-induced accident proved the existence of a merciful and involved "higher power," or whatever the skeptics called God Almighty these days. She jerked to a stop just a couple of feet from a scooter left in the drive, and only the absence of Cressida's van kept A.J. from getting a bawling out.

Portia snatched it up on her way to the door and propped it prominently beneath the doorbell. He'd never miss it. "*Silent sermons speak the loudest.*" How often had her father said that?

She bolted up the stairs, two at a time, without saying a word to anyone about her being back. Shower, fresh clothes, and some serious makeup—in that order. A text from Reese changed it. WISH YOUR DAD COULD COME. I THINK I LIKE HIM.

That began a flurry of texts about when they'd meet, what they'd do, and a disagreement over whether Duncan should come with them to dinner afterward. She was on the pro side—they'd taken him home early enough. Reese remained adamant.

NIGHT TERRORS AGAIN LAST NIGHT. HE NEEDS TO GO TO BED EARLY. TRUST ME.

A moment later, an addendum followed. I LOVE THAT YOU WANT HIM, THOUGH.

An argument erupted downstairs—kids, but it showed that Cressida and gang were back. Miranda's voice reached her just as she opened the door to head to the bathroom. "—just kids. Everything can't be a lesson!"

"They're also *my* kids. Don't interfere, 'Randa!"

Never had a shower been more welcome. The pounding water, the steam, the feeling of every germ she'd acquired at the hospital being annihilated by anti-bacterial soap… aaah.

Though not a consistent habit, she even sang in the shower. Inside forty minutes, she dashed downstairs, ready to meet Reese for that walk. That nice, long, *quiet*, argue-free walk.

Miranda caught her as she reached the front door. "Where

are you going?"

Only after Portia had admitted to the walk and then an outing at "Golf-n-Stuff" did she realize she shouldn't have answered. "Just text me if you need something."

"Putt-putt golf sounds fun. We'll go, too. What time?"

"Um..."

"Never mind. We can just go now. Let me—"

Like an automaton, she spouted out Reese's opinions on it being more fun after dark. Miranda concurred. "Good idea. We can go at five." She turned to go. "Don't be late. We want to get in before people get done with dinner. We'll give the kids snacks and eat something on the way back."

"I—"

But Miranda was gone. Portia started after her, but having given the name of the business, arguing wouldn't work. They'd all be there between five and five-thirty, depending on distance. And nothing she said or did would change that.

Better go break the news to Reese.

A dozen rehearsed explanations did little to settle her nerves, but seeing Reese did. His slow, lazy smile as she appeared sent her heart back into the kind of calisthenics she just wasn't accustomed to. Unlike any other time they'd met, he didn't move to meet her. He just stood there, leaning against his car, waiting... watching.

"Hi." Such an inadequate word. When another one didn't present itself, she just repeated it. "Hi..."

Still, he waited until she got close enough to pull into a quick... and then not-so-quick hug. "Missed you today. Is that weird?"

Portia stepped back... just enough to give her brain and emotions space enough to regulate. "It's nice... even if it is weird. Which, I don't know if it is. What do you think?"

His gaze never wavered from her face, even when she couldn't meet it any longer. It was still there, alerting her to its presence with every passing second. "I think you're right about the nice thing."

The gentle, tender touch of a man's hands—a man *not* her

father's hands… Even through her coat, Portia felt them. While both slid down her arms, only his right hand caught hers and laced their fingers together. Not soft… not calloused… a nice, happy medium.

I'm so pathetic.

"You're quiet."

"I'm mad." She hadn't meant to admit it. "Sorry."

"Did I do something I should apologize for?"

Ouch. It took trudging through soft, loose sand for half a minute before she managed to force herself to say, "No, I did. Or, I didn't, actually. Whatever. I have to apologize, Reese."

"What for?"

Just do it. Band-Aid. Rip that sucker off.

"Portia?"

Gripping his hand tighter to help prevent a fall, Portia closed her eyes and confessed. "My family is showing up at Golf-n-Stuff. I have to cancel."

"That's fine. Duncan wants to meet A.J. any—"

"No, Reese. I can't deal with them and you there. I can't. They're doing it and I can't stop them, but I can't go with you and be with them, too. There's no right answer, but I know…"

She couldn't finish, and Reese didn't pick up the conversational baton like she'd hoped. They'd made it to better-packed sand and strolled in silence halfway to the pier before Reese spoke again. "Question."

"Shoot."

"Are they an excuse not to go, or—"

"No! I got blindsided by Miranda, and no matter what I said, she'd do it. I'd almost convinced myself to beg you to do something else instead—find another place—anything. But then I'll have to hear it from Miranda. Forever."

Reese kept shaking his head. "Sorry, Portia. I'll do what I can to avoid you guys. I'll even try to go a little early if you want, but I can't take it away from Duncan. He's so excited."

Instinct insisted she push for that—early going. They could be done before the Spears clan arrived. But Reese continued.

"Any chance you'll still be up for dinner afterward?"

"Late?" Even as she spoke, Portia winced. "I know it sounds horrible, but if I rush off, they'll try to follow, and I just… I'm not ready for all that means."

His thumb traced the ridge of her knuckles as they walked. "I understand. I think."

Instinct took over again. She popped a quick kiss to his cheek and, upon realizing it, took off at a quicker clip. Reese didn't speed up. "Portia?" After her noncommittal mumble, something akin to a snickered chuckle reached her ears. "Someday you're going to do that, and I'm going to show you what a kiss really is."

I hope so…

"Just as soon as I figure out how to do that."

Despite his assurances that he "understood" Portia's reticence to introduce him to her family, he didn't. Not really. He could have rushed Duncan through washing hands and face after an early dinner. He could even have put a quicker kibosh on Duncan's near-meltdown over learning Portia was going with her family instead. Instead, he selfishly allowed his son to vent the feelings he couldn't express himself.

And at a quarter till five, they drove off. At the light at Seward, just before getting on the freeway, Duncan tapped his shoulder and signed, *"Riding is more fun with Portia. She can talk to me."*

A horn behind him nearly prompted him to floor it. Only a split second kept him from ramming into the real cause of the holdup—a stalled eighties BMW. Reese threw his car into park, hit the flashers, and signed for Duncan to stay put. *"I need to help him."*

"He" turned out to be a she much too old to be driving, in his opinion. But with the help of a guy in a business suit and a girl who looked scrawny enough to move a feather, they managed to push the car up over the overpass and into a gas station parking lot. Reese backed away, even as the car came to a slow stop. "I've gotta get back to my kid. Thanks for the help, guys." He gave featherweight an air high-five. "And you are one strong girl. Wow!"

All time advantage he'd gained… disappeared in that little workout. Duncan waited until he'd reached the door before unlocking it. *"I was safe."*

A grin filled his heart and reached his lips—he could feel it. *"Yes, you did good."*

By the time they reached Victoria Avenue and crossed the freeway again, he knew Portia's family had probably beaten them. So, as they parked in an only moderately full parking lot, he zipped a text. GOT TIED UP WITH A STALLED CAR. JUST ARRIVED. TRIED TO BE EARLIER. SORRY.

After he hit send, he wished it back. *It's not true, Lord. I am not sorry—not that I'm here now. I'm sorry she doesn't feel comfortable, but…*

Prayer, however, would have to wait. Duncan had a million questions—beginning with when they'd see Portia. *"Don't know if we will. She's with family. Don't bother her. We'll take her again some other time."*

A large party laughed and argued over who would go first just a couple of yards from the counter. It had to be them, but Reese couldn't see her anywhere. Still, he'd keep his word. *"Let's go. We'll get a head start, or we'll have to wait a lot."*

Waiting, not usually Duncan's favorite pastime, didn't seem to be something the boy would object to… today, anyway. Reese pushed onward and shut down a protest. *"We're here to have fun. You and me. Like always. If you argue, we can go home."*

A glance over his shoulder made up Duncan's mind it seemed. The boy stepped up, put his ball down, and gripped his putter like a cricket player with a bat. It happened every time they came. And on every hole. *Really have to consider Little League this year.*

By the fourth hole, Reese had received four texts and had

become convinced that Duncan was perfectly okay with it just being them. By the fifth, the boy had even tied them up—impressive… or pathetic, depending on how you looked at it. *Getting bested by an eight-year-old. Oh, brother.*

Portia's texts kept him amused—especially since he occasionally heard some of the conversation himself. MIRANDA JUST HIT A POP FLY THAT LANDED IN THE NEXT TRAP. HOW DOES A PERSON DO THAT WITHOUT TAKING OUT SOMEONE IN THE PROCESS? I WOULD HAVE BEEN CHARGED WITH "ASSAULT WITH A SPHERICAL WEAPON."

A couple of minutes later, another followed. YOU WANTED TO DO THIS TO HUMILIATE ME, DIDN'T YOU? I'M PATHETIC. #GOTA15ONTHATONE #NOJOKE

His laughter caught Duncan's attention, and he had to explain the texts. His son's interest should have been a warning. Should have. Reese was too occupied with the next hashtag, #DumbestGameEver and a picture of her granny swinging the narrow end of the putter to notice.

A ball whizzed past his head, barely missing him. Duncan's shock? Totally genuine. His delight when the group behind them clearly became agitated—also genuine and in all the wrong ways. *"What did you do?"*

"Hit the ball—went over there. You okay?"

A boy—he had to be A.J.—appeared with the little green golf ball. "Is this yours? My aunt says thanks. It knocked her ball into the hole finally. Best score she's had so far—only a four."

Duncan signed sorry, and A.J. opened his eyes wide. With a glance at Reese and back at Duncan, he spread his fingers and tapped his thumb on his chest in the "fine" sign.

Big mistake. Duncan's fingers and hand must have become a blur to the obviously confused boy. He blinked, glanced over his shoulders, and looked up at Reese. "I don't remember how to do, 'I don't understand.' You shake your head…"

Reese held up one finger to the side of his head and flicked it "on and off" like a light bulb. "Like that."

"Right!" A.J.—it had to be him—signed, *"I don't understand"* followed by, *"My name is A.J."*

Duncan repeated it. *"A.J.? Is your name?"*

Reese signed, *"It's his initials—it stands for something. Ask him. I'll translate."*

A.J. stood for Austin James like his dad. A.J. was, as Reese knew, eight and lived in Rosamond. *"That's an hour from us—closer than if he lived here."*

"Is he the boy Aunt Portia told me about? Are you his dad?" Voices began calling his name, and A.J. backed away. "He should come over. We could play a game. All my aunts sign. My mom does a little, too."

As Reese translated, he added, "I'll see what Portia says."

"I'll ask." He gave them a huge grin. "Aunt Portia always agrees if *we* ask."

Duncan's eyes grew huge as Reese translated that. He waved and turned back to Reese. *"I wasn't sure…"*

"When you hit that ball over into their hole?"

His only answer came in that endearing little gap-toothed grin that melted his heart every time he thought about yet another milestone into maturity. *I'm not ready for him to grow up, Lord.*

Approaching voices—A.J.'s at the top of them, of course—told him he needed to hurry. Reese hit a ball that rolled straight through the windmill hole and out on the other side. A two on the windmill—unheard of. And he'd done it because he needed out of there.

A glance over his shoulder showed Portia watching—jaw dangling. He winked and urged Duncan on before the boy saw her and ruined her night.

Yeah. I'm totally not okay with this. Don't like it at all.

Her text arrived just as Duncan sent a ball off into the shrubs. SHOW OFF.

He couldn't help teasing a bit. I HAD TO MAKE A GOOD IMPRESSION SOMEHOW…

As he watched his ball zig-zag through the odd maze at hole seven, a reply came. YOU DID THAT DAYS AGO.

Flirting. It did a man's heart good.

NINETEEN

Beside a well-lit pineapple palm tree, Reese waited for her, and the moment she pulled into the lot at Denny's, he strode toward the parking space she grabbed. While not the most romantic of restaurants, Denny's had one undeniable advantage—that beautiful, "OPEN 24-HOURS" sign.

As he opened the door and she stepped from the car, Portia thought for sure this would be it—her first, real kiss. *Let me take that back. Denny's is totally romantic.*

One thumb caressed her jaw, while the other hand pulled her close. "Sure wish I'd studied up on that kissing thing…"

Okay… it's just sorta romantic. But still…

"Sorry about tonight."

"I got to meet A.J. Duncan hasn't stopped talking about him." Reese looked awkward as he stepped back and pulled her with him. The door shut a moment later. "My mom wasn't discreet. She made some comment to Dad about how A.J. could be Duncan's cousin someday. Now Duncan is ticked off at my parents for only having one child. Somehow it never clicked that if I had siblings, he'd have cousins."

"If A.J. was his cousin, he'd likely end up with half a dozen or more, too. I mean, Cressida has three. Between Miranda, Jessica, and Tami, that's statistically at least six more." Right about then it hit her that by giving Duncan her as of yet unborn nieces and nephews for cousins, she'd just signed herself up for wife. "Um…"

They'd made it to the door, but Reese just rested his hand on the handle. "No."

"No what?"

As he pulled it open, he leaned close. "No, I'm not going to 'forget' that you just told me that you're not revolted at the idea of me for the long term."

It wasn't easy to admit, but after ruining their date, she had to give some sort of concession, so Portia said it. "Wouldn't be here if I was."

"That's what your dad said. I like him, by the way. We've been texting all day. I think he's bored." The hostess stepped forward to seat them, making it impossible for her to respond to that.

Reese, however, had different ideas than the booth right by the window. "We're going to be here a while—probably. What's the most out-of-the-way spot you can give us?"

"Of course!" A smile formed on the girl's face as Reese slipped an arm around Portia's waist and led her forward. She bounced to the left of where she'd been intending to seat them and called back, "Right this way."

"I'm so going to get you for that."

Not until they'd been seated in a semi-circle booth did Reese respond. He gave his drink order, she gave hers, and the moment the hostess left, he turned to her. "What'd I do to get on your bad side? I just wanted—"

"You assume 'get you' *must* be bad." Flirting… it didn't come freely, but when it did come, she liked it. "Bad assumption."

"I'll hold you to that." He flipped open his menu, gave it a cursory glance, and shut it again. "Larry says he gets to come home tomorrow." Something awkward—almost nervous—entered Reese's tone… his demeanor.

"Is that bad?"

"He also said he's looking forward to Sunday."

Her throat went dry, but Portia managed to croak out, "Oh."

"I talked to Mom and Dad. We're bringing dinner Sunday night—regardless. If you want to invite us to stay, we'll be thrilled, but we've only told Duncan we're making you guys food."

Her heart sank. The minute Reese saw the drama start up—and it would. It always did. That's when he'd decide she wasn't worth the hassle. "I can't—"

Those two words produced instant discouragement. Though almost imperceptible, Portia saw it in the way his shoulders just barely slumped. The way his jaw went a little rigid. The way he stared at his hands. "I'm not asking you to be ready today. I'm just hoping you might be by Sunday. That's all. Just by Sunday.

That's like asking me to build another Suez Canal by then. Where is the Suez Canal? Where's Suez?

"Portia?"

"Where's Suez?"

"Egypt, why?"

She shrugged. "Just curious."

"Why don't you want me to meet your family?"

She might have snapped at him if a server hadn't appeared, ready to take their order. And she didn't even know what she wanted. "Go ahead. I can't remember the dish name…" A quick flip through prompted a choice for spaghetti and meatballs.

Of course, the moment the server disappeared, he gave her a look. "You couldn't remember what spaghetti is called?"

"I didn't know if they had more than one kind, but that 'Brookly—'" It sounded even lamer aloud than it did in her head. "Okay. Fine," she sighed. "I wasn't ready, but I didn't want her coming back." She stared at her hands as they rested on the table. *Are my hands small? Big? Fat? Skinny? I don't know. Do I care?* Portia shot a glance at him. *Does he?*

"If I thought that was because you're just so anxious to be alone with me, I'd be thrilled, but I suspect something less flattering."

"Be flattered. It was at least part of it."

When the next few minutes passed without another reference to the day or her family, Portia relaxed. Literally—and she knew the proper use of that word—one second before he said, "I still would like to know why you don't want me to meet your family."

"Because I'm not ready for you to write me off yet." Her throat did that horrible insta-dry thing that always made it feel like it was sticking together. *Did I really say that, or did I just think it?*

When he just waited… watching her from the corner of his eyes… Portia grew comfortable again. *Thank you, Jesus!*

"Do you love your family?"

She jerked her head up and glared at him. Daggers would have shot forth from her pupils if she could have produced them. "Duh! They're my *family!*"

"Do I like you?"

That was the problem right there. Anyone with eyes and half a brain or so could see he did. Why? Well, she hadn't let herself go there—not yet. But here he was, asking a question with an answer that terrified her for reasons she wouldn't let herself explore.

Her silence must have gotten to him, because Reese slid his hand over, captured one of hers, and brought it close to his chest. *A novel would say, "To his heart…" And suddenly novels feel inadequate.*

"Here's a hint. I do."

Unwrap heart and let it melt all over the table.

What Reese started to say next, she didn't know. The server arrived with spaghetti and burger, and eyes that looked like the living personification of heart-eye emojis. "Enjoy your meal."

Understanding didn't dawn—it exploded on the screen of her mind in a fireball of destruction. "Oh, ugh."

"What?"

"She's going to be so disappointed."

Reese just elbowed Portia and promised to leave a good tip.

"No… she thinks this is a proposal. She's waiting to have all her heart-throbbing romantic wishes come true—by proxy."

"And that's ugh, huh?"

Seriously, the guy sounded devastated. A sidelong glance showed him staring at his burger as if he'd never seen anything more unappetizing. A deep sigh followed. Then he shrugged, picked up the burger, and said, "Oh, well. It is what it is."

A cold fear swept through her, tingling her fingers and toes. Just as she decided to excuse herself and walk back to Sandpiper House, Portia changed her mind and opted to roll with it. "Yep. It is." After a sidelong glance of her own, she added, "So, I have this friend in Rosamond. Gorgeous girl. Funny. I could teach her to sign…"

"Sounds like a great girl. I hope I get to meet her someday." Beneath his breath he added, "If we weren't in the middle of a restaurant, I'd have kissed that smirk right off your face for that."

"Ditto."

This time he looked at her. "Don't tempt me." Then he blinked. "Wait, would you?"

"You deserve it—messing with me like that."

A bite of burger saved one of them from his reply. Portia just wasn't sure *which* one of them. And once she took a bite of startlingly and unexpectedly-good spaghetti, nothing else mattered. "I think I forgot to eat today. Pretty sure I only had rice cakes this morning." The memory of a small bag of chips at the hospital amended that. "And chips. One of those dinky bags that is designed to make you spend your whole grocery budget just to get enough to stave off starvation."

"Is the spaghetti okay?"

"Good… I just can't decide if it's because it's *that* good, or if I'm *that* hungry. Either way, I don't need ranch, so that helps."

Reese dropped his burger. Sure, it landed on his plate, but it fell into a jumbled mess of burger elements—lettuce there, tomato half-clinging to that, patty cockeyed against one half of the bun, and pickles stuck willy-nilly to everything. The onions, rogues that they always are, skittered off the plate and onto the table.

As he reached for them, she growled. "Nuh, uh." At his questioning glance while he reassembled the all-American "sandwich," she said, "If you're going to keep threatening to kiss me, you need to quit with the raw onions."

"Duly noted." Not until the burger had been reassembled did Reese clear his throat and ask, "Did you really say *ranch* on your spaghetti?"

"Yep. Makes bad marinara palatable. You should try it sometime."

"I'll just trust you on that one."

"Skeptic."

"The world needs more. Just doing my part—especially with ranch and marinara. Definitely."

Perhaps it was the infusion of calories in a body desperate for *something*, or maybe just the ultra-comfortableness of *being* with Reese, but the next thing she said was, "I'll tell the family you guys are coming for and bringing dinner on Sunday."

Panic set in the moment the words left her lips. *Oh, no…*

Reese finished his bite, wiped his hands, and put arms around her. Squeezing her close, he whispered, "Thanks. It's a gift. I know that. So, thanks."

I'm doomed. Aloud, she just said, "I just hope you don't forget two things."

"Name 'em."

"One, I love my family…wouldn't trade them for anything. And two…" At a crack in her voice, Portia took a sip of water to steady herself and smooth it a bit. "I'm a packaged deal. So all the craziness and random drama comes with a hefty price for me, because anyone interested in me has to be able to put up with *them*." Her voice dropped. "Just like they have to put up with me."

Despite suggesting a stroll up and down Main Street for variety, Portia asked to go back to the beach. "There's something about it…"

And as they strolled along the shore, she said it again. "I think I might be a little jealous of you growing up with this."

"It was life. I didn't appreciate it until Duncan and I moved to Newhall. Not being able to come down here and think… pray. It made me feel like I'd been exiled to the desert or something."

"Um... Santa Clarita Valley? Isn't that like the bottom of the Mojave... what's that thing called? *Desert?*"

"I think it's actually a—"

Portia cut him off with a jab to his ribs. "Stop. It's near the edge of it, if not in it. And the point is, it's barren and needs water to make anything grow. It's a desert."

Why is something that should be annoying just fun with her? *I'd be irritated if Duncan said that—or even if Mom did.* Something a youth minister once said hit him.

"Just remember that what is cute today may be the very thing you despise in someone later. It's never right to complain about someone being who they always were."

"Reese?"

A glance her way shifted from one concern to another—for her. "Yeah?"

"What's wrong?"

"Just thinking."

Several yards passed—they'd almost reached the pier before Portia spoke again. "I've been thinking, too."

"Yeah?"

Here she came to a stop and folded her arms over her chest. "This person...?" She made a perfect game show hostess swipe of herself from top to bottom. "This is who I am. What I say? What I think? What I do? This is me."

"And that's a problem because..."

Though she turned to keep walking, Portia didn't unfold her arms. As if hugging herself, she plowed through sand with the grace of tea cup-crushing bovines. "This is why I'm nervous about you meeting the family, Reese. This is why I keep freaking out. Because you bring out the best in me. They don't—but they do. But it's a different best. They also bring out the worst in me."

Maybe it wasn't smart, but he wasn't willing to risk it. He told her about liking that she'd stood her ground on her opinion. "I don't know what's different from other people. Duncan, I can explain away because he'd be arguing with an adult—something he has a hard time understanding why it's not okay to do. But

Mom…"

"Your mom could be because you don't feel comfortable arguing with her because she *is* your mom?"

Reese had no way of knowing if that was right, but it sounded logical. Seeing how far they'd come past the pier, he reached for her hand and tugged her back again. "Let's head back."

Though Portia allowed herself to be led, she said nothing, and for the first time, the silence bothered him. "Dad said something at the time. He said that Ron—the minister—was right about being upset when people stayed exactly who they've always been. But I just remembered what else he said."

"What's that?" The voice—flat. Reese couldn't understand why.

"Well…" He hoped he wasn't being naive, but talking it out seemed to help. "Dad said that sometimes the same thing came out differently. He had an aunt that guffawed when she laughed. He hated it. Annoyed him to no end. But then he met my mom. It doesn't happen often, but if she's really cracking up, she does it, too."

Portia had an opinion on that, too. "Well, if it's not every time…"

"That's what I said."

"Not it?"

He shook his head. "Dad said no. He figured out that it was because Mom's *tone* was different somehow. It didn't strike a range that grated on his nerves like his aunt. Coming from Mom, it was funny—especially because she is always embarrassed by it. He thinks it's cute."

"I can see why, though…" Again, she whirled to face him. "Look, if I do stuff that usually annoys you and you're not annoyed, I need to know it. I need to be sure that you're not just putting up with stuff because you like some other part of me."

Hackles he didn't even know he had rose. "Well, I think we all do that to some extent."

"Maybe," she insisted. "But I'm willing to wait to find the

guy who likes me for most of me—not the one who puts up with me for that little part he thinks is great. That's a recipe for misery—for both of us."

"Won't do that." Reese pulled her hand from her coat pocket—when had she slipped them in?—and kept walking. "And I know you said that to protect you, but it also protects me. So thanks."

"Not sure what you mean."

A gull nearly dive-bombed them as it swooped in for something in the sand—what, he couldn't see. Reese pulled her a bit closer as he led her away, knowing the sight might be disgusting. As expected, she protested.

"What's he eating?"

"Probably something gross. You don't want to see it, I'm sure." Despite her leaning in for a better look, Reese pulled her back. "Trust me. The stuff I've seen…"

"They eat fries in the Walmart parking lot. So weird to see half a dozen of them fighting over one fry." She glanced back once before falling into step beside him again. "Sorry, what were we talking about?"

"I said you wanting to be chosen for yourself, as you are, means I'm protected, too. I don't get a sanitized version of you that I don't recognize later."

Portia didn't seem to agree… at first. However, her entire demeanor changed over the next fifty feet or so. "Yeah. I mean, everyone changes—or at least shows some other side that didn't have a chance to come out before—when you start living with them. But if you were actually *hiding* or *repressing* that part of you…"

"Exactly."

Just as they reached the place where he'd parked, her phone rang. "Oh…" A glance brought a sigh. "Hang on. It's Cressida."

From his side, it sounded like they wanted her home, but Reese kept her moving down the beach, away from the car, and toward his house this time. *Maybe she'll say no. I want her to say no…*

"Fine! I'll be there in just a few. I'm at the beach, so just hang on." With that, she shoved the phone in her pocket. "Everyone wants to go look at lights. We were supposed to the night Dad got hurt, so we haven't yet. Miranda found this 'light path' app that gives you a GPS route to all the best lighted neighborhoods."

Ask me to come.

She tried to turn, but Reese caught her other hand and walked backward, pulling her with him. "Just a little farther…"

"They'll get all mad—"

"You said beach. You didn't say what part. You didn't define 'a few.' So let's make it a few more…" When she hesitated, Reese took the opportunity to pull her close. The temptation to kiss her there—nearly irrepressible. He managed, though. *It'll feel like manipulation. Not doing that.*

She pointed to a nearby jetty. "That far. That's it."

"I'll take it."

"I love that you don't want me to go."

Ask me to come.

"I wish I could bring you."

Ask me to come…

"I'll probably have A.J. in the car—Tami, too. There's room for one more…"

Ask me. I'll come.

"But then everyone will hound A.J. and Tami for information. That's not fair to them. Still, it would have been a gentle introduction…"

I won't even hold your hand. Ask…

They reached the jetty, and to his delight, she turned to him, wrapped her arms around his waist, and rested her head on his chest. "I don't want to go."

"So…"

With a gentle squeeze, she stepped back and turned toward Vista del Mar and Sandpiper House. "Why does everything seem so fatalistic in movies, but in real life it's perfectly logical? If we were on TV, I'd be rolling my eyes at us."

His answer would earn him a mocking laugh, but Reese still had to say it. "I think it's because, until we've been there, we can't imagine how it *could* be that way. Then when it happens, we can finally appreciate it."

"Makes sense..." Her phone buzzed. She read the message, sighed, and turned it to face him.

HURRY UP. JESSICA'S COMING FOR A BIT WHEN WE GET BACK, AND WE'RE PLAYING REVERSE CHARADES.

"I'd better hurry before they all figure out I'm close and invade."

By the time they reached his car, she still hadn't asked. He tried to follow her up to Sandpiper House, but she'd only agree to as far as the other side of the overpass. "I'm not ready to deal with them over you. They'd insist you come and..."

What else she said, Reese didn't hear. *That was kind of the idea. They see me, they invite, you figure out that I'm not running because Miranda is uptight about the house, or because Jessica is a natural-born leader.*

At the other side of the overpass, she gave him a quick hug, thanked him for understanding, and once more, kissed his cheek before dashing away. He inched forward, watching... closer... still watching. Up near the house, still hidden by a large eucalyptus, Reese watched. And from there, he saw her race up the drive, pick up a little one, laugh, and call out greetings to the others.

You still have time, Portia. Ask...

Only when the cars began to fill with people did he give up and turn away. *I really wanted her to ask, Lord. Does it matter that she didn't?*

TWENTY

As if on a new routine, Reese bolted upright, flung the covers from himself, leaped across the room, wrapped Duncan in the familiar blanket burrito, and shushed him with soothing tones the boy could only feel—never hear. Most of the time, it didn't bother him—his son's lack of hearing. The familiar has the habit of making the unusual seem commonplace.

But at times when his son hurt the most, he ached to communicate in the way that best spoke *his* heart… through sound. "Oh, Duncan. I don't know how to take these away. What can I do?"

The door opened, and a path of light appeared across the floor. "He okay?"

"As okay as a terrified little boy can be. I don't know how to help him."

Mom stepped forward to hug them both and kiss Duncan's forehead. "Just wait until he's calm. He can't hear you if he's agitated."

His throat tightened with emotion, and his voice cracked as he rasped out, "Thanks, Mom."

That's all it took. Mom half-closed the door before settling herself against the pillow, too—the three of them squished on one twin-sized bed. "I'm so sorry, son. You've been out of sorts since you got home, and now this."

Nothing he tried to say conveyed what he needed it to. Instead, he sat tongue-tied, eyes closed, reveling in his mother's hold. Then the words came. "I should be too old to need my mommy's arms."

"You're never too old to need *someone's*, and since you don't have Portia..."

"Not sure she's ready for that job anyway." The words sounded harsher than he meant them to. "I just mean that she's never dated. I think it's made her insecure or something."

Duncan already slept, the little body growing heavier against him with each passing minute. His mother still sat there, holding him, and Reese let her. Until that moment, he didn't realize how much he liked—*craved*—that contact with someone who cared.

"Does she know you've never dated anyone but Audra?"

"Yes."

"Does she really? I mean, you can say it, but does she really understand that you and Corinne weren't a thing? It's hard to remember that when you see Duncan. Even for me."

He'd never heard her say that before. "Really?

A soft snore prompted her to tuck blankets even closer around Duncan's neck. "Our brains are wired to picture people with children as having been close with the other parent. It's the norm—the *overwhelming* norm. So yeah, I forget sometimes just how uninitiated even *you* are in the world of dating."

"Um... there was Audra..."

"Who had the world's most overprotective father on the planet. I know you never kissed her, but did you ever even hold her hand?"

He chuckled. "A few times—when she felt particularly rebellious."

"Does *Portia* know that?"

A shadow filled the doorway. "Family meeting and I'm missing it?"

Mom wrestled herself out of bed, kissed Reese's cheek, and moved to the door. "Tell your son that Portia might need reassurance that Reese isn't comparing her to the 'other girls' he's known."

"Is that what you meant? Why didn't you just say that?" He

must have stiffened or jerked, because Duncan stirred. Mom promised to talk more in the morning and pulled the door shut again.

Darkness wrapped Reese and Duncan in yet another blanket. Duncan struggled to free himself a moment later. He flung himself from the bed and touched the lamp on his side table. Warm light glowed as he scrambled up close again. Hands signed words—fears. But translation proved harder without seeing the facial expressions on his son's face.

When Duncan turned to watch him reply, Reese smiled. *"Hard to understand without seeing, isn't it? Can you imagine how hard it is for blind-deaf people?"*

"I shouldn't be so scared. I can see."

Sitting cross-legged, Reese signed assurances that everyone is afraid sometimes. *"That's why Psalms say to put our trust in God* when *we're afraid."* At when, Reese made an extra-large clock circle and pronounced touch of the fingers—at the beginning *and* end of the phrase. *"When. When you're afraid. Not if."*

His son nodded but seemed unconvinced. *"Okay."*

"You know I'm never leaving you, right?"

The reply came faster than expected. *"You could die."*

"Yes, I could. But that's not leaving. That's God saying it's time for me to go home. He knows best."

Duncan didn't like that at all, but Reese refused to back down. God was good and would only "take him away" if it was the *best* thing to do. *"And you'd still have Grandma and Grandpa. People who love you aren't going to leave you. Ever."*

Something shifted in Duncan at those words. He sat up a little straighter. The sleepiness and fear that had mingled in the little furrows and creases on his face disappeared. *"So… I just need to pray that Portia loves me. Then she won't go away. Right? I can do that."* A huge grin formed. *"Grandma says everyone loves me—eventually. They can't help it."*

Oh, great… Reese geared up to explain that things weren't quite that easy, but Duncan just settled under the blanket, kicked both feet under, and rolled over.

Every instinct said to stop that train of thought—then. Every one except the ones that said never to interfere with a child's sleep.

Or mine…

As Reese finally eased from the bed and back into his own, prayers formed in his heart. *He's so attached. She's so resistant. Was this a good idea? Is that what all this is supposed to tell me? To be careful?*

Sleep took over before he found an answer.

From the doorway of her parents' *downstairs* suite, something that would now prove to be a blessing, Portia watched as the kids decorated to welcome Grandpa home. She snapped a picture and zipped it to Reese. SOMEONE'S EXCITED FOR THEM TO GET HERE I THINK.

And a moment later, she added, MISS YOU. IS THAT SILLY? I'VE ASKED THAT BEFORE, HAVEN'T I? Her thumb hovered over the send button. Uncertainty made tapping it harder than it should have been, but a jostle from Charis took the decision out of her hands. *Made it* through *them is more like it. Ugh.*

"I think we need more balloons." A.J. eyed the enormous French doors with their valance of blown balloons. "I can still see white between those…"

She should have argued—of course she should. But she didn't. Portia promised to get a couple more and start blowing, but a horn blared from out front. "No time! They're here!"

All three kids charged for the door, but she stopped them. "What's the rule? What's the number one rule right now?"

Bella piped up first. "Don't touch Grandpa before asking."

"And why do we have to ask—even to give a tiny hug or kiss?"

A.J. sighed. In a near monotone, he recited, "Because-we-might-hurt-something-we-can't-see. Now can we go?"

From the corner of her eye, Portia saw Cressida appear in the entry way and stepped aside while Cressida hurried outside. Her phone buzzed just as she moved to follow.

A text from Reese, of course. IF SO, THEN WE'RE BOTH SILLY.

Portia couldn't resist. YOU MISS YOU, TOO?

By the time she made it out the front door, Dad was surrounded by sisters, grandkids, Mom, and Jessica wearing her Nurse Ratched persona. Portia began filming the grand return, for unknown reasons that might actually make sense someday.

"Back. Away!"

Forgetting the recording, she called back, "Calm down, Jessica. They're being careful not to touch him. Give them some credit."

"The only thing between him and a splenectomy is one wrong punch in the wrong spot. So, no. I'm not going to 'calm down.'"

From the look on her father's face, he'd had it. But whether with being in pain, with trying to make it up the steps when he usually rode for miles at breakneck speeds on his bicycle, or with Jessica, she couldn't be sure.

And to make things go from bad to worse, as things always did, Charis shot across his path. Dad stumbled.

In the middle of the ensuing argument, Portia caught sight of her hands holding her phone out to record it all for "posterity" and shut it off. The memory of Reese's obvious hurt over her reticence to include him in family stuff prompted another idea. *Well, maybe this would be easier, huh?* And before she could talk herself out of it, she sent the video with a short text.

NOW DO YOU SEE? CAN YOU DEAL WITH A STEADY DIET OF THIS?

Of all the replies she could have gotten back, his, SO, ARE YOU ASKING ME TO "GO STEADY"? wouldn't have ever registered.

What did register, was that he hadn't panicked. And something about that buoyed her flirtatious side. MAYBE…

The response popped up a minute later. DEAL.

And a minute after that, another came. She read it even as, one-handed, she scooped Bella up just before a collision with Grandpa's knees. Everyone seemed to wait for a reaction, but with Dad in the house and shuffling his way to his room, Jessica just took Bella and followed, pointing to how slow Grandpa walked, how he had to sit so carefully before rolling into bed.

Just like when he had his surgery—but worse. At least that was semi-planned.

Portia stood in the doorway, watching for kids growing too antsy, while Cressida urged Mom to get some food, take a shower, and go for a walk on the beach. Mom might have protested, but Portia beat her to it. "That's a great idea. You've been cooped up in the hospital, too. We'll get Dad down there in a day or two, but you should go now."

"I'll wait for him. It's okay…"

It probably wouldn't work, but Portia dropped her voice a bit and murmured, "You won't be any help to him if you don't refresh yourself, too."

Dad piped up. "Go on, Pat. I'm fine. I'll be asleep before you get done showering, anyway. Find me something."

That's all it took. Those three little words and a lifetime of finding one small thing to share after a walk or trip. Sometimes just a penny. Maybe a rock or a wildflower. They weren't the most romantic of couples, but something in their little ritual always hinted there was more to their relationship than they let on.

I want something different… She caught it—that look her parents sometimes shared. *But it works for them.*

A text message came.

NEED TO SEND YOU AN EMAIL. GOT ONE YOU CAN SHARE?

If he hadn't just joked about going steady, Portia would have taken it as a brush-off. With stomach clenching anyway, she sent back her personal email. HOPE I DON'T REGRET THIS. PORTIA.SPEARS@THELETTERSBOX.COM.

I HOPE YOU DON'T, EITHER.

The words reassured her, even as her stomach did a much less pleasant workout at the things her mind imagined.

With everyone settled, and her father half asleep already, Portia dragged herself upstairs and into her room. Whatever he'd send, she just "knew" it would be awful—somehow. *Friends. He wants to be just friends. Can you be "steady friends"? And what'll happen when Sunday comes, everyone meets him, and then nothing happens? Why'd I say they could stay? This is going to be so awkward.*

That did it. Portia tossed her phone on the bed and dug out her half-finished book. "And I was afraid I wouldn't have enough to make it through the week…"

Curled up on the bed, she should have managed to get through a chapter or two by the time her email chime came through the phone. She *should* have. Still, despite being on page eight, all she could remember was the main character's first name.

An email that seemed never to end filled the screen. Line by line, she scrolled. One moment happy—the next nervous again. The picture of Duncan waking up screaming, shaking, terrified of those he loved leaving him—it tore at her.

Reese's next words soothed and humbled.

It's hard to take risks when your son's heart and faith become the fallout. I was ready to decide that I could just wait a few years for a relationship and see if he gets over this, but Mom and Dad set me straight.

I reminded Duncan about how God says we're to trust Him when we're afraid. I wasn't trusting Him. So here it is on the line. Where my heart is waiting for me to give it the okay to step out.

That video? I don't think it's so crazy. I can see that the tension gets to you, but I can also see that you take part in it. You say what you *think. It's one of the things I like about you. And it's probably not like that "all the time," or if it is, it wouldn't matter, would it?*

If we do what people do, we'll fall in love. We'll get married. We'll give Duncan those cousins and hopefully a brother or sister or three. We'll have our own house and our own family and flaws all our own.

Because, isn't that what people do?

Throwing this out there, but that's what I want someday. I don't know for sure yet if I want that to be with you, but I do know I want a chance to find out. Even with your family and any other issues you think there might be. I want that chance. I hope you do, too.

Portia read it and reread it. Then she did the only rational thing. She screamed down the stairs for her mother. Five minutes later, she zipped back a text message.

I DO.

Half a second later, she panicked. WAIT! THAT'S NOT WHAT I MEAN. I MEAN THAT'S WHAT I WANT, TOO. UM. DON'T SUPPOSE YOU'LL FORGET THIS ONE?

Another half a second passed—or a few dozen of them—before his reply hit her inbox. SINCE I'M TRYING TO CONVINCE YOU TO GIVE US A CHANCE, YES. THIS TIME.

Squeals raced past her door. Somewhere downstairs, Miranda asked who spilled juice on the carpet. The cinematic explosions of an action movie grew louder and louder before being silenced at the close of a door.

Portia, however, sat on her bed, feet straight out, toes pointed. The words danced on her fingertips until she gathered the courage to type them. MY HERO.

The game dragged on—Monopoly. Why he'd agreed to play, Reese didn't know. While Duncan and Dad duked it out over Mom's St. James Place, Reese made a decision. "Do you guys have plans tomorrow?"

"I need to get some groceries," his mom admitted. "Why?"

"Thought I might see if Portia wants to go up behind Ojai with Duncan and me. You guys could bring a car if you wanted. It's been a while since we've all gone."

A slow smile told him she'd refuse—but that she didn't want to. "I really do need groceries, and I was thinking about maybe taking down the tree early. Dad agreed to that new couch finally, so I'm considering going over on Saturday to see if the floor sample is still for sale. It'll save us a few hundred dollars."

That's a lot of talking. She's nervous. About what? It occurred to Reese that maybe his nerves played off on her or something.

Duncan scored the sale and rolled. While he counted, Reese put forth his next idea. "Would it be… I don't know, *wrong* of me to ask Portia tonight so Duncan knows before he sleeps? I thought maybe it would keep the nightmares at bay."

"Can't hurt." Mom caught his gaze and held it. "Tell her up front. You're asking because you want to spend time with her. You're asking *now* because you want to test this with Duncan."

His turn over, Duncan looked up and pointed to Mom. *"Your turn."*

Three more rounds followed until Duncan managed to snag Tennessee Avenue. The building began, and Reese took that moment to zip a text to Portia. IS TOMORROW FREE? MORNING OR AFTERNOON? BOTH? WANTED TO TAKE YOU UP BEHIND OJAI. A.J. COULD COME?

He'd rolled twice before he remembered his mother's admonition to tell her about his test. I WOULD WAIT UNTIL TOMORROW TO ASK, BUT I WANTED TO TEST AND SEE IF KNOWING HE'D SEE YOU TOMORROW WOULD HELP DUNCAN SLEEP BETTER. THOUGHT I SHOULD BE UPFRONT ABOUT THAT.

The wait began as the game wound down. As always, the minute Duncan got hotels on all the orange properties, the game ended. That kid had serious Monopoly skills. "We should get him in business school."

"He'll probably want to be a piano tuner or something," his father muttered. "And he'll prove it can be done. You know it."

"Probably already has been," Reese muttered.

As usual, Duncan volunteered to put away the game. Every bill was counted and straightened—put in exactly the right direction. Classic stall tactic, of course. For once, Reese didn't care. Portia hadn't responded yet.

He tried another note. I JUST REALIZED YOU MIGHT BE "DOING CHRISTMAS" TOMORROW. WE COULD JUST PLAY FRISBEE ON THE BEACH FOR AN HOUR? GO DOWN TO MARINA PARK?

Desperation dripped from every word, and he knew it. Still,

Reese sent one more. YES, THIS IS MOSTLY FOR ME. I MISS YOU. WE COULD MEET AT THE ENTRANCE AND TAKE A WALK TO TALK ABOUT IT IF YOU WANTED. I WOULDN'T COMPLAIN. BUT EVEN A CHANCE TO SEE YOU FOR A FEW MINUTES WILL ALSO GIVE ME AN IDEA ABOUT DUNCAN. DOES THAT MAKE YOU FEEL USED?

The game had been put away, Duncan showered and ready for bed, with two glasses of water and extra hugs for his grandparents, before Reese gave up and tucked him in. Less than a minute after he pulled the door shut, a reply came.

WISH I COULD COME DOWN NOW. WE'RE IN THE MIDDLE OF A MOVIE. LATER? AND CRESSIDA SAID YES TO OJAI. THAT'S WHAT TOOK SO LONG. I WAS WAITING FOR AN ANSWER. SHE HAD TO ASK AUSTIN. ROUND AND ROUND... WHAT TIME SHOULD WE BE READY? IS THERE ROOM FOR TAMI?

A smile formed, despite every effort to suppress it. ALWAYS ROOM FOR HER. TEXT ME WHEN YOU CAN MEET. I'LL COME GET YOU. THANKS FOR UNDERSTANDING.

Reese stepped into his old room and snapped on the light. Duncan lay there, eyes wide open. He knew that pose—the, *I'm not going to let myself fall asleep* one. With a prayer for success in his heart, he signed the news. *"We're taking Portia, Tami, and A.J. to Ojai tomorrow. Portia just sent a message saying they could go. Surprise!"*

Immediately, Duncan signed back, *"What time?"*

"As soon after breakfast as they can be ready, but before lunch. I want to take them to Javier's Tacos."

How the boy managed to fling the covers back and propel himself into Reese's arms in one movement? Who knew? But it did bode well for the success of the plan.

Now, if we can just convince him to trust You *like this, Lord...*

TWENTY-ONE

Maybe it wasn't fair of her—okay, it *probably* wasn't, actually. However, Portia had hoped to keep her new... She swallowed hard. Even in *feelings,* rather than specific thoughts, she found it hard to identify what she had with Reese as a relationship. *But it is. And I didn't really want to share that with everyone. Not yet. I thought it was about the family, and maybe part of it was. But...*

"You okay?"

They sat at Javier's Tacos, inhaling the best tacos she'd ever eaten—chicken and crispy flour tortillas. Who did that? At Reese's furrowing eyebrows, she leaned against him and gave him a half-smile. "Yes. Just thinking."

"About me?"

Instant burning face? Check!

A knowing smile formed on Tami's face, and Portia shot her a *Don't you even think about texting anyone about this* look.

The smile only grew more smug.

Portia tried to give Reese a hint that she'd talk to him about it later. It missed him by the proverbial mile. True to her kind and helpful nature, Tami decided to explain. "She's trying to tell you that she'll talk to you when we're not around to hear her."

"Oh..." Reese's leg pressed against hers for a moment before he picked up his third taco and prepared to take a bite. "She probably *really* loves those tacos then."

"It's chicken. Of course she does."

As he chewed, he watched her—not that *that* was awkward or anything. After a quick sip of his Mountain Dew, he eyed the plate again and said, "Do you *really* like chicken that much?"

"Love chicken. I just don't like *fish*." She screwed up her face and wrinkled her nose as he started to take another bite of batter-fried fish tacos. "Gross."

That stopped him. "We will have to come to an agreement on this one. Fish tacos are a non-negotiable in my life. *Fish* is a non-negotiable. However, if you don't object to having an every-man-woman-and-child-for-himself night once every couple of weeks, we'll be good until death by mercury do us part."

Tami's eyes widened at the same time Portia's response shifted from delighted amusement to panic at the realization Tami had just heard that. "I—"

"I think that's smart." Tami kicked her under the table. "We should do that now. It would get rid of leftovers, and then we could have alfredo more than once or twice a year."

"She loves alfredo, doesn't she?"

How is it that he remembers that? And why does him knowing feel like the most romantic thing that has ever happened to me?

"Yeah, but Dad hates it. So we never get it. But if we did this, then sometimes it could be alfredo night for us. He could make frozen pizza or something."

What else could she do? "I'll talk to Mom. I think it's a good idea—leftovers especially. Good idea."

The boys ate their food in record time. Reese finished up and took them outside to walk around while Tami and Portia ate the rest of their food. The moment the door closed, Portia pounced. "Did you *have* to do that?"

"Let him know you like him? Yeah." Tami wadded up her mess and carried her tray to the garbage. When she returned for her drink, she winked and said, "Someone has to, and it's obvious that you won't."

Oh, help.

If that wasn't bad enough, and as far as Portia was concerned it was the worst it could be… When Tami stepped outside, Reese pounced. "Grilling her about it, I bet. So not fair. So, so, so not fair."

"Excuse me?"

A teen with pimply skin and braces stared at her. Portia waved him off. "Just talking to myself."

Conversing on the climb up into the hills behind Ojai? Just as choppy as conversing on the way *to* Ojai. Every third sentence seemed to be interrupted by, "Portia, how do you sign volleyball? How do you sign…?"

Maybe it should have been more obvious. Frankly, he couldn't help but flush at the look on her face when the idea hit her, but one minute they'd been interrupted… *again,* and the next, she held out her hand. "Phone?"

"Phone? For…?"

"Just give it here." And with both phones in hand, she passed them back. "When you guys can't remember how to sign something, type it. And whatever you do, have him sign it for you so you can learn for next time."

He kept it low, but Reese murmured, "Thanks."

"I can't get a thought out without being interrupted. It's making me crazy. They're worse than preschoolers!"

When no protests came from the back, Reese took a chance. "So… is this a 'hands-off' trip or…"

It might have been presumptuous, but when he saw Portia set her bottle into the door, freeing her left hand, he took that as agreement and laced their fingers together. A glance or two in the rearview mirror showed no reaction. "Don't think anyone noticed."

"Good. Trust me, that's a good thing… but so is this."

Keeping the car climbing the winding, twisting roads with his least-dominant hand—not so easy. The warm pressure of her fingers squeezing his—totally worth it. Totally worth every second of it.

Their favorite turnout was empty. At that particular spot, the creek had large enough rocks to get across it without getting wet, and hiking on the other side was a slow, easy climb. Kids tumbled out of the car almost the moment it stopped. Reese turned to her, and without thinking, asked, "Is this what it would be like?"

"What?"

"Having a bunch of kids. Going places." Their eyes locked, and his next words came out in an emotion-laden whisper. "*Being* together."

She didn't answer. She just climbed from the car and came around to meet him at the back. Without a word, she slipped her hand into his and followed the kids.

Just as they reached the water, what he'd said… what he'd *implied*, became clear. A lump formed. "Portia?"

"Hmm?"

"Too much? I—"

She squeezed his hand before dropping it to start across the water. "Don't over-think it. It's just a question. And, yeah… this is a lot like what I remember when I was a kid."

The kids had made it up the embankment and waved back at them. Tami called out, "Can we climb up a ways? I'll keep an eye on them." Before he could tell them to wait up, Portia asked about phones. "I've got mine. Yours and Reese's are in the car."

"Go ahead, then. I'll get phones. Don't go far, and call if you even *think* you don't know where you are."

Reese would have protested, but Tami signed, *"Let's go"* and led the boys up the hill.

"Is that safe?"

"She'll be fine as long as we have our phones."

Dad would approve of that. Stuffing down a bit of panic, Reese jogged back to retrieve said phones and returned hers with a flourish. "I'm trusting you."

That caught her attention. Portia blinked up at him—way up. Standing on an incline did wonders for his height, and to his disgust, he kind of liked the sensation of being significantly taller. *What a totally caveman attitude! If she knew…*

"You're a lot taller standing there." Pink cheeks turned a bit blotchy as she added, "You weren't okay with them climbing? They didn't have to, I guess."

"You're good for my over-protective side. You know more about kids than I do." The more he rambled, the better he felt, so Reese kept going. "I mean, you've got siblings and students and stuff. I just have a panicked idea of having a kid who can't communicate easily so…" Now he flushed. "I hover."

He took a step closer, and so did she. Only once they'd met on even ground did it feel *right* again. "There you are…"

"Huh?"

It was right—he could feel it. Had the kids not been close enough to return and become an instant audience, Reese would have taken the opportunity. "If we were alone—"

"We *are* alone."

"Without any chance of being interrupted," he continued, "I'd be kissing you right now. You should know that."

"The chances of interruption are slim with A.J. in that group. Tami will have to drag him back at some point." A slow smile formed. "But I admit that I don't like the idea of having my first kiss interrupted by a little sister who would use it for blackmail. Not the memory you dream of, you know?"

With the creek bubbling past, the trees rustling in a chilling breeze, and birds twittering about something or another, Reese slid one hand along her jaw, leaned forward, and pressed his forehead against hers. "I just can't believe you're going to let me be that guy."

Squeals and calls proved all fears are not unfounded. He stepped back. "You called that one. Let's go see what horrible thing they've seen."

"Or smell if they've tangled with a skunk."

They crossed the creek and met the trio a few yards from it. Tami grinned. "There's this tree back there. It's like *all* mistletoe. I've never seen anything like it. With berries!"

Reese lunged forward, but Portia caught him. "Just note. If you ever want that kiss thing to happen," she whispered under her breath. "You'd better get me some of that mistletoe. Tomorrow we're doing Christmas, so…"

He grinned. "As long as I get some for… you know, just in case, then yeah. I can make that happen."

Tami hadn't exaggerated. The tree stood tall, with outreaching branches. Each branch had enormous balls and an almost square brick of mistletoe hanging from them. Portia stopped short and stared. "Wow… that's like God hung kissing balls right on the tree! There's more vegetation in the mistletoe than there is on that tree."

"It's winter. Doesn't that stand to reason?"

She whacked at him without even looking to see if he was near enough to hit. He wasn't—not on the side she "attacked." "Don't interfere with my awe."

Duncan grabbed at his sleeve. *"Tami wants some. They're having Christmas tomorrow. Can you get it?"*

Agreeing—easy. Desire—overwhelming. Who wouldn't want to make the Spears girls happy? Actually climbing the tree and procuring said mistletoe without breaking his neck, on the other hand, not so easy and oh, so overwhelming. Never had Reese fought so hard to push down the temptation to scream and run away like a little girl from a wriggling snake. *Forget that. I'd squeal and run. Portia would probably take it home and use it as an object lesson for Adam and Eve or something.*

Two branches broke on his way to the nearest bunch of mistletoe. He tried the other side of the tree, and there they seemed stronger—just higher, too. "I think that half of the tree is dead. Going for that bunch."

"Good! It has berries. It's prettier."

Of course, it was. "Would you have said that before or after I killed myself trying to get the other stuff?"

"After we were home and you wouldn't risk your neck again." A glance down showed her right below the tree, as if she'd be able to catch him if he fell. "Oh, and you should know something else."

Reese tested another branch and swung his leg over it once he saw it didn't creak like the others had. "What's that?"

"If you fall and break your neck, I'm not dragging you back to the car. You can be dead all alone, for all I care. Oh, and I'm not going to your funeral."

A glance down mid-threat showed that she wasn't signing a translation for Duncan. One at Tami and then A.J. just showed them grinning. *A normal threat. I can work with that.* He ignored her for a minute and inched closer to the center of the branch, where he hoped to grab the giant ball of hanging parasite and rip a bunch from it.

Just as he reached out, Reese called down, "I'll be sure to come back and haunt you like the ghost in that old movie." He missed.

"Wha—you know *The Ghost and Mrs. Muir?*"

Reese scooted out a few more inches and prepared to try again. Was it a lie to say yes if he only half-remembered bits of it from when he was about A.J.'s age? *Chicken pox, wasn't it?* Reese decided not. "Yeah… I'm the guy who quoted Miss Bates, after all."

"True. That's settled then."

"What is?" When she didn't answer, he glanced down again and saw her ordering the kids to stick their fingers in their ears.

A chorus of "La-la-las" followed before she called up, "Check your phone when you can do it without dying."

"Why'd you tell them to do that, then?"

Her grin—he could see as clear as if she stood right beside him. "Gotta torment them somehow, right?"

And you know they'll have my phone on the way back, right? Duncan probably wouldn't think to look at my texts, but Tami would… and probably would.

Three seconds later, half the mistletoe ball lay on the ground and Reese almost tumbled after it. Instead, he hung monkey-style from the branch and inched his way back to the trunk. By the time he reached it, Reese wanted nothing more than a hot bath, a cup of coffee, and the obvious reward for procuring enough mistletoe to inspire a few hundred new romances. In reverse order, please.

His phone blipped halfway down, and Reese *almost* stopped and read it right there. In fact, he tried to, but a slipped foot produced a scraped hand and stomach and his heart pounding harder than it ever had in his life—not that he'd admit that to Portia, who now stood at the base of the tree, screaming orders for him to stay alive.

Do you realize you just shouted for me not to die before you get that first kiss? Do you see your little sister grinning like the Cheshire Cat's twin sister? Do you realize A.J. is not as discreet as she might be persuaded to be?

If doubts had tried to resurface, the contrary things, her orders to keep that kiss possible would have driven them back again. Still, he took twice as long as he wanted and ended up a rather scraped and bleeding mess by the time he dropped the last six or so feet to the ground.

Portia hugged him even before he'd managed to become fully upright. "I told you not to die!"

"I didn't, although there was a moment there where I wondered…"

"I had about fifty of those, thank-you-very-much. If I was a cat, I'd be owing the grim reaper for an overdraw on lives right now."

Duncan hugged him next, laughing at the antics. The boy was completely unaware it hadn't been one of his usual jokes, pretending to get hurt while doing something—cutting off a thumb while fixing a toy or making a sandwich. *I hope I can keep it that way.*

Tami hugged him next. "Thanks." She glanced over to where Portia had moved to assure A.J. that everything was good. "I don't think she realizes that she said that out loud. She'll be embarrassed if she does."

"I'm pretty sure she didn't. If you can keep A.J.—"

"He'll remember better from you than me. That's what I wanted to tell you. If you tell him not to tell, he won't." She gave another glance at Portia before leaning in to whisper, "Tell him he can tell the story at your wedding, but only if he keeps it a secret now. Trust me, he'll do it."

A smile formed. "I knew I liked you."

"If I didn't like you, I'd totally tell everyone when I got home. Even Portia's wrath would be worth it, but you're too nice. And you're nice to her."

"Who's he nice to?"

Too smooth—Tami was way too smooth for his comfort. She turned to Portia and said, "You. I mean, he just risked life and that poor tree's limb to get you mistletoe."

"Well, let's gather it up and take it to the car." Portia examined his hand, and at the way he jumped when she brushed her elbow against his stomach, she stopped and jerked up his shirt, too. "Ouch! Got first aid in the car?"

And here we become every cheesy black and white movie. She'll doctor me. I'll yowl at the pain of getting my wounds clean. She'll call me a baby. Sounded a bit wonderful, actually. "Yep."

"Let's go."

Portia led the way, arms full of life-sucking tree parasites that promised love, relational fulfillment, and… well, it promised their first kiss, and he'd take it. Her text message, however, promised more. Much more. From that, he got a hint of the kind of love, relational fulfillment, and many more kisses that a life with Portia could bring.

I'M SO GOING TO DO EVERYTHING I CAN TO MAKE YOU WANT TO MARRY ME. SOMEHOW. CONSIDER THIS YOUR WARNING.

Reese caught her around the waist as she shoved in the mistletoe and retrieved the first aid kit from the back of the car. Heedless of those big ears the old storybooks always talked about, he murmured, "Challenge accepted."

"What challenge?"

Reese showed her the phone. "That one."

As she buried her face in his shoulder, he winked at Tami and sent a silent message. *Make sure you read that text, too.*

Tami's nod was all he needed.

"So, are you going to torture me or what?"

"Thanks a lot!" Portia jerked back and scowled at him. But when he raised his shirt and eyed her, the scowl turned to a flaming, mortified face. "Oh. Yeah. Torture. Let's get to it."

TWENTY-TWO

Christmas morning. December twenty-ninth. Those two things didn't work well together, but there it was. Four-thirty, no less. And Portia had been awake for half an hour. *I wonder if he's ever up this early.*

That thought prompted another. *Has there been a day that I've been here that I haven't seen him?*

Rather than try to figure that out, she zipped him a text message, rolled over, and tried to go back to sleep. But a minute later, a reply came. NOT ONE SINCE THAT DAY WE MET ON THE BEACH, ANYWAY.

A few seconds later, another text followed. YOUR FAMILY DOES EARLY CHRISTMAS. WOW!

She shot back a reply and flung back the covers in anticipation of his next response or two. If she got dressed, the family would be suspicious, so Portia pulled on her thick, fuzzy sleep pants that added ten pounds but kept her toasty on chilly nights and reached for her coat.

That next reply came just as she reached the front door. WELL, IF YOU CAN'T SLEEP, WHY DON'T WE MEET AT THE BEACH? I COULD BRING COFFEE IF YOU GIVE ME FIVE.

She'd give him fifteen if he insisted. DEAL. JUST MAKE SURE THERE'S CREAM AND SUGAR OF SOME KIND AND I'M GOOD. THANKS. After she'd reached the bottom of the driveway, Portia thought of something else. OH, AND MERRY CHRISTMAS! ONLY THE SPEARS WOULD BE THAT LATE WITH AN ENTIRE HOLIDAY.

At home, the air would have been crisp—biting. But as Portia stepped out, a different kind of cold swooped over her. She couldn't call it damp… but it was. Being colder seemed to temper the scent of salt, but the closer she grew to shore, the stronger it became.

Walking *to* the beach in the darkness of morning—a new experience. *Did Reese do this all the time when he lived here? I love walking along the shore at night… what about morning?*

A jogger passed. "Morning."

She hadn't expected it—not down here. "Good morning!"

The cries of gulls greeted her as she stepped onto the sand. Well, Portia rather suspected that they actually threatened her with poop bombs if she didn't get off their territory. "You guys are just like those obnoxious birds in *Finding Nemo*! The world isn't yours!"

Once she'd reached the water line, Portia realized that Reese wouldn't know to look for her so far from their usual meeting spot and turned to go wait for him. If the shadow up by the road was who she thought it was, he stood at the top of the dunes, watching. *Probably trying to see if it's me.* She waved.

A second later, it raced toward her—as quickly as someone can race through the loose sands along the entrance to the beach. *He'll scald his hands if he's not careful.* He deserved it, she decided. If he was going to try to run through *sand*, then he deserved every burn he got.

Only when she recalled his scraped hands from the previous afternoon did she change her tune. "Ouch! Stop!"

He didn't.

Reese reached her side, shoved two travel mugs into the sand, and wrapped arms around her. "Morning."

"Morning! But why are you running around like—"

"Didn't like thinking of you down there alone." He reached down and eyed the cups. "Uh, oh. I don't remember which mine is, now."

"Sugar in yours?"

"Not much."

Portia took a chance. She reached for the closest one, took

a sip, and scowled. "That better be yours." A sip of the second one changed everything. She swallowed, eyes closed, and inhaled a fresh whiff of the caffeine-infused perfection. "Oh, yeah… I'm definitely marrying you. If for no other reason than so you can make me coffee every day. This is *good*."

Another sip prompted just a bit more gushing—something she knew she did and, frankly, didn't care. "Yeah. You should quit your day job and make coffee. You'd put Starbucks out of business."

Reese's chuckle might have annoyed her if the coffee hadn't already worked its magic and beaten back the bad-attitude invaders. "So… I think maybe someone was *really* craving coffee? Because that isn't great coffee. This I know."

"Is to me."

"As long as you keep thinking that, I'll keep making it. "Til death or a dearth of coffee cherries do us part."

"Plant me a tree?" Portia knew she sounded ridiculous, but she didn't care. Early morning walk on the beach + guy she was rapidly falling for + delicious coffee equaled perfection in her book.

"Of course." He reached over, slid an arm around her waist, and leaned in to kiss her temple. "*Now* it's a good morning."

It wasn't the kiss she'd begun to anticipate more than the average girlfriend looks forward to that little hunk of precious metal known as an engagement ring, but it would do. "I'm going to throw this out there while I'm feeling fearless and happy."

"What's that?"

Head resting on his arm, Portia took another sip of her coffee and sighed. "I think I'd marry you even if you didn't make me coffee. Isn't that weird?"

"I think it'd be weird if coffee *was* the deciding factor." He pulled her closer—if that was even possible. "Glad to hear I don't need to be nervous about that proposal I was planning."

At that point, she would normally have been *done* with the teasing. Just in case. But with waves rolling in and rocking her nerves into a stupor, caffeine doing its best to give her mind clarity and happiness, and that feeling of connectedness with a guy she realized she *could* love someday, Portia didn't care. Not a whit.

"Just make sure it's not public. I'm not into those. Love to watch them. Don't want to be watched."

"What about a friend to record it for us?"

"Nope." She turned and gazed into his eyes. "Sometimes, a memory needs to be enough—and maybe a selfie afterward, but otherwise—memory."

When his lips moved closer, she almost regretted it—not having that mistletoe there. A second thought sent her gaze up, but no green ball of romance hung over their heads. "Portia?"

She snapped back to proper attention and waited for that kiss. It landed, a second and a half later, on her nose. "I forgot the mistletoe. I think I want to wait for that."

Despite the momentary disappointment, she nodded. "I agree. Blast it."

"Blast it?"

She shrugged. "I read it in a book once. I liked it. Kind of fit the Spears and our propensity to 'blast' each other. Clever, don't you think?"

"If you say so." He swatted at her fuzzy pants and teased a bit. "So eager to see me that you couldn't take a minute to get dressed?"

Where it came from, Portia didn't even know. But a second later, she heard herself say, "No… I just thought I'd drive over and try to get on that site that does the weird Walmart photos."

Reese's laughter boomed out, scaring a few gulls that, she suspected, had decided to try to steal their coffee. "Won't happen unless they've decided to take their site in a new direction—like the most adorable shopper." He reached up and smoothed a hand over her hair. "Then again, that mop might just—"

"Oh, ugh…" Portia held up her phone and checked out the hair she hadn't even looked at, much less brushed out. "Talk about mortifying."

"Still beautiful, as far as I'm concerned."

Where her caution and discretion had gone, Portia didn't

quite know. However, when she heard herself say, "That's why I'm going to marry you," Portia put a BOLO out on them right away.

"Will you wear your hair like that at the wedding?"

"I'll do my best, but this is a one-of-a-kind style. It comes out differently every time."

Reese took a swig of coffee, pulled her into a full hug and murmured into her hair, "Like those 'fling paint at the canvas' paintings?"

"Exactly like those."

"Deal."

With her cheek pressed to his chest and one arm around him, the surf providing ambiance and accompaniment, and the gulls adding their own riffs here and there, it couldn't have been a more perfect morning. "Is it expensive to live here?"

"Yeah—not as bad as L.A. or Santa Barbara, but yeah."

"Blast it."

"I've got a shot at a job in Ojai with my company. Just thirty minutes away. Meiners Oaks is right there, and a lot cheaper than Ojai or Ventura… and half an hour away."

Her heart sank. Ojai was a lot farther than Santa Clarita and Newhall. "When's that happening?"

"Not sure it is."

She snapped her head up and eyed him. "Why not?"

"Well…" Even in the darkness, she could see the emotion in his eyes—emotion that terrified and delighted her all at once. "I met this girl, you see…"

"You did, huh? Should I be jealous?"

"Insanely." Again, he pressed his forehead to hers. "Because I'm pretty sure I'm falling for her. Ojai is too far away for a baby relationship."

Her heart had chased down those words, "I'm falling for her" and captured them. In the process, she missed part of his next sentence. Confused, though still soaring toward the infamous cloud nine, she stuttered, "—you want to have a—baby with—our relationship?"

"You need to go to bed. You're not awake."

Clarity formed just as she was about to protest that he would be doing "no such thing." With a choke on another gulp of coffee, she snorted. "You do not want to know what I almost said that time."

Laughter rang out half a minute later. "Oh, yeah. I just figured that one out. Good one."

"For you, maybe."

She needed to change subjects—fast. "What are you guys doing today?"

"Probably give Duncan a few more macro-derm-abrasions until time to pick you up for the movie." He stepped away and laced their fingers together, turning toward "his" side of the beach. "Thanks for doing that, by the way. He slept again all night. I'm trying to figure out how to get him comfortable before we all go, or we'll be right back there when we hit home."

"Maybe not," she argued. "I mean, I'm associated with *here* in his mind, right? So, as long as I come whenever you visit your parents, maybe it'll be fine."

"Is that a hint for an invite?"

"Nooo…" Portia grinned into her cup as she took her last gulp. "There was no hint about that at all. That was me inviting myself, of course."

"Done."

If only all of this flirting and teasing could be real. Another thought made the last seem almost pathetic. *The best part is it can be… someday. Maybe.*

They'd made it almost to the first house before she spoke again. "I wish I could invite you to Christmas this morning."

His silence asked more clearly than any question of why she couldn't. Portia obliged. "It's just that I was pretty vocal about how ticked off I was that they were bringing their guys to this so-called 'family only' thing. Tami wanted to bring a friend so she could have something to do, but no… *family only*. So when I found out the guys were coming—well, Damon, mostly. I mean, Gavin will *be* family in four months. That's family enough for me. But

Damon hadn't proposed before we planned this, and I don't actually think he has still."

"Really?"

Portia shrugged. "She's not wearing that ring, but he's not gone, either."

It sounded strained, but after a couple of houses, Reese cleared his throat and said, "I think you're smart. Of course, I want to be there, but they've never even met me. I don't have the connection with your family that even Damon does. I get that."

It wouldn't happen, of that, Portia had no doubt. Still, by way of concession both to him and her own heart, she made a promise. "If they say even one thing about how I should have invited you, I'm texting. Bring Duncan or not, but if you're not busy, come."

This time, he stood there, searching her face in the moonlight. "Do you mean that?"

"Mean what?"

"You really want me there?"

I'm such a jerk. She couldn't explain it. She didn't quite know how to make it make sense, even to herself, but Portia knew one thing. "Yes. I definitely *want* you there. I just don't know if I want to *share* you there."

"I'll be waiting… and probably praying, for that text."

The first text came as he began scrambling eggs for breakfast. GET THIS. EVERYONE'S UP BUT A.J. KID IS OUT LIKE A LIGHT.

Ten minutes later, the next came. BELLA "ACCIDENT-IC-LY" WOKE HIM UP BY FLINGING HERSELF ACROSS THE WRONG BED. HIS. THEY NOW HAVE MATCHING GOOSE EGGS.

A picture followed.

Toast popped up just as he shut off the eggs—perfection in

breakfast timing. *Make a note. That'll never happen again.*

Duncan appeared, and Reese passed over the phone. *"They're doing Christmas today since Portia's dad was in the hospital on Christmas Day."*

Mom entered a moment later. "That smells good… what're you doing up so early?"

"Took a pre-dawn walk with Portia. She couldn't sleep."

By the time he'd dished up food, his father had appeared, and everyone had read the messages. Mom piped up. "There's another one."

"Read it to me."

"Okay…" Just as he realized that might not be a good idea, his mom's voice softened to that tone that meant extreme happiness and she read, "'Miss you. I should have invited you. I'm sorry.'"

Duncan signed wildly, wanting to know where they should have been invited and asking why they couldn't go now. *"Isn't that an invite?"*

While his mother explained simple rules of etiquette, Reese popped more toast in the toaster for his father and poured a cup of coffee as well. Dad just accepted it with a *look*. Those things were usually his mother's purview—when he'd gone overboard or something. However, when his father entered the game, they usually took on heavier meaning.

"Son, are things moving a little… fast?"

"I haven't even kissed her, Dad. We joke, but I think we're both a little skittish, too."

Dad shifted so his back was to Duncan before adding, "Just remember that you have a boy who is already attached to her. You need to be extra careful."

"I will be."

Duncan shoved the phone between them before Reese could even look that way. *"She says A.J. got my pirate ship for Christmas!"*

"You guys will have to compare notes on how hard it is to put together."

"He likes my ship in a bottle. Tami found a picture for him." Then,

as if asking for a stick of bubble gum, Duncan added, *"He wants one. Can we get it for him?"*

His usual caution with making promises nearly flew out the window. He opened his mouth, but Mom tapped Duncan on the shoulder and signed, *"I don't think that would be a good idea. It's expensive. Maybe something else would be better."*

Those words surprised Reese. "It's expensive?"

"I checked it out when I saw all the pieces. It's over fifty dollars. If you bought that for A.J., you'd need to bring something for Tami and the little girls, too. That's a lot of money."

Reese couldn't get past the price tag. "She spent that much money on a kid she'd only met a couple of times?" He sank into the chair and stared at his steaming eggs. "Do you think they're rich?"

"They rented out Sandpiper House. Probably."

His mother had a point. It had to be a couple hundred dollars a night, at least—off season. If it was June more like five hundred at least. Times two weeks… easily three thousand dollars for the trip. Then again, all those people would need at least four hotel rooms. Maybe five. Even cheaper ones at a hundred dollars a night would cost more. "Maybe…"

Dad spoke up, stating just that. "With that many people, it's probably less expensive than moderately priced hotel rooms. And didn't you say she bought it Christmas Eve?"

"Yeah…" Reese speared a forkful of eggs. "Why?"

"I just thought maybe it was the most affordable thing left on the shelves or something. I've heard people talking about how understocked stores were this year."

All of that made more sense than wealthy. Portia's Buick wasn't exactly a luxury car, and she couldn't make much running a church preschool. Before he could throw out those ideas, a new text came in—complete with picture. Apparently, A.J. got more than a goose egg from the encounter. He now had a matching missing tooth to Duncan's. He wanted Duncan to see.

One by one, pictures came through. Bella with a princess dress. Jessica with a set of silicone zip top bags. Tami with art supplies. And in each photo, a stack of books by one corner of the couch rose higher and higher. He flipped through and showed his mom. "I think that gift card I got her to Price & Bradbury Booksellers was a good idea."

"Oh! I forgot to tell you!" Mom hopped up and returned with two familiar wrapped packages. "I found these under the back of the tree skirt." She eyed Duncan with exaggerated suspicion and signed as she said, "I suspect they were hidden to try to keep her here longer."

Duncan fingered the little wrapped box that held the gift card that suddenly felt more personal than it had originally. "I just got it because I knew she read books on her phone, but now that I see books are really her *thing*…"

His mom shook the wrapped Pringles tube and frowned. "I still can't figure out what's in it. It's *not* Pringles."

"We'll find out tonight. I'll take them with us to the movie." Once more, he smoothed the tie of the bow on the box. "Can't believe we forgot about these…"

Here, Dad piped up again. "Well, you *were* otherwise engaged."

"Doing what?"

Together, his parents blurted out, "*Flirting!*"

"Oh… that." A smile refused to be repressed. "Yeah. Flirting."

TWENTY-THREE

Overcast skies killed any chance of a moon as the three of them strolled from the old-town Ventura Theater to the car. However, the lights and Christmas decor along the streets shone even brighter because of it. Despite almost being New Year's, in the air, there was definitely a "feeling of Christmas." In fact, Portia could almost hear the song playing through the streets.

Duncan walked between them, occasionally catching one or both of their hands before dropping them to sign something else. A pang struck her so hard, she gasped at the force. Reese glanced over. "You okay?"

"Yeah… just thinking. Do you hear 'Silver Bells'?"

"Probably from that guy over there."

Sure enough, diagonally across from them, a man played a violin under a street light. Portia dug into her purse, fished out a five-dollar bill and dashed across the street with it.

On her return, she watched as Reese explained to Duncan and shook his head at her at the same time. "Heads up next time might be nice. I was ready to grab you!"

"That'd be the second time you tried to play a father role in my life. Hint. I've got a daddy. Looking for a different kind of relationship with a man." She winked at him before adding, "Just thought I'd set that straight."

They'd only gone a few steps before Reese murmured, "That wasn't all, was it?"

"No." Telling him might be a bit much, but not… It seemed so petty. "It just felt like when I walk with one of the girls and Bella or Charis is between us. We walk, we swing the girls—it's fun. I'll never get to do that with him."

Saying who she meant by "him"? Not necessary. Still, when they reached the car, he unlocked the doors and waited for Duncan to climb in before pulling her close and murmuring, "I do love that it matters to you. Maybe someday…"

Portia's breath caught, and to her surprised relief, he didn't finish. *He's right. Too much of that kind of flirting might just be too much. It's fun, but…*

However, when he slid behind the wheel, Reese gripped it with knuckles that glowed white, even in the weak parking lot lighting. For a moment, she thought he'd say the same thing, but instead he said, "Who am I kidding? We keep joking and teasing, but there's seriousness beneath it all, too. I *do* hope something happens so someday we *can* do that. It just won't be with Duncan. *His* kids, maybe."

Or ours. Despite his honesty, she wasn't ready to admit she'd even thought it. Instead, she just nodded. "I hope…" she began with a bit of trepidation. "I hope that no matter what happens between us, we'll at least be friends when he is old enough to have kids for us to swing between us."

Reese backed out of the parking slot and pulled out of the lot a moment later. They'd made it nearly to Pierpont before he spoke again, and the hard edge and stiffness of his voice and words almost hinted of anger or hurt. "Are you hinting that friendship is all you're interested in? I don't want to—"

"No!" Grateful for a dark car, Portia willed the heat to leave her face, even as she pressed one cheek to the window in an effort to speed that along. "I just—"

All the *hurt*—that's what it had been, hurt. It all disappeared from Reese's tone. "Okay. I just needed to know. You'll tell me, though, right? If you decide *we* are not what you're looking for? You'll say something?"

"Of course!" Logic said to make the same request. The

words, however, refused to form. *You are so too invested in this already.*

Reese passed her his phone. "Can you send Duncan a message?"

"What's that?"

"Ask him if he remembers what he's supposed to do at home."

She typed it in and passed it back. No cellphone or even signing communication was necessary. Duncan's entire body quivered with agreement. "I think that's a yes."

"I'd say so. Even I saw that."

"What's he doing?"

But Reese wouldn't tell her. He just kept saying, "You'll see."

He drove over the Seward Avenue overpass, showed where they'd pushed a car over it the night of the Golf-n-Stuff outing, and turned right at Pierpont. In front of his parents' house, he flipped a U-turn and parked. Duncan flew from the vehicle and up the walk. Reese turned off the ignition and came around to open her door.

"We're going in?" He hadn't mentioned that. Why she thought it, she couldn't say, but she'd just assumed they'd drive back to the no-entrance sign and walk along the beach for a bit.

"No..."

The front door banged open and Duncan raced down the walk with the wrapped Pringles can she'd brought for Reese on Christmas in one hand and a smaller box in the other. He passed them to his father, flung his arms around her, and kissed her cheek with the abandon of a toddler instead of a too-old-for-that-nonsense eight-year-old.

When he stepped back, he signed, *"I love you,"* and dashed back into the house before she could respond.

Portia fumbled for her phone. She thrust it at Reese. "Put your mom's number in there. Hurry."

"Wha—?"

"Just *do* it." And to give his hands free range of motion, she took the packages. She popped them onto the hood of his car and moved until she thought the street light could capture her. "Okay, now take a video."

"Oookaaay..."

It took three tries, but a short video of her signing, *"I love you, too, Duncan"* whizzed its way to Kendra Whitaker's phone. "Thanks."

He just eyed her. "You know how they say that the way to a man's heart is through his stomach?"

"Yeah?"

"Total lie." Reese snatched up the gifts and tucked them under his arm and in his pocket. With his other hand, he took hers and led her toward Bangor Lane. "At least for me. Every time I think you've totally captivated me, you show some kindness to my kid, and I get smitten all over again." A groan escaped. "I can't believe I just used the word 'smitten.'"

"I like it."

He snorted. "You would, little miss bookworm."

"I prefer bluestocking. Worms are gross." Portia couldn't have explained where *that* idea came from. She'd never thought of either thing before. Still, Reese laughed, and Portia found that she really liked making him laugh.

The path to Reese's beach had already become familiar. She knew just when the short road curved to the right, how many steps there were up to the sand, how he'd pause there and take a long, slow, deep breath. "I love this place," she admitted. "I love how all the houses are different."

"They used to look more different. On the other side of Seward, about halfway to Marina Park, there's one that looks like an English cottage with a 'thatched roof' and everything. I mean, I think it's some kind of fake thatching, but it looks right out of one of those paintings from the Cotswolds."

"Oh, I want to see that!"

"Remind me." He pushed the small box at her. It could be anything from a bracelet to a gift card in one of those boxes they sometimes provide for them. "Open it. Mom found them yesterday. She thinks Duncan hid them so you'd have to stay longer."

"Or come back..."

If the air Reese sucked in right then meant what she thought it did, she'd nailed it. He stopped her just as she'd untied the ribbon. "I want to say something."

"Okay..."

"When I saw the pictures you sent this morning, I was glad that I'd bought that, but I also know that, knowing you better now, I'd have done something different, too. It's generic. You're so not generic."

She just waited until he looked ready to sweat bullets. "Are you done?"

"Yeah."

"Good. Can I open it now?" Without waiting for an answer, she tore the paper off in one movement and grinned. "Price & Bradbury. Awesome! I love books."

He caught her around the waist as she threw her arms around him and hugged him. "Yeah, I kind of figured that out today."

That prompted her to jump back, and the sand took her down. Flat on her backside, Portia stared up at him "Wait, you figured that out *today*, but you bought this back on, what, Christmas Eve?"

"Well, I got it then because we met for the second time when you went down to the beach to 'read' and not to meet me or anything. It was supposed to be teasing you, but the joke's on me."

"That's oddly romantic." Portia put the card, box, paper, and all in her full coat pocket and held out her hand for him to help her up. "And much more thoughtful than the lame gift I got you."

Reese gripped her hand and pulled her close enough to hold... to kiss, even. Any moment, she expected to see a ball of mistletoe appear and that kiss to finally happen. His eyes held hers in a gaze so intense it stole her breath and refused to give it back. "This vacation is almost over."

What air remained in her lungs released in a whoosh. "I know. I hate that."

"Let me see your 'lame' gift."

In what seemed like half a second, he'd pried the lid from the can without even unwrapping it at all. Bow, paper, and lid dropped to the ground, followed by the can itself as he pulled out the Target bag. He extracted the wadded up shirt from within and held it up, shifting this way and that to read it. "'Nice.'"

"I'm starting to think I should have gotten the 'naughty' one."

"Curious… love it, by the way, but curious."

"Why?"

He picked up the can and wrappings and shoved it all back in the can. The shirt, however, was another story. He shrugged out of his jacket, let it fall in the sand, and pulled the T-shirt on over his button-down oxford. Then, with a minimal shake, he put his jacket on again. "There. And yeah, what made you choose that?"

"I was looking at *everything* in Target while we were trying to find stocking stuffers. Everything I liked just reminded me of how much I don't know about you. Do you like video games? Board games? Movies? Books? Outdoors stuff?" She gave him an awkward smile. "I even looked up cryptocurrency to see if anything was cheap enough as kind of a curiosity thing. But that stuff's pricey."

"Yeah… I have a friend who invests heavily. I'm just not so sure."

"Right? Anyway, I was just about to give up and go buy you a package of socks as a gag gift, when I walked past those Christmas T-shirts. There were lots about mistletoe—should've gotten one of those in retrospect—but then I saw the 'Nice' one and went, 'That's perfect. That's exactly what I *do* know about him. He's nice.' So I hid it under a couple of things, and Tami doesn't even know I got it."

"It's my new favorite shirt."

Hers, too, if she were honest. Still, she couldn't tell him that. How awkward. So, she tried to alleviate that misery with something a little more subtle. "Still, now that I know you didn't see it for days more… I kind of wish I'd gotten the mistletoe one."

"After I risked my life to get you some of the real thing? The ingratitude. Besides," he added. "My parents insist the magic is in the real thing. They're very pleased."

Still determined, Portia continued her protest. "I wouldn't know about that. It's never been tested."

"Is that a complaint?"

"I'll let you know once I have verification of the validity of the argument."

Reese reached into her pocket and extracted the gift card.

"Hey!"

"You do not need more books. After a sentence like that, I'm quite positive you are erudite enough."

She snorted. "Says the man who just used the word, 'erudite.'"

Everything shifted in that word. He'd started to lead her down the beach. She felt it. But at that, he turned and steered her back toward the stairs. "I'm sorry, but I really think we'd better go back."

"Did I say something?"

Not until they'd reached the corner of Bangor and Pierpont did Reese answer her. "I know my limits—or at least one of them, anyway. And staying longer would have been too much. Sorry."

They'd reached his car before Portia could answer that. "I never imagined a guy telling me that he had to take me home could be so flattering—romantic, even."

TWENTY-FOUR

Reese's day began at nine-thirty when Duncan jerked him out of sleep with his phone shoved in his face. "Wha—?"

"Portia messages."

He tried to suggest that next time Duncan wait until he woke up before giving him the message. *"I didn't sleep well last night."*

Duncan's almost owlishly wise nod preceded, *"Portia? I know. But you'll see her today. That helps."*

He would have argued that no, it wasn't a fear of not seeing Portia again that kept him awake all night, but his son did have a point. *"I was thinking about her."*

Again, the wise nod. *"Grandma says that's what people in love do."*

A protest formed. *"I'm not in love with her."* His son's disappointment filled the room almost instantly. Reese backed down a little. *"Not yet. I might be. Soon. I sure hope so."*

That seemed to be enough for Duncan. If Dad wanted her, then it was just a matter of time. *And such is the mind of a child. Whatever adults want, they get. If life were only that easy.*

Before he could try to explain why it didn't quite work that way, Duncan took off, leaving Reese dying for more sleep and a peek at those messages. The first had come at six.

I CAN'T SLEEP. ANY CHANCE YOU'RE UP?

Half an hour later, another followed. I GUESS NOT. AND HERE I THOUGHT I'D HAVE ANOTHER SHOT AT THAT SAND AND MISTLETOE THING. MAYBE I BETTER GO BUY THAT SHIRT AFTER ALL—FOR ME. I'LL WEAR IT. DARE YOU TO IGNORE IT.

Just a minute or so later, the next one said, I THINK I SHOULD NOT HAVE DARED YOU. MAYBE I WON'T GET IT.

Right then, Reese made a decision. He'd go find a mistletoe T-shirt if it took all day. Well, unless the plans she'd texted him about when she got home the previous night had changed. GONE. ALL DAY. TO SOLVANG AND BUELTON. WHY WE HAVE TO GO TO SOME PEA SOUP RESTAURANT WHEN NONE OF US LIKE IT, I DON'T KNOW. JESSICA SAYS WE MUST, SO WE MUST. BET SHE COMPLAINS THE LOUDEST, she'd written.

Another text message had come in at eight o'clock. HEADING OUT. MOM INSISTS THAT WE'RE HOME BY FIVE. SHE WANTS ME TO HAVE TIME TO GET READY. OF COURSE, SHE DIDN'T TELL THE OTHERS THAT. She went on to tell him how her mother had used the excuse that they didn't know what time the Whitaker family ate as the reason to be home by five. When Portia had started to say something, that "mom look" had shushed her. THAT'S WHEN I KNEW SHE WANTED ME TO HAVE A CHANCE TO CLEAN UP AFTER ALL DAY WALKING AROUND.

Halfway to Solvang, the next text had come. THIS IS BEAUTIFUL. I WANT TO COME HERE WITH YOU AND DUNCAN. WHEN ARE YOU FREE?

Did that mean she liked it but wanted it with different company, or that she just wanted company with him and had found an excuse? He didn't know. But it did prompt him to flip it up to the last message.

I HAVE THREE OUTFITS SITTING ON MY BED AT HOME. WHAT'S YOUR FAVORITE? RED, GREEN, OR BROWN?

That one he could answer in a heartbeat. THE ONE YOU'RE WEARING, OF COURSE.

Her reply shot back immediately. YOU'RE UP! AND I WON'T BE WEARING ANY IF YOU DON'T GIVE ME A COLOR.

That prompted a snicker. Reese waited. "Five... four... three..."

I DID NOT MEAN THAT THE WAY IT CAME OUT. JUST FOR THAT, I'M WEARING BLUE. MORE CASUAL, BUT I'D NEVER LOOK AT YOU WITH A STRAIGHT FACE IN ANY OF THOSE. SO, THANKS...

I GUESS.

The messages and pictures continued all day. For all her complaints about her family and her sisters, the photos told a different story. They might get on each other's nerves sometimes, but love exuded in all of them—even the one where Miranda, almost cut out of the picture, looked ready to deck someone.

Lord, I'm not used to this kind of dynamic. I bet I could be really judgmental. Keep Your hand over my mouth? I'd appreciate that.

At five o'clock, he was put on mashed potato duty. At six, everything was ready to pile in his car. At six-fifteen, they pulled into the drive at Sandpiper House and stared at each other. Dad spoke first. "Well, this is awkward."

"Right?" Reese sank against the seat. "What are we doing?"

"You've wanted to meet her family for days. Let's get in there and do this thing."

Duncan took the initiative, though. He watched them for a moment, and when no one translated, he flung open the door and dashed to ring the doorbell. Reese groaned. "Well, that solves that problem. Better get out and get the food."

"Go up with Duncan, Reese. We'll get this."

He might have protested, but Portia flung open the door just as he stepped from the car. Though she flung her arms around Duncan and signed a welcome, her eyes never left his. A.J. appeared, and the two boys disappeared into the house.

Reese, however, stood there like an idiot, watching as she approached. "Hey. How can I help?"

"I don't know what those other shirts looked like, but that's my favorite. That right there."

"Thanks?" She gave him a quick hug. "I'm so nervous."

Nothing she could have said would have put him more at ease. "You've already won me over. My turn to be nervous."

"But you're not. I can tell."

"I was, though. C'mon. Let's get the food. Mom made enough for two of your families, at least."

She looked skeptical, but when his father passed over the third roast, Portia's eyes grew wide. "Three?"

Mom sighed. "Four. I knew it wouldn't be enough. I should—"

"It's *more* than enough. Trust me." Portia led the way. Entering the house, she called out, "Food's in the trunk. They're feeding us until we leave, so hurry while it's hot."

His parents tried to argue—and lost.

The moment they'd set everything down, she grabbed his hand and his mother's hand and led them to the living room where Pat and Larry Spears stood to greet them. "Mom, Dad. This is Kendra, Brian, and Reese. Duncan disappeared somewhere with A.J."

While his mom had to drop her hand to shake hands, Reese didn't. She might have let go, but he held on. "It's great to meet you finally. How are you feeling, Larry?"

"Weak. Like an idiot, and weak."

Pat Spears looked nothing like what he'd expected. The Spears girls were tall and athletically built—like their father. Mrs. Spears couldn't have been rounder. Face, hands, body. If Mrs. Claus had a sister, it would have been Pat Spears—right down to the rimless, round "spectacles."

"Happy to meet you at last. Portia's been keeping you close to her chest." The woman's eyes shut. "Okay, that came out wrong. Let's try it again."

"Maybe it's true, Pat. How do we know?" Larry gave him a look that would have sent most men shivering in boots that they weren't even wearing.

"Good point." Pat eyed him. "Should we ask?"

"She's twenty-five…"

Again, Pat nodded and said, "Good point. So, have you—"

"Mom! Dad! Seriously, they're going to go run screaming from here!"

Larry elbowed his wife. "She let that go on way longer than I thought she would."

"Right?"

Reese's parents looked at each other, at him, at the Spears, and promptly cracked up. Portia's red face hinted that she was not amused. Not yet, anyway. Before he could even try to come up with a suitable come back, females invaded the room. Cressida, Miranda, Jessica, Tami. Bella and Charis appeared. Duncan and A.J. Off to one side, Austin smiled, said it was nice to meet them, and bustled his girls from the room.

While he had a chance, Reese pulled Duncan close and made introductions. Pat tried to imitate the, *'Nice to meet you"* sign, with understandable success. Larry winced. "All I know how to do is flail my fingers around, which Portia is terrified I'll do. She says it's an insult."

It was, too—if meant to be. He said as much. "If someone knows you're trying to say you can't sign, most don't usually get offended, but it's safer just to learn, *'I don't understand,'* so you're safe."

That one he *did* seem to know. Duncan grinned and asked Reese for his phone. Reese pulled up Larry's contact information and tapped it. As he passed it back, he warned Larry. "Duncan relies way too much on predictive text. It can get… interesting."

Sisters bombarded him with one question after another. How long had he lived in Ventura—oh, he didn't live there now? Where did he live? What did he do? His job gave both Portia a start and him a star in Jessica's book. She pounced on it immediately.

"You're in sustainable waste management? Really? Do you see that as a poss—"

Miranda ordered her to stuff it. "Grill him on the fate of the planet later. Food's getting cold."

That, no one could argue with. The crowd converged on the kitchen, and his family was ordered to fill plates first. Portia snickered as she climbed in line behind him. "And we mean *fill.* When we leave here, you're getting whatever's leftover back, so if you don't want to eat this until next year—literally, I guess…"

"With tomorrow being the thirty-first, yeah, I'd say so," Cressida joked. "Good one."

"Wasn't intentional, but I'll take it." Portia's voice dropped to an almost impossible-to-hear level. "I didn't know you were in waste management."

"Didn't realize we hadn't discussed it until I told her. Is it a problem?"

"No!"

The entire family leaned in. Reese couldn't see it, of course, but he felt it—every puff of breath on his neck as they all craned to hear whatever had set Portia off.

Chaos—everyone talking at once. Portia helping with the little kids between bites of her own food. A.J. shouting across the island to Duncan before remembering Duncan couldn't hear. Mrs. Spears laughing at something someone said. Mr. Spears making a joke. Miranda and Jessica muttering under their breaths—opinions on him, if he'd caught one or two of the words right.

Reese watched his parents out of one corner of his eye and the rest out of the other. *Anyone looking at me must think I have out-crossed eyes or something.*

"Had enough already?"

"Are you kidding? It's awesome."

Even as he said it, Reese realized it was true. A twenty-four-seven diet of the melee would be more than he could handle, but compared to his family's ultra-quiet evenings, where the TV provided most of the noise, and the nights at home alone with Duncan when he sometimes didn't hear a word from the minute he picked his son up to the time he dropped Duncan off in the morning, it had appeal.

"It's not usually *this* loud. But dinner, everyone wanting to get to know everyone…"

Habits form quickly. Without thinking, Reese slipped an arm around her waist and leaned in to whisper, "Stop apologizing. You have nothing to apologize for."

The conversation quieted to only Bella and Charis asking their mother questions, but even they hushed after a moment. Jessica raised one eyebrow, and if the disgusted expression on Portia's face meant what he thought it did, she couldn't do that. And she wanted that skill—badly.

"Is there a problem?" What made him say it, Reese didn't know. Portia choked. Jessica gaped. And then they all erupted in laughter. Pat squeezed his arm as she passed. "You'll fit in well."

Before he could answer that, the doorbell rang. Portia gave him a weak smile. "Enter the guys. They went on a wine run."

"Will they be offended when we don't drink any?"

"Most of us don't. No worries."

His mother shot him a look when each man entered with wine bottle carriers hanging from each hand. *Just when I thought things were going so well…*

Kendra's expression made Portia rethink her decision not to protest the wine run. *Are you nervous that you'll offend* us, *or are you offended? What approach do I take?*

Mom to the rescue. Bypassing the food, Mom went for the glasses cupboard and called out, "Number off for wine glasses… and go!" Five called out numbers in succession.

"And let's see… four children for regular drinks. Larry and me…" She glanced over her shoulder. "I didn't hear you guys, so the three Whitakers for something else? Portia… Tami… Cressida… That leaves…" She counted each glass. "One for everyone. Grab your glass and drinks are in the fridge, in the cooler there at the end of the island, and there's coffee, if you prefer, over on that coffee bar."

It worked. The shell-shocked look on Kendra's face melted into her usual pleasant lines, and a smile formed. She whispered to Portia as she passed, "I feel silly. I was so sure someone would say something. They usually do."

Well, if Dad had his way, the stuff would never enter the house, but still. Only Damon would say anything, and even he wouldn't tonight. The truth of that thawed her toward him… just a bit. *He does try if he knows it is important. He just doesn't always seem to take the time to find out what is important.*

Guilt hit a moment later. *Then again, I don't find out what's important to him, either. Maybe if I did…*

She and Reese found spots at the dining table with both sets of parents, Austin, Cressida, and Charis. The other kids sat in the breakfast nook with Tami, and the rest of the adults stood around the island, talking and laughing.

And staying out of my hair. I owe them.

Austin asked intelligent questions about Reese's job—things she'd want to know if she'd thought to ask them. Cressida asked about Sinagpore's "landfill island" and if it was really as great as the Facebook videos made it out to be.

Portia, on the other hand, sat there waiting for something terrible to happen—something that would make Reese stand up, drop his napkin in his chair, and say, "This is it, I can't deal with these people. I'm done."

A semi-heated debate began over the NIV versus the ESV, and Kendra put in her preference for KJV, giving her bonus points in Austin's eyes. "It may not be the most accurate with the latest manuscripts," he argued when Brian protested, "but it is the longest lasting. For a Bible translation to still be beloved while not being proven *in*accurate for five hundred years, that's pretty solid."

"And 'Easter' in the Bible is 'accurate' to you?"

"Brian!" Kendra looked ready to melt through the floor.

Austin held his ground. "Do you know what they mean?"

Brian grinned. "I like you. Exactly my point. I may not prefer it, but I get tired of hearing it maligned. Kendra is a lover of older fiction and Shakespeare—"

The Spears shouted, "Hear, hear!" as if some kind of family chant. She'd never understood it, but her voice joined the others.

As if uninterrupted, Brian continued. "—so I think it only makes sense that she'd appreciate it, but she does get a lot of flak for it."

It happened over and over—politics, points of doctrine, books, movies, you name it, if the topic came up, Portia stiffened, waiting for the argument that would force her to choose between the guy she could see herself falling for in the next year, six months, month, week, day or two… And the family who loved her—despite her deficiencies… and theirs.

Twice, Reese reached under the table and squeezed her hand. "It's okay. They like each other. I like them. They like you. This is good."

She almost believed him. Okay, she *did* believe him. Right up to the moment when Jessica popped her head in the door and said, "That was amazing roast. Seriously, I want to know how you cooked it. Oh, we're about to start Reverse Charades, so hurry!"

"Oh, help…"

Four shouting matches, five insults that she couldn't chalk up to game play, two times when she nearly burst into tears at the look on Kendra's face, and a lost game of charades later, the Whitaker's said their goodbyes, carried a sleepy Duncan to Reese's car and drove him home. Only promises that she'd be at their New Year's Eve party the next night kept the boy from a complete meltdown.

Nothing, however, kept Miranda from dragging her into the game room and having her own meltdown. "What do you think you're doing? New Year's Eve—*family*."

"And what are we doing, exactly? Because on the itinerary I was given, there is a big, fat *blank* on New Year's Eve."

"We were trying to find out what kind of options there were first. We *always*—"

Here, Portia broke in. "Do our own thing at New Year's, and you know it. So why would I assume otherwise? Especially since you guys have been making up the rules as you go anyway. I'm going to their house. Period. So I can spend all day with them or just for the party. That'll be up to you, but I'm not sitting around to get dumped on all day just because you had plans you didn't bother to tell me about."

She would have stormed from the room, but a few slow claps behind her stopped her. Portia whirled in place, ready to blast her sister, but Miranda flung herself at her. "Yes. Good girl.

You did it. Now keep standing up for yourself like that all the time, and you might get a little more respect. Go out with your guy. I like him."

"That's just because he let you have 'jumper' for 'parachutist.' That was a stretch and you know it."

"Still… he's nice. And cute. And he's obviously totally into you."

There, Portia couldn't let it go. "You think?"

"Definitely." Miranda winked. "And I *know* you like him, because you fought for that time. You *never* fight. I didn't even have to bring in the kids."

That made no sense. Bringing in the kids would have made her *more* likely to stay, but before she could argue it, Miranda shot that down. "Just trust me. I was ready for it, but you didn't need that. You still would have said no. I didn't even have to bother. Now go for that walk before he bursts in here to rescue you from the evil not-step-sister."

"Is Jessica waiting to pounce and run me through some kind of test, too?"

As if on cue, Jessica pulled open one of the game room doors and poked her head in. "Did she stick to her guns, or do I need to come tell her what an idiot she'd be to let this guy go?"

"She's going. Now *and* tomorrow."

"Good. Now get out there. I don't know how long I can keep him there before I scare him off."

Still stunned, Portia found Reese by the front door, holding her coat. "Want to take a walk?"

"Definitely. Why are you—? Oh. Right. Thanks."

"Are you okay?"

Portia gave him a look. "I don't know. But, for what it's worth," she added as he helped her into the coat. "*All* of my sisters like you."

"I like them, too." Once outside the door, he added, "You're right, though. They do argue—a lot."

Here it comes.

They made it to the end of the drive before he took her hand.

"I don't quite know what to make of it. They obviously love each other—you all do. But there are your parents, just laughing and joking, and in the other room, they're duking it out with words over stuff that makes no sense. Your mom walks in, and it settles a bit until she leaves."

"Old habits. We weren't allowed to 'fight.' We could 'discuss,' but no getting loud and ugly. So… we learned to go somewhere she couldn't hear us. I think she regrets not making us sit on the couch and say exactly what we wanted to in calm, pleasant tones or something. The arguing stresses her out."

"I think I saw it a couple of times." He pulled her a bit closer. "It stresses you, too."

"But not enough to shut me up."

Down Vista del Mar, under the overpass, across Harbor Boulevard—just as she had that first day. They walked through the "no entrance" gate and fought their way across the sand to the harder packed stuff.

Reese spoke then. "Left or right?"

"Pier. I want to walk on it again."

As they turned right and started the half-mile trek to the pier, Reese spoke again. "I think I understand more now. You wanted them to like me. That's why you didn't want them to meet me."

"That doesn't make sense. How can they—"

"Listen. Think about it. If we don't meet, we can't disagree. If we don't disagree, we won't dislike each other. If we don't dislike each other, you don't have to make a choice."

How does he know what I was thinking?

She couldn't ask.

Instead, they walked along, hand-in-hand, allowing the gentle rolls of the tide to wash away the noise and chaos of the night. Even as they climbed the steps to the pier and walked along the rough planks, the anxiety of the past week and a half seemed to dissolve. Waves crashed against the pilings, gulls cleaned the boards of the day's remnants, and the crescent moon shone down, brighter than expected for so little left of it.

"The moon'll be just a sliver tomorrow night—almost

completely gone on Wednesday—like us."

Reese pulled her close, his arm around one shoulder as they gazed out over the dappled light, what little there was of it, on the water. "I suppose meeting next weekend is too soon. We should wait until the twelfth?"

"You looked up dates already." The statement came out as an accusation, but Portia didn't bother apologizing. He'd understand.

"Guilty. As much as this coming Saturday sounds better…"

"We should at least try it. Maybe I could come down for Wednesday night Bible Study, or something, if it gets to be too long. Or Sunday night church. We do an afternoon service, so I'm free Sunday nights."

They'd worked out a crazy schedule of ways to spend time "together," if not actually together, when Reese stepped back and shoved his hands in his pockets. Portia's heart sank. *This is it. He's decided it's too much—maybe for Duncan. Steady…*

"This is really happening, right?"

She blinked. "Huh?"

"This—us. It's happening. We're really going to do this, right?" When she didn't respond, he continued. "We're not going to go home and just let it fade into nothing, are we?"

Maybe it was kind of pathetic. Portia suspected as much, but she also suspected that she didn't really care. Hearing the fear in his voice—the fear that they might *not* get together again—reassured all the little insecure places in her heart. They'd empty out again, and he'd have to refill them at some point, but for now, they sat happy and full.

"You're not getting rid of me that easily."

He took her hand again and led her back up the pier. "Whew. I just had this picture of you not knowing how to tell me that your family actually hated me and you're done or something. Pathetic, but there it is."

"No… they like you. Did I tell you that Miranda hauling me off to ream me for going to your house tomorrow was to *make* me go…?"

TWENTY-FIVE

Thirteen texts. Either the luckiest number on the planet or the *un*luckiest. He didn't know which. Portia and her sisters had gotten it into their heads that nothing she owned would be appropriate for the annual Whitaker New Year's Eve party—the one he suspected they thought was larger than the twenty or so people who would come in and out of the house open-house style all night.

Nine of those texts had sported different tops and dresses. Five of them with her in them. At first, he tried to figure out which might be cheapest, but his mother shot that down. "The simplest outfits are usually the most expensive. Just go with what you like on her. I think that black dress is cute."

"Isn't it a bit dressy?"

"Everything she's sent is. We'll just dress up a bit more, too. I've got that new top I bought with nowhere to wear it."

He protested. "Everyone who shows up will be underdressed then."

"I've got this. Just go iron your gray shirt and black slacks."

"What about Duncan?"

There, Mom drew a line. "No one expects a kid to dress up for New Year's Eve when he's just going to fall asleep behind the couch anyway."

The couch—*that's* why she'd been adamant about the floor model. It would get Dad to agree and get her the new couch before the party. *And it worked. The couch looks great.*

Five minutes later, a group text message arrived. WE HAVE GUESTS COMING WHO MAY DRESS UP A LITTLE MORE THAN WE USUALLY DO FOR THE PARTY, SO THE WHITAKERS WILL BE WEARING SOMETHING A BIT MORE FESTIVE THIS YEAR. PLEASE FEEL FREE TO COME AS YOU USUALLY DO, BUT IF ANYONE ELSE IS WILLING TO DRESS UP A LITTLE, THAT WOULD BE WONDERFUL—JUST SO OUR GUESTS DON'T FEEL OUT OF PLACE. THANKS ALL. LOOKING FORWARD TO SEEING YOU TONIGHT.

So, when Reese went to pick up Portia, and she opened the door wearing the black dress he'd liked best, he thought he'd be prepared. After all, he'd already seen it on her. But Portia of the department store and Portia of the "ready to go to the party" were two very different Portias.

"Wow is inadequate, a whistle is inappropriate, and I don't know what else to say."

"How about, 'Hi'?" She tried to smile and failed. "You look great, by the way. Gray is your color."

"How about I take that but change it to black—except the other day it was blue. And there was a brown once—and green…"

That produced a smile—a real one this time. Still dazzled, Reese couldn't have said when they left her house and entered his. He just knew that out of the blue, there they were in his living room, and he was introducing her to friends his parents had known for most of their married lives. "—is my girlfriend, Portia Spears."

Panic set in as the word *girlfriend* reverberated through the room. Every person present turned to stare—including a friend he'd forgotten he'd invited. Portia didn't even miss a beat. If anything, she stepped up and took charge. "Nice to meet you… was that Amy and Joe?"

"Sandy and Joe," he corrected automatically. "Hey, sorry guys, but Shawn just got here. I want to introduce her."

As they wove through the tiny living room and into the kitchen where Shawn had gone to say hi to his parents, Portia elbowed him. "I should get you for that."

"Sorry. It just came out so naturally. I should have asked first or something."

She froze, nearly knocking into the minister's wife, which would have certainly tossed Mom's nice orange punch onto the even nicer dove gray couch. "That wasn't a joke? You weren't just messing with me?"

He winced. "It just came out."

Instead of following him into the kitchen, Portia dragged him out the front door. Once it shut behind her, she stood rubbing her hands on her bare arms as she asked, "Is that what you want?"

"Well, yeah. It's what we've been talking about."

"Around, Reese. We've been talking *around* it—not *about* it."

She had a point—semantics, perhaps, but when she'd never had a boyfriend… "I guess I should have asked. Can I introduce you as my girlfriend, or should I go tell Joe and Sandy that I was presumptuous."

"Yeah… I'll totally take girlfriend." She'd started to add something, but her teeth chattered.

Reese spun her in place. "We'll figure the rest out later. You're going to freeze…"

Talking about it? Brilliant. He'd have to remember that little trick. If they hadn't, he wouldn't have done it again until later, and seeing his mom's face as he introduced Shawn to his *girlfriend*—well, there wasn't much he'd rather see.

Except someday… wife might be nice.

Reese waited for a moment of panic… uncertainty… even just a hitch. He got none. *Yeah… someday. That's a great way of saying it. It's a when… maybe… instead of an if… maybe.* A smile formed as she swept the room and found him standing there… watching her. *Definite maybe.*

Their planned walk along the beach after the party ended the moment Joe and Sandy presented the Whitakers with four tickets to Disneyland for the day. They offered to buy one for Portia, apologizing profusely for not knowing, but she refused. Her family might want her to assert herself, but an entire day gone when the vacation was almost over? Not hardly.

So, Reese walked her up the drive to Sandpiper House, feet dragging. "I wish I could just send Mom and Dad with Duncan."

"It's a gift."

"And that's why I can't. It would hurt their feelings. I had a hard enough time keeping Sandy from being hurt that they couldn't buy you one."

"Really?"

He squeezed her hand tucked in his coat pocket. "Oh, yeah. Sandy's love language is gifts. You can imagine."

"She's not mad?" Portia winced at the way he stiffened. "Sorry. You said she'd be hurt, so…"

"Hurt isn't always a nice way of saying mad. Sometimes it's just hurt." Portia might have protested that idea, but he stopped under the porch light and gazed at her. "I've said it before. I'll probably say it until you're sick of hearing it, but you are so beautiful."

One of those rare but decidedly indelicate snorts made a very unwelcome appearance right then. Portia closed her eyes and groaned. "What I was *going* to say before I mortified myself—"

"I thought it was cute."

"Whatever." He started to speak again, but she shushed him. "Again, *as I was saying*, I don't know anyone who would get tired of hearing that someone they respect thinks they're…" she couldn't bring herself to say it. "Well, that they look nice."

Reese shook his head. "Nope. That's not it. You always look nice. But once in a while, you do something that says, 'Hey. Don't forget. I'm not just an awesome girl with a wicked sense of humor and a kindness to children. I'm also gorgeous.'"

"Yeah… that's not something I'd say."

"But you do… Every time we're together, somehow, you do." He did that thing again—that thing where he moved in close… and slow… and made her think and hope and wish for that kiss. As usual, a brush of his lips on her forehead this time—that was it. "Forgot that stupid mistletoe. It's New Year's Eve, too."

"Day, now. Another year. My sisters were taking bets on how close to thirty I'd be before I had a boyfriend. I made it before twenty-five without even trying." She wrinkled her nose. "I can't decide if I should be embarrassed or proud."

"I'm just glad you waited around for me."

That she could get into. "Hadn't thought of it that way. I'll take it."

"If we don't get home too late, I'll text you." Reese sighed. "Who am I kidding? I'll text you even if we do. And while waiting in line, and—"

Portia stopped him. "No, don't. Really. I mean, if you want to on the way home, if Duncan's asleep or something, sure. But make tomorrow just for you guys. I'll try to stay awake. Maybe I'll take a nap tomorrow afternoon so I can. I just need to be able to get to bed in time to drive home on Wednesday. I don't want to be tired driving in traffic. Ugh."

It could have been an hour—or even just fifteen minutes. But when Portia's feet couldn't take another minute in the heels she'd bought, she knew it was time to go in. "I have to go."

"I know. Me, too." Once more, Reese kissed her cheek. "Tomorrow—Wednesday at the latest. I'm getting that real kiss."

"Yeah… I've heard that one before."

Reese did it again—leaned in, his eyes shifting from hers to her lips and back again. Portia's breath caught. And centimeters away, he whispered. "I always keep my promises. See you tomorrow—I hope."

The shift of curtains warned her of an impending pounce as she opened the door. "I see you back there. Thanks for ruining the chance of my first kiss."

Miranda stepped out. "I didn't…"

As much as she wanted to play it up a bit, the stricken look on her sister's face wouldn't let her do it. "No… but you could have."

"You're so dead! Was it fun?"

"Actually, yes. I mean, I knew it was going to be a lot of his parents' friends and people from church, but it turned out to be really nice. He had a couple of old friends stop in, but the others really were the most fun. They knew all the great stories about him as a kid. One lady even knew his old girlfriend."

"Yeah?"

Remembering Sandy's story of a girl who wasn't allowed to go to the store by herself at twenty-one, Portia kind of felt sorry for her. "She was happy when they broke up. It was kind of an uncomfortable situation with the future in-laws."

"Like anyone who marries into the Spears family, huh?"

"That'll be the one time Jessica will *love* Mom's hands-off philosophy. She won't be interfering in our marriages."

The shock on Miranda's face told her that her sister hadn't thought of that yet. "You have a point. And Jessica will really like that. Especially if it's Damon."

Tami came downstairs in a now-rare bout of sleepwalking. It became the perfect opportunity to get Portia upstairs, out of the dress, and into comfy sleep pants. Once she was certain Tami was asleep again, she hurried through a nighttime routine that often earned her complaints and teasing by the rest of the family.

The clock read one-thirty by the time she climbed under the sheets and pulled her phone close. A text message from Reese waited.

YOU SHOULD KNOW THAT IT WAS REALLY HARD NOT TO TRY TO CONVINCE YOU TO COME. I'M ALREADY REGRETTING THE DAY WE'RE MISSING.

She shot back a reply. I'M ALMOST REGRETTING NOT JUST DOING IT. BUT I HAD A GREAT CONVO WITH MIRANDA. I NEED TO STAY HERE AND ENGAGE WITH THE FAMILY. I THINK I'M BEING SELFISH. HAVE FUN. AND TAKE PICTURES.

Sleep refused to come until she tried praying for the Lord to make things work out well or to slam the door shut on any relationship. Then, as usual, prayer put her right to sleep.

TWENTY-SIX

At breakfast, Portia snapped at Tami for asking how the party went. Okay, breakfast was more like barely brunch—or mostly lunch, depending on how you looked at it. However, she managed to get her food on her plate and to the table before noon, so in her book, it counted.

During nap time, Portia snapped at Jessica for not keeping the noise down. Hearing Jessica's not-so-kind response to that objection should have prompted a bit of remorse. After all, she'd deserved it. Instead, she jumped up from the couch, grabbed her book and stormed off to the door, calling back, "You oughtta know. You've got a PhD in it."

Sitting at the beach, knowing Reese wasn't going to come along, didn't make her snappier, to her relief. However, it did explain some of her angst when she woke up a couple of hours later. "Ugh. I should just go home and go to bed."

A.J. was scootering around the drive when she strolled up, ready to try a shower to get the sand out of her hair. He took one look at who had arrived and bolted inside. *Ugh, was I that bad?* Apologies. She'd have to make some. Just what she needed when she already had to fight a bad mood.

Cressida met her at the door. "Forgot the sunscreen, huh? Is it that bad out there?"

Dread churned her gut into a brick of butter. "What?"

Without trying to explain, Cressida took her upstairs. "I'll go get aloe. You take a shower and rinse that face in cool water."

And that's when the pain started.

One look in the mirror of her bedroom prompted tears—pain, frustration, embarrassment… *I'm going to be hideous when he kisses me. And he'll do it. Even if he doesn't want to now, he will. Just to keep his word. He'd* better *get home in time tonight. Moonlight—there won't be any. Perfect.*

That prompted a text. I TOLD YOU TO IGNORE YOUR PHONE TODAY, BUT I HOPE YOU GET THIS. WHEN YOU GET BACK, I REALLY WANT TO HEAR ABOUT ALL THE FUN YOU HAD. I WANT TO SEE DUNCAN, TOO. THINGS ARE UP IN THE AIR ABOUT WHEN WE LEAVE ON WEDNESDAY, SO I HOPE YOU GET BACK IN TIME TONIGHT.

Yes, it was a tiny stretch of the truth and the exact truth both. She had no idea when she'd leave. They just had to be out of the house by noon. Her parents had already volunteered to take Tami so she could stay as long as she wanted. But if the burn didn't go by then.

Lord, I know it's pride, but c'mon… is it awful for me not *to want to look like this when we say goodbye?*

A reply came a few minutes later. In the form of a picture. From his mom. Words followed. REESE WON'T REPLY. HE SAID HE PROMISED, AND HE WANTS TO PROVE HE KEEPS HIS PROMISES. BUT, THERE IS NOTHING IN THE BYLAWS THAT SAYS I CAN'T SEND THIS PICTURE I GOT OF YOU GUYS TONIGHT. I'M NOT SUPPOSED TO TELL YOU THAT IT'S HIS PHONE WALLPAPER, SO I WON'T. WISH YOU WERE HERE.

As soon as she'd showered and Cressida returned with aloe, the skin repair began. She guzzled water, slathered aloe, and guzzled more. The moment the aloe became sticky, she rinsed it off in cool water and slathered more. Lying flat on her back nearly drove her nuts, but every time she sat up, the aloe wanted to slither off.

Might be using too much…

At the two hour mark, it looked no better—and probably worse, if she were honest with herself. Portia was not. "I think it's helping."

Cressida snorted. "You think that."

The next coating she did thinner and sat up to read.

A door slammed down the hall—Jessica's if Portia guessed right. That wasn't completely unusual. However, that kind of physical response without a correlating shouting match? *That* was odd.

Her burning face offered the perfect out. Conviction argued that there was never an out from doing right. Conviction won.

Despite the nudge down the hall, Portia crossed to the bathroom, first. She rinsed the sticky aloe goo from her face, patted it dry, and slathered on a fresh coating. A glance out the bathroom door showed nothing. No one had come upstairs.

Okay… going in. Keep me safe. Let Reese know how much I liked him if I don't make it out alive.

A knock earned her a, "What?!"

If she answered, someone might hear. If she just walked in, everyone would likely hear—unless Jessica had cooled off a bit. Portia opted for the latter. She pushed the door open a bit and asked in a low tone, "You okay?"

Jessica rolled over to face her, a retort on her lips no doubt, and froze. "Ouch! Better than you. I thought Cressida was exaggerating."

That's all it took. Portia slipped into the room, pushed the door shut behind her, and leaned against it. "Life at the beach tip for ya. Don't fall asleep without sunscreen, a hat, and an umbrella or two."

"Do you need aloe?"

"I've got some, but thanks." She inched forward to the empty twin bed beside Jessica's. "What's wrong?"

That's when she saw it—evidence of crying.

However, before Portia could respond, Jessica drew her

knees up to her chest and flung her phone aside as she wrapped her arms around her legs. "Stress—work, family, friends…"

"Boyfriends?"

A sigh—Jessica's only response.

"He loves you. That's got to count for something."

"He does, and it does, but for all the wrong stuff. He keeps trying to propose. I'm going crazy making sure it can't happen."

She doesn't want to marry him? Yes! Figuring that might not be the most tactful thing to say, Portia attempted a more socially acceptable response. "You know?"

"He's come up with five so far—one when you were at the hospital. Barely got out of that one."

There, Portia winced. "That's my fault. Sorry. We talked, I felt bad for being so hard on him, so I tried to help."

"Next time, ask. You know how I hate surprises."

There, Jessica had a point. Still, she couldn't help but wonder why her sister would stay with someone if marriage wasn't an option. "Why don't you want to marry him?"

"Who said I don't?" A wry smile followed. "I guess I sound like it. It's not that. It's just too soon. I'm not ready, but if I say no, he's going to get offended, and we'll probably break up."

That seemed like a perfectly splendid reason *not* to marry someone, but maybe she hadn't told *him* that. "Does he know you're not ready?"

"Do you really think I'd keep an opinion like that to myself?"

"You've got a point…." Portia moved closer, or, rather, conviction propelled her to Jessica's side. A hug, a wince at her cheek scraping across Jessica's sweater—an apology. "Sorry about this week. I didn't want to come."

"No… Couldn't tell at all."

"But I agreed to. I should have tried to enjoy it."

That prompted a snicker. "I'd say you enjoyed it quite well, actually."

Portia couldn't repress a smile if she tried. So she didn't. "I did. Except for Dad falling, arguing with you and Miranda—even Cressida—snapping at people, making Tami cry…"

The longer she talked, the worse everything sounded.

"It wasn't exactly unprovoked. I've been taking frustrations out on everyone." Their eyes met and Jessica added, "You guys are safe. You'll love me even when I just lose it."

"I know. And we will."

Jessica flopped back on the pillows. "Mom always says that it's wrong the way we treat those we love the most the worst."

"We do it, though. We all do. Maybe it's wrong, but you've got a point. It's safe." Portia shifted her legs into a pathetic excuse for a lotus position and tried to force her back straight. "I wonder what Bible verse fits here."

"I know which one. I just don't like it."

"Tell me. At least we can not like it together." Portia winced. "I think I'm glad Mom didn't hear that."

"You should be. If she could make us write verses still, I bet that's one she'd do."

"You still haven't told me which one."

Jessica's eyes closed. "'*If I speak with the tongues of men and of angels, but do not have love, I have become a noisy gong or a clanging cymbal...*'"

A smile formed. They'd memorized the chapter when Portia had turned ten. She picked up the next verse. "'*If I have the gift of prophecy, and know all mysteries and all knowledge; and if I have all faith, so as to remove mountains, but do not have love, I am nothing.*'"

"'*And if I give all my possessions to feed the poor, and if I surrender my body to be burned, but do not have love, it profits me nothing.*'"

They joined in the rest together, but Jessica's voice broke when they got to, "'*...does not seek its own, is not provoked, does not take into account a wrong suffered...*'"

And when Portia got to, "'*...bears all things, believes all things, hopes all things, endures all things...*'" she couldn't help but notice how fitting the words were for their relationship. "I don't endure anything—don't *bear* anything like I should. I just get 'easily provoked' and keep that 'record of wrongs' like Dad put it that time."

"You're not the only one.

A thought occurred to her. Portia pulled up the verses on her phone and counted. When the idea didn't work out like she wanted, she almost put it aside, but another idea hit her. That one worked. "Each set of things… between commas, you know?"

"Yeah?"

"There's thirteen of them. At least in the NASB, there are thirteen."

Jessica didn't respond to that. She just stared up at the ceiling. A second look showed weariness that Portia hadn't seen before. "Why is saying you're sorry so hard?"

"Pride." At Jessica's sharp look, she shrugged. "Didn't we hear it *all the time* when we were kids? I know the right answer, but I'm still workin' on that one."

"The song says God's still working on it."

They'd sang it as girls. "*…working on me…*"

"Yeah. Well, He is. All of us."

A minute or two passed. Jessica lying on the bed, eyes riveted to the ceiling. Portia fighting to keep her back straight and her inner thighs from burning as hot as her face. *It shouldn't hurt to* sit*!*

But somewhere in that ninety seconds or so, Portia had a bit of an epiphany. Jessica wanted to apologize. *And that's enough for me.* She'd just started to say so when it occurred to her that she'd never actually asked for forgiveness herself.

"Hey, Jess?"

"Yeah?"

"I meant it. I'm sorry. I hope you'll forgive me."

A snicker—she expected it, too—preceded Jessica's response. "Of course, I will. But Mom'd get you for not *asking* for it. Telling me what you want…"

"…is not *asking*. I know. Will you?"

"Yeah. And the same goes for me, too."

It might not be the most loquacious of apologies—on either of their parts, in fact—but it might just have been the most genuine they'd ever given each other. *And that's what matters most.*

A new thought occurred to Portia just as she was about to excuse herself and give Jessica some privacy. "Hey, can I toss out my opinion on the Damon thing?"

"Dump his sorry butt?"

"No… although, I wouldn't complain…" She winked. "Just go downstairs and tell him. It's what you do best. You're a lawyer. Make a case for him waiting until he knows you're ready. Tell him you know he's been trying, and you're sick of thwarting those efforts and hoping he doesn't sneak one past you. You don't want to lose him. Just tell him."

"Maybe…"

Hugs… tears… embarrassment. Aaah… what were sisters for? Best of all, Jessica followed her down the hall and made for the stairs. "Wish me luck. I'm doing it."

"I'll do you one better. I'll pray."

The book still sat unread as Portia sat on the bed, thanking the Lord for restoration, asking for a heart to love the man who might become a brother, asking for favor for a sister who had once been her hero. *She's still an amazing person. I've got to quit holding things against her. That's wrong… And You don't keep that record of* my *wrongs. The Psalms… or is it Isaiah? One of them says You don't remember our sins anymore.*

Jerked from her prayer by new thoughts, Portia called up I Corinthians 13 on her phone again. She reread it. "Patient… that's God all over. Kind—duh. Not jealous? Well, that's a tough one. He says He's a jealous God. I wonder if it's the same kind?"

The next words were easier. "God doesn't brag—doesn't have to. And He's not arrogant. Of course, He doesn't act unbecomingly or seek His own. He seeks the *lost.* The next two were harder to reconcile—especially not provoked—but Portia couldn't imagine that her provocations and wrongs suffered were anywhere on par with what God endured. It probably had something to do with that.

"But you do bear all things, hope all things, believe all things, and You already endured all things for us… Wow. I Corinthians 13—a how to guide to becoming godly… That's exhausting just to think about."

By eight o'clock, she couldn't stay awake. Her face burned,

her eyes refused to stay open, and the bed called. She zipped a text message to Reese. TEXT ME WHEN YOU GET IN IF YOU'RE UP TO MEETING. I'M TURNING ON MY NOTIFICATIONS SO I'LL HEAR IT IF YOU DO. I'M JUST TIRED.

With some of her mother's rich facial moisturizing cream massaged into the screaming skin, Portia turned out the lights, climbed into bed, and slept until dawn.

Not sending a text when they got home at eleven-thirty—hardest thing he'd ever done. But if Portia had gone to bed that early, he figured she needed the rest. However, the minute he awoke, he made coffee, grabbed the mistletoe ball his mother had made for them and something he'd gotten her at Disneyland, and headed down the beach. There, in the same spot he'd met her, Reese drank his coffee and waited for the day to break.

The minute the sun peeked over the horizon, he sent the first text. ARE YOU AWAKE?

No reply.

Just in case, he sent another. MISSED YOU YESTERDAY. DUNCAN SPENT ALL DAY SAYING, "PORTIA WOULD LIKE THIS. PORTIA SHOULD SEE THAT." I THINK WE'RE GOING TO HAVE TO MAKE DISNEY A PRIORITY.

Again, no reply.

He tried again. THAT'S A THOUGHT. I DON'T KNOW. DO YOU LIKE ROLLER COASTERS? I'M KIND OF AFRAID OF THAT ANSWER. WHAT'LL I DO IF YOU DON'T?

By the fifth text, he wondered if she'd gotten upset at him. By the seventh, he finally got a reply.

JUST GETTING READY. MAKEUP, HAIR, ALL THAT STUFF.

Reese would have thrown something if it would have done any good. I'VE SEEN YOU WITH BED HEAD. YOU WERE GORGEOUS THEN. YOU'LL BE GORGEOUS NOW."

THAT'S WHAT YOU THINK.

Something about it didn't feel right, but Reese couldn't put his finger on what. He tried flirting. HOW ABOUT YOU COME DOWN HERE AND LET ME BE THE JUDGE. IF I THINK YOU NEED A LITTLE WORK, I'LL SEND YOU BACK.

Her reply came almost without hesitation—as if she'd been anticipating it. I'M SAVING ME A WASTED TRIP.

Again, something felt off. WHAT'S WRONG?

WHY DOES ANYTHING HAVE TO BE WRONG?

Something was definitely not right. Of that, he had no doubt. With nothing else to do, he began a guessing game. BAD HAIRCUT?

NO.

Reese tried again. BAD HAIR DYE? DID SOMEONE CALL YOU "CARROTS?"

This time, the reply took longer *Oh, no…*

Then his phone pinged. I THINK I JUST FELL IN LOVE WITH YOU. YOU KNOW ANNE.

For the first time in his life, Reese was thankful for his mother's obsession with period and literary adaptations. IF I LET YOU CALL ME GILBERT, WILL YOU TELL ME?

NO.

"It's bad." There wasn't any way around it now. Something, at least in Portia's mind, was terribly wrong. Probably with her hair. Reese tried again. HOW ABOUT IF "CARROTS" BECOMES MY NEW PET NAME FOR YOU?

This time, her reply took a bit longer, but still not helpful—sort of. GREAT NAME. I LOVE IT. BUT NO. A minute passed before another reply. WILL YOU STILL LIKE ME IF I'M HIDEOUS?

He tried again. ARE WE TALKING MICK JAGGER OR MEDUSA?

While he waited, Reese tried another approach and sent Larry a text. WHAT'S WRONG WITH PORTIA? I'M CONCERNED.

A single reply followed. SUNBURN.

"Oh, no… Okay. I can work with that. Poor girl."

Her reply followed before he could come up with something. DEFINITELY MEDUSA.

The obvious came first, of course. WILL YOU TURN ME TO STONE IF I LOOK AT YOU?

NO. BUT YOU MIGHT WISH IT. SHE'S PRETTY HIDEOUS.

That'd work. SO WHAT YOU'RE SAYING IS THAT YOU'RE GREEN. NOT HAIR… SKIN. I'VE ALWAYS PICTURED MEDUSA AS GREEN—PROBABLY ALL THOSE SNAKES.

A full minute passed before she replied this time. WHAT ABOUT COPPERHEADS?

That one he could answer blindfolded. I LIKE COPPERHEADS. YOU'RE ONE, AFTER ALL. A moment later, he added, HAIR WISE, I MEAN.

The confession came at last. SKIN WISE NOW, TOO.

This time, he hit the call button. She answered, and if he knew voices like he thought he did, she had to fight back tears. "Portia?"

"Yeah?"

"Just remember that I've seen you blush. I won't pretend it's your best look, but I still loved being with you."

"Blushes go away faster." A sigh followed. "And this'll probably earn me a couple dozen more freckles, too."

It was a risk, but one he couldn't resist. "Well, at least there's makeup for that…"

"Let me guess. You adore freckles."

"It's more like I couldn't care less…" Reese did a Google search as he kept talking. "For the record, almost no guy I ever knew does either." Results were inconclusive, but he went with it. "Well, there's Stan and his dermataphobia…"

"If you tell me that's a fear of freckles…"

The strain had gone from her voice, and a chuckle entered. Reese couldn't help but laugh with her. "Hey… it's a thing. Or, rather, it's more like that's where it fits." He had to give her an out, but he didn't want her to stress, either.

"Look, if you're going to feel better with makeup and hair and heels and pearls, then do it. But I'd just as soon see you in fuzzy sleep pants and bed head than wait another minute."

A gull cried overhead, and Portia gasped. "Wait, are you

already down there?"

"Yep."

"Fine. I'll put on more of Mom's old lady cream—"

"I bet she'd kill you if she heard you say that."

Her laughter—finally something felt right. "You don't know my mom. But I'll get it on to save my skin, grab Cressida's obscenely huge sun hat, and be right down."

"I have coffee."

Portia groaned. "Seriously? You couldn't have said that up front?"

She hadn't been joking. Under the overpass, he saw it—a hat that made sombreros look undersized barreling down the hill toward him. The way she flung herself at him only made it impossible to see if she was really as burned as she seemed to think.

"I missed you."

"If I promise not to look at you, will you please tell me you're okay?"

A sound—could have been a choked laugh or a sob, he didn't know which—preceded her wail. "I missed you yesterday, and I was grumpy. Kept snapping at everyone, so I took off for the beach. Fell asleep for a couple of hours. The side of my face that was turned toward the water got the worst of it, of course. Serves me right for being a jerk."

The moment they reached "their spot," Reese took over. If he waited for her to give in and "let" him see her, it would never happen. Irrational as it might have been, he also had a feeling that she would use it as an excuse not to see him until it was gone, and by then…

With his coffee nestled in sand and the Disneyland bag beside it, Reese turned to her and pulled her close. "Now, this is going to hurt you way more than it hurts me. So, do you want fast or slow?"

"Oh, rip the dumb hat off if you must."

He did. Before he could stop himself, Reese sucked in his breath. "Ouch! Are you okay?" The back of his hand on her cheek told him all he needed to know. The skin still burned hot. "Oh, man… I'm so sorry."

"Me, too. I look awful."

"You *feel* awful, you mean." Reese would have pressed his cheek to hers in an effort to cool it, but a memory stopped him. "I have to go home."

Shock registered. She'd believed him that it wouldn't matter. *Good.*

"I—"

Without a word, he took her hand and brushed it against his face. She didn't get it. "If I come near you with stubble, you'll be in so much pain you'll never speak to me again. Mom did once—almost had the neighbors calling the cops when Dad tried to kiss her goodbye. Give me ten. Just drink your coffee. I'll bring you a fresh one when I come back."

"You *are* coming back? I didn't humiliate myself for nothing?"

If he couldn't see that she really believed it, Reese might have been annoyed. But her genuine mortification made it easier to swallow. "I'm not missing out on this…" Reese pulled the mistletoe from his pocket and handed it to her. "For anything."

He jogged halfway home and ran the rest. It would require a changed shirt, but Reese decided it was worth it. A quick shave… and an even quicker double shave, lots of lotion afterward—he smelled like almond-cherry, thanks to his mother's lotion—and a fresh shirt. Inside ten minutes, he was on his way back. Without the coffee.

Halfway there, he remembered. Hesitation cost him a few more seconds, but he ran back to the house. He'd promised, and he'd promised to keep those promises. *Be careful what you promise, eh, Lord?*

By the time he made it close enough to see, Portia paced up and down the walkway. Twice, she inched a bit too close to the road for his comfort. The third time, she saw him. Her smile, despite the grimace it became as her skin stretched and tugged—most beautiful thing he'd seen in ages. "Hi…"

Something about a clean-shaven Reese carrying that silly travel mug of coffee told Portia she'd found the real thing. *I'm going to marry this guy someday. Weird how I just know that…*

"Portia?"

She took a sip of the coffee, the heat burning her lips, and tried not to wince. *That kiss is going to hurt anyway. Ugh.* Unwilling to let him see her squirm, Portia tried another smile. "Thanks. I'm sorry I freaked out. I'm not *that* vain. But it feels like you shouldn't know me well enough not to care what I look like yet."

"I do."

Again, she smiled. "Yeah. I figured that out."

They sat together, her slightly-less burned cheek almost resting on his arm. Almost. It was more like an odd neck lean that just propped everything into place. Anyone who didn't see the red might not notice, but Portia did.

I'm missing out because I was stupid. I was stupid because I was a jerk. I was a jerk because…

Reese pointed at a sailboat off in the distance. "Have you ever sailed?"

"No… have you?"

"Nope. Lived here most of my life and never climbed into a sailboat once—motor… but no sails."

It seemed an odd thing to mention until an idea hit her. "Are you stalling?"

A sigh answered before he did. "Yep. I figure the longer I keep you out here, the longer it is until we say goodbye."

"When do you need to leave for home?"

"If I leave by three, I'll miss the traffic."

Three would get her home by five-thirty. She could deal with that. "So… what do you want to do until three, then?"

Reese's grin should have warned her. "Well, an hour ago, I would have said that it might just be enough time to break in that mistletoe, but I'm thinking that's overkill now."

For the first time in her life, blushing didn't bother Portia Spears. She let it try to mortify her, but it failed. "Maybe not until *three.*"

"Okay, not even close, but admit it. You blushed under that red skin."

"Prove it."

This time, Reese did press his cheek against hers. The skin, cooled by ocean breezes, felt good… for a few seconds, anyway. "Thanks for that… shaving, I mean. I didn't think about that."

He pulled a fresh tube of beeswax lip balm from his pocket and passed it to her. "Saw that on the way out and grabbed it. Thought it might help keep your lips from cracking. Mom's did badly when she burned her face."

"Thanks! I was going to stop for some on the way home. I don't like Mom's granny cream on them, and the aloe doesn't last long. Seeps down the corners or tries to seep into my mouth. Gross."

For a minute there, she thought he'd finally make use of that stupid mistletoe ball. But instead, he reached for the Disneyland bag and passed it to her. "That thing was crazy hard to keep from crushing yesterday, but I managed."

Inside the bag—a cut-off wrapping paper roll. "What?"

"I put it inside that when I got home—to keep it safe. I could just see me crushing it on the way here after all that work."

Portia unrolled a sketch. "Wha—?"

"At California Adventureland, you can go to the Animation Studio and they show you how to do a sketch. We did Goofy. So…"

It looked impressive to her. She recognized the character immediately. "He's so cute." The caption below it was cute, too. *I'm Goofy for you.*

"It's true… spent all day yesterday thinking of you. Dad says I haven't had a 'crush' like this since I was ten." Reese swallowed so hard she could hear it. "Yeah, I've never felt like this. And my rational mind says that maybe I won't after a month, or three or ten… but I don't think so."

"I know…" Portia gave it one last glance before rolling the sketch back up and sliding it in the makeshift tube. The kiss to his cheek happened before she realized she'd done it, and it didn't even hurt. "Thank you. I love it. I'll stop in Lancaster and get a frame on the way home."

He rose and held out his hand. "C'mon. Let's walk a ways."

She tried to guess where he'd take her, but down by the water, he turned right instead of left, and by the time they reached the pier, he pulled up short near the pilings. The area—deserted on an early Wednesday morning. Standing under it almost gave an air of privacy.

Reese pulled the mistletoe ball from his pocket again. She hadn't even seen him put it back, but there it hung over their heads. His other hand reached for her, but he held back. "I don't want to hurt you."

I don't think I care. Sort of.

The ball slipped from his fingers and landed in the sand. He bent to pick it up, but Portia stopped him. "Wait… that's pretty." She fumbled for her phone and snapped a picture.

Reese pulled her close. One second she stood gazing into those eyes—pale brown… they really were—and the next, burned cheeks, lips, and all, Reese stomped every kiss she'd ever read about, ever watched and re-watched, ever *dreamed* about.

In that kiss were locked a thousand promises, and he'd unlock them all… one at a time.

TWENTY-SEVEN

He'd been home four hours—just five since he kissed her goodbye. Again. She'd followed him all the way to the Newhall Avenue exit, off the freeway, and he'd pulled into the Chevron station. There, in front of God and everyone, Reese kissed her goodbye once more.

Duncan kept him occupied, setting up a Skype chat, planning their lunches the next day, even practicing memory work for Sunday school. But the moment his son crawled into bed and fell asleep, Reese paced.

The first text went to his father. I MISS HER.

A reply came back in less than a minute. THEN TELL HER. WHY TELL ME?

AM I RIDICULOUS?

This time, less than thirty seconds passed before the reply came. YOU ALWAYS HAVE BEEN...

He tried his mom. HOW AM I GOING TO MAKE IT TEN DAYS WITHOUT SEEING HER?

Mom proved more encouraging. WHO SAYS YOU HAVE TO WAIT? JUST GO SEE HER. IT'S AN HOUR. MOST PEOPLE COMMUTE THAT LONG.

His father's next reply came on the heels of his mother's. I THINK YOU SHIFTING TO MOM ANSWERS A LOT OF QUESTIONS, DON'T YOU? CALL HER.

Reese started with a text. YOU UP?

YES. DOING LAUNDRY. WHAT'RE YOU DOING?

That's all he needed. Portia answered on the first ring. "Hey… I was just sitting here missing you."

"How does Saturday look for you?"

Though she said, "I thought we were waiting until *next* Saturday," the snicker beneath the words told him she'd been thinking the same thing.

"Friday?"

"You just said Saturday!"

Never had Reese felt more pathetic—and alive, excited, *optimistic* about life—than when he amended it once more. "Maybe tomorrow night after work?"

The world stood still—even the cars stopped driving past his house for a few minutes while he waited. "I drove around Acton on my way home," Portia said at last. "They have a sushi place…"

"You hate fish."

A few more agonizing seconds passed until her voice came through again. "Yeah… but I like you."

An hour later, he lay in his bed, hands behind his head, staring at a dark ceiling. And in that darkness, he decided four things. They'd spend so much time together people would worry. They'd fall in love. They'd get married. They'd have children—adopt a few, even.

After all, she was willing to endure sushi for him. *And I'll find a new, romantic adaptation of some book or another to endure for her. Because that's the kind of couple we'll be.*

AUTHOR'S NOTE

Sand & Mistletoe... It all began the fall of 2016. Two of our daughters suggested Christmas at a beach house in San Diego—one last hurrah with everyone together before the kids all started going their separate ways.

We didn't end up at the beach, but we did end up in an enormous house on a hill with an infinity pool and jacuzzi overlooking a valley—and no railing. On Christmas Adam, while I was finalizing edits for *New Year's Revolutions*, my kids came tearing into the house. My husband had fallen fifteen to twenty feet down a boulder-lined hill. Only the fence around the property kept him from going down for hundreds of feet.

Getting him back up—not so easy. He has a bad back and there was no light. Flashlights? We used cellphones because while the house probably had them, we didn't know where.

Kevin and I spent Christmas Eve in the ER to discover that, unlike this story, he wasn't injured beyond deep tissue bruising—possible bone bruising as well. Still, I couldn't let us all go through the concern, the moments of panic, and the hours of praying (and weeks of healing) for nothing.

Add to that the fact that few of us actually wanted to do Christmas away from home, and I had a story in the making. Things like that in this story are true.

While we were at the ER, my girls did go shopping for food and stocking stuffers. There was tension because we'd brought non-family members to be a part of our celebration. And there was a lot of tension because when people are concerned, it sometimes comes out as friction.

Well, and let's face it. When Mom won't push Dad to do something that you think is important, it can be frustrating. I'm still not sorry I didn't insist my grown man of a husband (of twenty-eight years then!) go to the hospital. I'm also not sorry that he chose to go the next day to soothe our daughter's concern. Sometimes you need to make those decisions, too. Note: our girl wasn't ugly or demanding. Just persuasively persistent. 😉

However, with all the little similarities, there are huge differences. For one, not one of the daughters portrayed in this book are exactly like any one of our girls. I tended to combine faults and virtues willy nilly. We have seven daughters, but I chose to go with five, and I left the boys out entirely. I also trimmed our grandchildren to three instead of five.

For the curious, our family is nowhere near this dramatic. We're rather boring, actually. I'd say my husband and I are reasonably similar to our characters in the book, but not exactly. Still, in this story, I have hyperbolized and exaggerated everything. Personalities (the good and the bad), actual events, logical assumptions of what someone would or wouldn't do—all of it.

Why did I share all of that? Well, because friends and family who do know us will recognize bits. People who have read my newsletter will recall the accident. I just didn't want to malign the characters of my real family. My daughters are strong, beautiful women—inside and out. They're flawed, yes. But so am I. They learned from a master at making mistakes, I assure you. However, who you see on these pages is not an accurate representation of any of them. I wouldn't want anyone to think it was. This is fiction—inspired quite loosely by a few small facts, events, and personality quirks. That's all.

Merry Christmas.

Stay tuned for a Spears wedding in *Sand & Lilies.*

CHAUTONA HAVIG'S BOOKS

The Rockland Chronicles

Aggie's Inheritance Series

Ready or Not
For Keeps
Here We Come
Ante Up!

Past Forward: A Serial Novel (Six Volumes)

Volume One
Volume Two
Volume Three
Volume Four
Volume Five
Volume Six

HearthLand Series**:** A Serial Novel (Six Volumes)

Volume One
Volume Two
Volume Three
Volume Four
Volume Five
Volume Six

The Hartfield Mysteries

Manuscript for Murder

Crime of Fashion
Two o'Clock Slump
Front Window
Silenced Knight (A Christmas Mystery "Noella")

Noble Pursuits
Argosy Junction
Discovering Hope
Not a Word
Speak Now
A Bird Died
Thirty Days Hath…
Confessions of a De-cluttering Junkie
Corner Booth
New Year's Revolutions
Premeditated Serendipity

The Agency Files
Justified Means
Mismatched
Effective Immediately
A Forgotten Truth

The Vintage Wren (A serial novel beginning 2016)
January (Vol 1.)
February (Vol. 2)
March (Vol. 3)

Sight Unseen Series
None So Blind
Will Not See
Ties that Blind

Christmas Fiction
Advent
31 Kisses

Tarnished Silver
The Matchmakers of Holly Circle
Carol and the Belles
Christmas Stalkings
Christmas Embers
The Second Noel
Silenced Knight
Merri's Christmas Mission
Sand & Mistletoe
Tangoed in Tinsel
The Ghosts of New Cheltenham

* * *

<u>Meddlin' Madeline Mysteries</u>
Sweet on You (Book1)
Such a Tease (Book 2)
Fine Print (Book 3)

* * *

<u>Ballads from the Hearth</u>
Jack

* * *

<u>Legacy of the Vines</u>

Deepest Roots of the Heart

* * *

<u>Journey of Dreams Series</u>

Prairie
Highlands

* * *

Heart of Warwickshire Series

Allerednic

* * *

The Annals of Wynnewood

Shadows & Secrets
Cloaked in Secrets
Beneath the Cloak

* * *

Not-So-Fairy Tales

Princess Paisley
Everard

* * *

Legends of the Vengeance

The First Adventure

Made in the USA
Columbia, SC
20 August 2020

15881269R00137